BEHIND the Yarrow

T.J. DEAL

ISBN:979-8-9907007-5-8

Cover design by: Sarah Hansen © Okay Creations

Editing: Sam Moon @acourtofbooksandcats13

To the audacious and badass women who aren't afraid to put their own happiness first, who stand firm in their boundaries, and who allow themselves the grace to forgive—not just others, but most importantly, themselves.

To the audacious and badass women who aren't afraid to put their own happiness first, who stand firm in their boundaries, and who allow themselves the grace to forgive—not just others, but most importantly, themselves.

Prologue

Drew

Present Day—

"So, I think it'd be best if you told Liv about what happened at the house." I joke to Isla as we pull out of her driveway. She had called me less than fifteen minutes ago, rattled by a noise she heard in her bedroom while Everett was at work.

Isla shoots me a side-eye, the corner of her mouth quirking up. "Lovely! Can't wait to tell *your* baby mama that her *other* baby daddy is haunting her old house."

Just then, my phone buzzes with an incoming call.

"Think her ears are burning?" I ask, raising an eyebrow as I reach for the button to connect Olivia's call. "We were just talkin' about ya, Boots! Isla's with me; we'll be there in a few minutes."

She sniffles and says, "Okay," then adds "Can you hurry?" My body goes tense, instinctively alert at the tone of her voice.

"What happened?" I demand, a little too forcefully as I put more pressure on the gas.

"I—" she falters, and I can picture her biting her lip, trying to hold herself together. "I don't know," she admits. "Pops called; Levi's on his way to hang out with the kids. Something happened to Odessa—she's being transported to Bend." Her words land like lead weights, quiet and devastating. Odessa's as much of a sister as my actual sister Charlie is to me.

"Isla's with me. We'll be there in a minute," I say, forcing calmness into my voice while the needle on the speedometer climbs higher.

In the background, I catch snippets of Olivia speaking softly to the kids, her voice only slightly trembling as she explains our sudden departure.

I hit the turn into our driveway a little too fast, feeling the truck's back end slide. "Sorry," I mumble to Isla, casting her a quick glance. She waves a hand dismissively, leaning forward with anticipation; I can see the same worry etched on her face as mine.

Before I even put the truck in park, Isla flings her door open and bolts toward Olivia, who's standing with her purse in one hand and her phone in the other. I quickly trail behind, catching the tail end of Olivia leaving a message for Charlie.

Levi pulls in behind us, jumping out of his truck and joining the frantic scene in front of the house.

"What's going on, Vi?!" Olivia's voice sharpens as she spots Levi approaching.

He raises his hands defensively, shaking his head, just as confused as the rest of us. "I don't know much. Pops called about five minutes ago and told me to haul ass here."

The distinct sound of rotary blades cuts through the otherwise quiet air, pulling our attention skyward. The familiar green and tan of the Cascadia County Sheriff Department helicopter flies south toward the hospital in Bend.

Olivia gasps, "Is that—?"

Isla's the only one who moves, instinctively gliding toward the distant helicopter. Everett's the only pilot on the force; it has to be him flying it. *Coincidence? Or is he the one flying his sister to the hospital?*

Levi seems to share my anxiety; he kicks at nothing on the ground in frustration, shouting, "Fuck!" His fingers rattle through his short hair before his hands drop. He closes his eyes briefly, trying to steady himself. If anyone understands the weight of dealing with siblings in crisis, it's him.

Instinctively, my hand reaches out to squeeze his shoulder. He shakes his head, and I see the pain in his eyes. "You good?" I ask, even though we both know he isn't.

He nods, looking back at the distant dot of the helicopter. "I got the kids. Text me updates."

"Come on, time to go." I lace my fingers through Olivia's and start to pull her along.

Glancing behind me, I notice Isla hasn't moved from where she stands, her body visibly shaking.

"Isla!" I shout, not out of anger, but to snap her out of it. The sound startles her and I instantly feel bad. "Sorry. Levi's got the kids; we need to go."

As I pull out of the driveway, Olivia's phone rings with a call from Charlie. She answers, her voice shaking slightly as she begins to explain the situation. We all hear the shocked gasps from Charlie echo through the truck.

"Hey," I hear Hayes take the phone from her. "What's going on?" His tone drops, serious and probing. It doesn't take long for Olivia to explain the situation again to Hayes but in the background, Charlie's muffled sobs cut through—heartbreaking. I glance at Olivia and Isla, who mirror the same distress, their faces reflecting a mix of worry and despair.

Reaching out, I place my hand on Liv's lap, trying to instill some confidence. "It'll be okay. She'll be okay."

When she nods, I take the phone from her hands. "Hey, mom there?"

He exhales deeply, a sound heavy with concern. "Yeah, think she's taking a nap. I'll find her, we'll meet you there."

As Hayes leaves to get Connie, I pass the phone back to Liv. The tension rises when Charlie's voice bursts through again, frantic. "I don't understand! How does no one know what's happening?!"

We hear drawers slamming in frustration. "Fuck," she groans, irritation mingling with panic. "I forgot to repack the diaper bag when we got home. I can't find anything!"

It hits me then—she's planning to bring August with them.

"Wait, Charlie, are you sure you want to bring a baby to the hospital?" I ask, urgency threading my voice.

"What?!" Charlie gasps, disbelief clear in her tone.

"Charlie, he's tiny! There are germs, infections, fucking bright lights, and shit."

Charlie hesitates, my point sinking in.

Olivia jumps in. "Levi's at my house! He's great with babies."

Hayes must have returned because he agrees, determination rising in his voice. "Drew's right, Sunshine. Let me call him."

Charlie hesitates for only a moment before yielding. "Fine. We'll see you there," she says, her voice heavy with sorrow. Then, raising her voice, she demands, "Drive safe," before hanging up the phone.

I'm almost to the turnoff for the highway when lights and sirens blare in front of us. Three marked Cascadia County

Sheriff cruisers and one unmarked vehicle fly toward Bend. My arms go rigid, but I pull out immediately behind them, following as they break every speed limit. Our own little police escort into the unknown.

The drive gives me time to shift into mission mode. It's been a long time since I was in the field, but the adrenaline surging through my veins feels familiar—like a rush that sharpens my focus, allowing me to see everything through a wide-angled lens.

Olivia has been taking calls and answering texts, working to piece together who knows what. It helps that she knows everyone at the Sheriff Department and throughout Three Sisters. Meanwhile, Isla sits silently in the back seat, gripping her phone tightly and staring at it, waiting for any word from Everett.

By now, he's likely landed at the heliport and gotten Odessa into the emergency department. The real question is what he'll do next. He can't leave the helicopter there for long, in case Airlink needs to land as well. Which means he'll park it at the private airfield just a few miles away, but someone will need to fetch him and bring him back to the hospital. I mentally start mapping out a route to drop the girls off before heading to get him. I wouldn't put it past him to run to the hospital if nobody arrives quickly enough.

Three of the cruisers head directly to the hospital, but one speeds on, not slowing down.

Glancing at Olivia, I ask, "Do you know who was in that one?"

My gut tells me whoever is driving that cruiser is picking up Everett wherever he's touched down, but I don't want to be wrong and leave Everett stranded out there.

"Will."

"Can you call him for me? Speaker, please." I ask gently, my voice barely above a whisper.

She nods, her fingers trembling as she holds the phone out toward me. We wait in silence, the ringing tones filling the air.

He answers on the first ring as I pull into the hospital parking lot.

"Olivia—"

"She's here too. You picking up Everett?"

"Affirmative."

"Thanks. See you soon." Olivia ends the call just as I throw the truck into the first available parking space. We rush into the Emergency Department, the usual thirty-minute drive condensed into twenty adrenaline-fueled minutes.

A few deputies I recognize from around town stand at the front desk as we storm in. Olivia approaches them, and they motion for us to follow as the medical assistant leads us through two sets of locked doors and down a dimly lit hallway.

We enter a separate waiting room, sealed off from the rest of the department. "You can wait here until we have more information," she says before retreating back the way we came.

"Luke!" Olivia suddenly shouts as I follow her inside. She rushes to him, kneeling in front of his chair and taking his hand in hers. Sweat and dirt cover his entire body, but his vacant stare is focused on a single tile in front of him, lost in his own world.

"Are you okay?" Olivia asks, her voice trembling with concern. "What happened? Were you with Odessa?"

Luke doesn't flinch at her barrage of questions; he doesn't even look at her. His gaze remains fixed on a single tile he's been staring at since we entered the waiting room.

He's clearly in shock, but at least he doesn't seem to have any visible injuries. Mentally, though, he looks like he's been through the wringer. Guilt? Is he blaming himself for Odessa's injuries? My gut tells me that's not it, but something is definitely weighing on him.

I catch the eye of Corbin, one of the deputies I've hung out with at Ponderosa Pine Tavern before, and gesture toward the hallway.

He follows me and steps to the side so that we have privacy.

"Any idea what's going on?"

He runs a finger along his jaw, considering his words. "We don't know much. Turner called us individually and asked us to come, to be here for whatever Luke may need. Said Odessa was being transported by Astor to the hospital, and we needed to be here. LT Will went to pick him up from Powell Butte Road."

"Anything else," I plead, desperate for more information.

"Sorry, man. Nothing. He's keeping everything under wraps."

"That's about what we know too. Thanks."

We walk back into the private waiting room, where Olivia sits on one side of Luke and Isla on the other. Olivia gently rubs circles on his back, a soothing gesture that once would have sent me spiraling. If this situation weren't so intense, I might chuckle at my former worry about something more between them. I know better now than to think Luke is attracted to Olivia. Especially now, looking at the devastation etched across his features, as if he's just had his heart ripped out and stomped on. But I still can't figure out why? Last I heard he couldn't even be in the same room as Odessa.

I lean against the doorframe for a few minutes, analyzing the situation, when a commotion behind me catches my attention.

Everett barrels down the hallway, nearly sprinting past our room. How he got past the keycard doors, I have no idea.

"Astor!" I call out, reaching for his arm and spinning him

around before he can pass. Fury ignites in his eyes, and he pulls back his fist, ready to throw a punch.

It takes just a moment for him to snap out of it and relax, but my patience is wearing thin.

"What the hell's going on, man?" I ask, urgency creeping into my voice.

"Odessa was fucking bit by a goddamn rattlesnake!" he shouts, frustration spilling over.

"A rattlesnake?" I challenged, as loud gasps rippled through the waiting room behind me. "It's March!"

"I know!" he shot back, a tense standoff hanging in the air between us. After a moment, he inhaled sharply and stammered, "I think. Shit! I don't know. Doctor Lewis was speaking in tongues. I dropped her off with Luke; he'll know."

I gesture toward Luke, and Everett's eyes widen as he steps into the room. "Luke! What the hell's going on?" *Just said that.* "Where's Odessa? Is she okay?"

Luke remains motionless, as if he hasn't even heard him. Isla's shoulders sag, shaking her head in disbelief. Tears stream down Olivia's face, and when she looks at me, I try to offer a sympathetic smile, though it's hard to maintain.

Everett glances between the three of them before turning his questioning gaze back to me.

"He hasn't moved since we got here—ten minutes ago—not even an inch."

His mouth opens and closes, but nothing comes out. The situation has us all off-kilter.

"Okay, so what do we do? Just wait?"

I nod. "The doctor will be out any minute to give us an update."

Frustrated, he huffs and takes a seat next to Isla, the tension radiating off him like heat from a fire. Sensing his distress, she gently places a hand on his arm, offering quiet comfort amid the chaos.

Corbin and the other two deputies greet Everett quietly from where they're standing off to the side. He asks them the same questions I did, everyone trying to piece together what's going on but still not having enough information.

"We saw you fly by the house," Isla offers during a quiet moment. "Drew had picked me up, and we had just gotten back to their house when you went by."

His head shifts, confused. "Why was Drew picking you up?"

Isla's gaze nervously bounces between me and Olivia, unknowingly sending mixed signals about our relationship. Fortunately, Everett knows me better than that.

Finally, she says, "I heard a noise and called him."

"Why didn't you call me?" A chuckle escapes me at the hint of jealousy in his tone, knowing I'd probably feel the same.

"You were working!" she replies, exasperated.

"Okay, fine. What was the noise?" He turns to me, his eyes searching for answers, so I glance at Olivia to see if she's listening. *And of course she is.*

Clearing my throat, I say, "Your safe popped open."

"No way," he admonishes the idea right away. "It's one of the best. Even if the batteries died, it wouldn't open by itself."

I shrug, trying to avoid that rabbit hole while we're in the hospital.

"Was anything missing?" he asks, his brow furrowing with concern.

"Not sure—Your Korth and SIG were in there. As well as two envelopes and a little cash."

Isla adds, "Well, one envelope had fallen out."

"What? Back up. What do you mean one had fallen out?"

Isla sighs and then explains everything in detail, starting from the beginning.

Everett's only response is a dismissive "humph."

"What?"

"Math ain't mathin'," he shrugs casually. "Someone had to have opened the safe, which means someone was either in our house or—" I can see the moment he connects the dots with the rest of us. His eyes go comically wide, and he draws in a sharp breath, raising his shoulders. "You don't think—?"

I glance at Olivia, who looks between us, clearly anxious. "Think what?" she prompts gently.

Thankfully, Isla steps in. "It was probably just a fluke, but the only other, not really reasonable thought is... uh, well, ha, a ghost?"

Olivia's head reels back in confusion. "You're joking—" Then she quickly adds, "You're not joking?!"

We all sit in an awkward silence as she glances between us like we're crazy. "I lived in that house for almost a decade and there was nothing ever that weir—OH MY GOD! You think it's DAN!" Her shriek has us all cringing with guilt. It really is crazy to think Dan would be haunting us. *Right?*

Low voices suddenly drift in from the hallway, and I take full advantage of the opportunity to step out and avoid that conversation. I greet Charlie, Hayes, and Connie, filling them in on what little we know and buying myself some time before walking back in.

By the time we all go back in there, the conversation is steered back to Odessa.

For another twenty minutes, questions are rapid fired through out the room, everyone—except Luke—trying to piece it all together.

"Rattlesnake bite?"

"In March?"
"Is that even possible?"
"Was Luke with her the whole time?"
"Maybe they ran into each other?"
*"Who just runs into someone at the end of
    March hiking alone?"*
"Do they even talk?"
"They're not even friends!"
"Why haven't we gotten an update?"

Every person has a different hypothesis, a different question, but I haven't said much or even really paid much attention to who's talking.

I only stare at the still, unmoving man before us. I have seen this man during crisis' and not once has he ever shown any sign of weakness or vulnerability. A rattlesnake bite for what should be acquaintance at most? He's the Sheriff of a small town he grew up in—this should be nothing to him. Yet, here he is—poke him and he'd topple over, statuesque, Luke.

"Seriously, where is the doctor? Or a nurse?"
"Do we need to call anyone else?"
*"She mentioned she was hooking up with
    someone casually, but not who."*
"Hooking up with someone? Since when?"
"Was anyone else there?"
"Dog."
"Dog was there?! Where is he now?"
"Claire and Will have him."
"Wait, who was she dating?"
"Casually seeing. Not dating."
*"What does that mean? She's hooking up with
    someone?"*

"No!" Luke's rough voice suddenly booms through the chaos, and the room falls silent.

"No, what?!" Everett demands, the tension in the room escalating.

"We're—it's—" Luke stumbles over his words, his chest heaving as he struggles to gather his thoughts. "Complicated."

"When the hell did that happen?"

He leans forward, taking a moment to catch his breath, his forearms resting heavily on his thighs. His eyes dart around the room, searching for the right words. "At the beginning of January, we..."

Chapter One

Luke

Three months prior—

My finger hovers an inch from the button that calls the front desk staff to unlock the first door of the secured building. Today is Sunday, so it's probably Rachel on the other side—unless she's too hungover again, in which case it might be Daphne. Daphne's getting married in a few months and going on a once-in-a-lifetime honeymoon that she's trying to save for. The thing about coming here so often is that you start to know the ins-and-outs of not just the place but of the people in it.

To get in and out, two locked doors stand between me and the hallway beyond, each requiring staff assistance to open. I take a deep breath and press the button, not releasing the breath until I hear a satisfying buzz and the lock clicks free.

Once I'm through both doors, the hallway stretches before me, bursting with vibrant artwork and cheerful decorations. It's quiet right now; most residents are either in the dining room for breakfast or still tucked away in their rooms. The aroma of freshly brewed coffee weaves through the air, mingling with faint floral notes from small bouquets positioned carefully on tables. As I reach the dining area, familiar faces bustle about, plates of food being distributed with care at tables draped in colorful tablecloths. My eyes scan the room until they settle on Maddy, sitting in her usual corner spot—the one she picks because she knows I don't like to have my back to the crowd. If I can't blend in, I need to see everything. *Old habits die hard, but they could also save your life.*

Her steel blue eyes seem to twinkle as she glances up, a smile radiating across her face at the sight of me. My heart should be soaring, but instead, it's a dull ache that begins to weigh me down. Instinctively I rub my chest, my boots scuffing softly against the floor as I move toward her.

A few family members of the residents nod hello but mostly keep to themselves, absorbed in their conversations. A pang of jealousy hits as I glimpse their easy interactions.

Maddy nearly jumps from her seat, her long blonde hair cascading around her shoulders. Her makeup, perfectly applied as always, highlights her cheeks with a rosy glow. The leather skirt she wears clings to her confidently, paired with a button-up blouse that hints at her flirtatious side, a few buttons casually left undone. In this moment, she feels like the same Maddy I've always known, unapologetically herself despite the whirlwind of change surrounding us.

"Hi, baby!" She nearly squeals in my ear, her voice full of delight. *Guess it's a good day.*

Before I can dodge her advance, she's trying to wrap her body around mine and kissing me like we aren't in a crowded room. I awkwardly pat her back, trying to subtly push her away, but she only latches on tighter. The familiar scent of her perfume overwhelms me, bringing back memories of easier days. It'd be easy to get lost in the moment with her, but it wouldn't be fair to either of us—or the people in the dining room that are surely staring at us.

It's not often she shows this level of affection, and each time it happens, a pang of guilt creeps in for not fully reciprocating. *She doesn't remember.*

A little bit more forcefully, I untangle her hands from around my neck and set her down. I catch a flicker of disbelief in her eyes before they turn hard, but I remind myself it's for the best.

Quickly, I mask my reaction with a soft smile. "You hungry? It smells amazing in here."

She nods enthusiastically and moves to the buffet, piling fruit and scrambled egg whites onto her plate before selecting a Greek yogurt—the same breakfast she has every day. I grab a cup of black coffee and a muffin, then follow her back to our table, the familiar rhythm settling around us.

"What's on your agenda for the day?" Maddy asks, her grin so casual it stabs me with guilt that makes me feel nauseous. *The same question—every morning. Every. Single. Morning.*

Some days, she's aware of the passing time yet has no recollection of how we got here. Other days, she denies the accident entirely and pleads with me to take her home, insisting it was all a mistake.

"Back to work," I reply, my voice flat.

Her eyes tighten briefly as she chews her eggs, but then she brightens, "You just work sooo much, ya know? It's really admirable how dedicated you are, but—"

I brace myself, sensing the shift in the air that signals this conversation is about to dig into the past.

"What's the point of it all? You know things are going to shift, who'll get the promotion. Why waste your energy?"

She doesn't remember—I chant it like a mantra, hoping to silence the chaos bubbling inside me. Taking my silence as agreement, she continues, but I hold my ground, refusing to engage with her negativity. It wasn't worth the emotional toll to argue with her before the accident, and now it certainly wouldn't be.

"Your friends will always be around," she says, "but I don't get why you're still in Three Sisters when you could be in Bend. You have so much potential and opportunity here."

I can't even muster a smile. She has no idea how wrong she is—how everything has changed in ways that elude her. I want to scream it at her, to let her feel the weight of my misery, because that's how it feels every day. But I don't. I've become an expert at burying my feelings. Unleashing them now would do no good. Instead, I trace my thumb along the plain white mug, staring into its half-empty contents.

"I'll think about it, Mads," I murmur, attempting an encouraging tone, but I can see she knows I won't.

"What are your plans for the day?" I ask, desperate to shift the topic.

In an instant, the disapproval melts from her face like the conversation never happened. A smile blossoms as she excitedly shares her plans—the paperwork to tackle at the office, a house showing for a couple later, and a dinner meeting with a client.

It's the same spiel she gives nearly every day, a routine we've repeated for the past two years and eight months. It echoes the last conversation we had before she left her phone on the table, where I glimpsed a text from that "client" she was meeting for dinner. Just one message from that thread was enough to unravel the facade she had so carefully constructed, exposing a web of lies I never anticipated.

But, of course, she doesn't remember any of this—neither our last breakfast together on that Wednesday morning nor how I left her house without a word. She has no memory of my refusal to argue on the phone or my insistence that we meet to talk in person the next day.

She doesn't remember the deer that darted in front of her car on her way to meet me. She doesn't recall swerving into a semi-truck, the impact crumpling her vehicle like a tin can. She has no recollection of the heartbreak that followed when the doctors told us she may not survive, may never wake up from the coma.

Because when she finally did wake up, it was to a reality fraught with the consequences of a severe traumatic brain injury that led to anterograde amnesia—the real-life version of 'Fifty First Dates.' Only, in this scenario, I'm not Adam Sandler. *I'm the guy she can't forget.*

Chapter Two

Odessa

Winter in Three Sisters is nothing like winter in the city. In fact, nothing in Central Oregon resembles New York at all. Here, the air is crisp with the scent of pine, and the silence is broken only by the soft crunch of snow beneath your boots—a stark contrast to the cacophony of honking horns and hurried footsteps echoing through bustling streets.

But the best part? No one here knows me for my work. It feels like high school all over again, where I'm simply "Everett's little sister." I never thought I'd miss those days as much as I do; yet every time a local greets me and mentions how much they admire my brother, it warms my heart—cold as it has become. While Everett has been off serving in the Army for the last decade, I've been busy building a modeling portfolio, rarely finding ourselves on the same continent, let alone in the same city.

That is, until he decided to move to the small town of Three Sisters, go through the police academy, and settle down among the friends we had grown up with. Suddenly, the distance that separated us began to shrink, and I found myself feeling majorly left out of all the fun they were having.

So when I heard about the "incident" at his work—how he saved a friend named Isla but ended up killing her abusive boyfriend, which led to a standard officer-involved shooting investigation—I didn't hesitate. I chartered a flight and headed straight here.

That was nearly four weeks ago, and as soon as I arrived, I knew I didn't want to leave. After years of traveling, grinding through long hours, and adhering to a rigorous diet and workout schedule, I had forgotten what a normal life felt like— one filled with simple pleasures and genuine connections. Not the kind I had left behind in New York, where friendships often felt more like transactions than true bonds.

That's exactly why I decided to buy a house here. In Three Sisters, despite the turmoil surrounding my brother, I found myself immersed in love and support. Family dinners, laughter around the table—things I hadn't realized how much I missed. It made the past year of surface-level friendships and constant hustle feel meaningless. I finally understood what Charlie had been raving about since she moved here: Three Sisters feels like *home*.

However, there is one relationship I will miss—Eddie and his wife, Monica. Eddie has been my head of security for nearly a decade, taking care of me and treating me like a daughter. When Eddie started working for me, his wife, Monica, became my house manager. Everett and I had just inherited our grand-parents' brownstone, and I had no business taking care of a large property by myself. It made sense to move them both in, renovate a suite for them, and have them live on-site to continue their roles. They quickly became like family to me— the only trusted people I had left in the city. Thankfully, they'll still be there to look after the property while I'm living here. But I've heard nothing but grumbles from Eddie about my safety and not having any of the team with me. When I referred to it as his "practice retirement," he nearly spun off the axle—despite nearing seventy, I think he'd work until he drops if I let him.

When they called before Christmas, I almost booked a flight back to the city right then and there. If Ev hadn't teased me about chartering so many flights and ruining the environment, I likely would have flown back just to spend a few hours with them.

Since then, the holidays have felt like a whirlwind. I spent Christmas Day surrounded by my entire family—a love-filled chaos that was both strange and wonderfully comforting. Then came New Year's Day, which I celebrated with Drew and Hayes—my non-biological brothers, but brothers all the same— racing down the mountain on snowboards. They brought along their team from the agency they started—Elite Forces Security and Contracting. It was mostly a group of Navy SEALs, with a few from other special operations units mixed in.

I may have been the only girl on the slopes, foolishly trying to keep up, but the adrenaline rush was worth every second. Between the friendly banter, my competitive spirit, and the breathtaking views of the snow-covered mountains, I felt more alive than I had in years. Even better was the confidence I felt when I got home. While the guys gave me a hard time, it was all in good fun and never behind my back. I know without a doubt they'd never say a fraction of the things that *she*-who-shall-not- be-named said about me a few weeks ago.

That day solidified everything about my move here and reaffirmed all I stand to gain by stepping back from modeling. Now, the only thing missing is my own space. Charlie and

Hayes have graciously let me stay with them, even though I offered to find a hotel. But with Baby Carrington due next month, I don't want to be a burden during such an important time. Fortunately, I'll be closing on my house just a week before he arrives, and then Connie, Hayes's mother, will move in with them to help.

Until then, I've been driving around a lot, telling everyone I'm getting familiar with the area—even though it's really just an excuse to get out of their hair. There's only so much to see in a town of 2,500 people, so I've started venturing further out to explore the surrounding little towns. That's how I ended up in an even smaller town, where every Sunday I grab coffee at the Little Corner Coffeehouse and sit outside in the freezing cold, yet still sunny weather.

The cutest family walks out the door in their Sunday best, the little girl gushing about getting to church. The mom nods and hurries her along, carrying a coffee and some baked goods, while the dad hoists a laughing toddler onto his shoulders. Their Sunday ritual, at least for the three Sundays I've been here.

I watch as they continue their short walk, tracking them across the road and into a beautiful old white country church. It's a quintessential small-town place, reminding me so much of the church Hayes's parents used to drag us to back when we lived in South Carolina.

Before I know it, my feet are moving on their own, following the family toward the church. I haven't been to a service in so many years that I'm convinced I've forgotten how to behave. But as I step inside, the familiar smell of stale coffee and the sound of hymns wash over me, rekindling memories of childhood Sundays spent with the Carringtons and Reynolds. It's a comforting feeling—one I wouldn't have experienced without Everett, Drew, and Hayes becoming friends when we moved to Heartsville. *My parents would probably catch on fire if they entered a church.*

Without thinking, I lower my head and find a pew near the back; it's much smaller than the others and, thankfully, empty. Looking down, I notice my jeans and silently scold myself for not wearing something nicer. However, as I scan the room, I see a mix of casual and formal attire, which reassures me that I don't stand out too much.

As the anxiety of not knowing the hymn begins to creep in, I spot a projector displaying the lyrics on the wall behind where the pastor will stand. Yet, I can't seem to make my lips move to sing along. *What am I doing here?*

Despite my nerves, I refuse to give up. Out of sheer determination not to cower, I stand tall and try to muster the confidence a world-renowned model should have. Thankfully, when the next song begins, I recognize it and manage to mumble a few "Holy's" on key.

An older man, presumably the pastor, stands at the front of the church in a neatly pressed button-up shirt, tie, and slacks. He introduces himself as Pastor Joseph and welcomes everyone to the service. With his balding head and wisps of gray hair framing his kind, weathered face, he has a warm smile and a gentle demeanor that radiate a lovable, tired grandpa vibe, instantly putting everyone in the congregation at ease. As he invites us to sit, it's clear he has a deep affection for his flock—his voice is soft yet steady, carrying the comfort of someone who has dedicated a lifetime to caring for others.

Glancing around, I see that the church is now full, with nearly every pew occupied except for the small one where I sit.

I settle into my spot, listening as Pastor Joseph briefly discusses upcoming church events before asking us to bow our heads for the prayer list.

With my head lowered, I become vaguely aware of a presence sitting at the end of my pew. My eyes involuntarily flutter open at the intrusion, and my entire body freezes when I catch a glimpse of familiar, square-toed, dark brown, worn-out cowboy boots.

My eyes snap shut, pinching together as tightly as possible as I silently pray, "Please, Lord, anyone but the one man in this area who loathes the sight of me."

I fight the urge to look at the stranger, trying to refocus on Pastor Joseph's words, but I can't. I'm too preoccupied with the realization that it might be Luke Haynes, the sheriff of Cascadia County, sitting next to me—the man who refuses to look at me, talk to me, or acknowledge my presence, despite my never having said two words to him. Oh, and he's best friends with my friends and family—and also my brother's boss!

Only when I hear Pastor Joseph say "Amen," followed by the congregation, do I dare to open my eyes again and sneak a glance out of the corner of my eye. Even with a couple of feet between us, I recognize his large, brooding form, and I feel my breathing turn shaky.

Luke is a force to be reckoned with, standing six feet three, rugged and gruff—Thor-looking, god of sour looks and menace. He won't even look at me, and yet I can barely keep my eyes off him—*but I do, 'cause Connie ain't raise no bitch.*

I'm surprised he chose to sit next to me; not that there are many options, but based on our past encounters, he'd rather stand barefoot on hot coals than be in the same room as me.

Unless... he doesn't know it's me.

Panic begins to set in at the thought that once he realizes who I am, he'll be furious. Not that he'd ever say anything; that would require a conversation. But I can already picture the way his shoulders would stiffen, the brief flicker of anguish in his eyes before they harden, his jaw clenching tight, muscles tensing. Then, as if nothing had happened, he'd look away and avoid eye contact like he has since we met at Charlie and Hayes's wedding. When he looked at me as if I'd ripped his heart out on the dance floor and stomped on it, even though I'd never met him before.

I simply resemble the love of his life—the one he lost in a car accident, even though she didn't actually die.

Chapter Three

Luke

I'm late.

I'm never late to church; I attend the last service to ensure just that. I should have had more than enough time to see Maddy and make it here. Hell, I'm often the first one in the parking lot, waiting to go in. But today, I lingered in my truck a little longer than usual in the Memory Care Facility parking lot.

My conversation with Maddy, though brief, left me unsettled. It's always been *the way* she says things that bothers me. She never outright claimed I wouldn't become sheriff because of Dan's connections to the town and his father being the sheriff, but her comments had a way of insinuating that. It's as if she's trying to coax me into bending to her will. Sometimes I wonder how different things would have been if I *had* moved away, fully committed to Maddy and married her. I would have been miserable, but maybe everyone else would have gotten their happy endings.

Ten minutes late, I finally find parking on the street and climb out of my truck, hurrying toward the church. I hear the familiar sound of the pastor's voice as I enter the room, and thankfully, no one seems to notice my late arrival. My gaze quickly sweeps over the crowd, scanning the faces in the rows ahead, but everything seems per usual.

Quietly, I follow the back wall toward the pew I always choose—the small one at the back, where I can keep my back to the wall. Because of its size, it's almost always empty, except for the occasional passerby wanting to avoid the onlookers.

Thus the reason for my surprise when my sight lands on the last person I ever expected to see here: Odessa Astor. Her white-blonde hair is pulled back into a tie, though it still spills down the back of her berry-colored sweater. There's an effortless grace to her posture as she bows her head in prayer, giving me a tantalizing moment to admire her flawless face and how the dark pink of her sweater compliments her ivory skin.

She's the one woman in nearly three years—longer, if I'm honest—who can make my heart race and my palms sweat. My weakness—an Achilles heel if you will.

The one who makes my skin crawl and tingle at the same time.

The one I can't wait to see yet dread running into all at once.

The one who unknowingly holds the power to unravel the carefully constructed walls I've built around my heart.

The one who could be the twin of my haunting past.

She's gorgeous—an actual supermodel coveted by every man who would do anything to be in her presence. Yet, simply looking at her threatens to send me to my knees—either to beg for her attention or to plead for forgiveness for wanting her.

I sit on the worn bench seat, staring at the back of the head in front of me, pretending to pay attention to the prayer rather than the vixen beside me. I've spent years training my facial expression to remain impassive and my body language neutral, but every time she's near, I feel like a live wire on the verge of short-circuiting.

What is she doing here? Is it for me?

Most people from town either go to the church in Three Sisters or stay close by on Sundays. It's a small town, so most know I attend this one, but it's not often discussed. This church is closer to Bend, so there's no real reason for her to be here unless she's intentionally seeking me out.

But I doubt that. Based on her demeanor at Christmas, she seems to have given up on trying to talk to me. *Why does that thought cut so deep?*

Despite hearing from her friends that she looks like Maddy, I wasn't prepared for the flood of emotions that hit me when I first saw her. The first time we met was a year ago at Charlie and Hayes's wedding—her childhood friends. She walked right up to me, trying to introduce herself, but when I saw her, it nearly knocked the wind out of me. I couldn't even find the words; I just nodded and quickly made my escape. Up until Christmas, it was much the same. If she commented on something I'd said while we were with friends, I'd give a curt nod and avoid looking her way.

Christmas, though? Not once did I feel her gaze. It was as if I didn't exist. The silence between us was both a relief and a torment—a paradox I thought I craved. Not that it matters; she'll be gone soon anyway. Once her brother, a deputy at my department, is cleared of any wrongdoing, she'll return to traveling the world and gracing the covers of magazines.

The prayer ends and Odessa slowly opens her eyes. Her chin lifts defiantly, and in that moment, I know she recognizes that I'm sitting next to her. It's a small but powerful connection, and I can almost feel the tension crackling in the air between us. I've gone from being unable to be around Odessa because she reminded me of Maddy to now struggling with my attraction to her because she's nothing like her—yet I crave to know more. *A line I'm not willing to cross.*

I barely listen to the announcement that they need a few minutes to set up and suggest we introduce ourselves to the person next to us. Laughter ripples through the room, a familiar sound among the same faces every Sunday. Except today.

I turn my shoulders and angle my knees toward her, encroaching on the space between us.

Yet she remains painfully still, staring ahead as if she's trying to make herself invisible—like a rabbit caught in a snare, praying the fox doesn't see her. *For some reason, that really pisses me off.*

"Odessa," I say, keeping my voice low, but it feels charged, like a match struck in the dark.

She gasps, her lips parting in surprise, as if she didn't think I knew her name. Then again, I've never spoken a word to her, let alone said her name.

When she regains her composure, it's with a curt "Luke," the sharpness of her tone almost makes me smile.

"There a reason you're here?" I ask, the question edged with what sounds like irritation, masking my genuine curiosity.

She glances around the room slowly, as if implying I should already know why. Her eyes dart back to me, piercing and defiant—daring me to question her. *It's attractive as hell.*

"You followin' me, darlin'?" I can't help the teasing lilt in my words, even as I struggle to discern whether I'm being bitter or flirty.

That earns me a full stare-down, her lip curling in disgust. "Don't ever call me that again—I'm not my daddy's darlin' and I'm *definitely* not yours."

Something about the venom in her voice ignites a fire within me, tempting me to burn the world down for her, to unleash all the anger brewing inside just to see her smile.

But then, like flipping a switch, she tips her chin up, indifference sliding into place like armor—one I'm quite used to adopting myself.

"And no, I'm not following you." She rolls her eyes dramatically, scoffing as if I'm the most ridiculous thing she's ever seen. "Besides, I was here first."

"Today," I drawl, teasing but with my heart pounding faster. "Technically."

"So? Why does that matter?" She shoots back, crossing her arms defensively.

"This is my church. My safe place. It's where I've gone for years to escape town and the prying eyes, where I can just be Luke Haynes, the person—not Sheriff Luke Haynes, the guy who deals with everyone else's problems." The weight of my words hangs heavily in the air between us.

For a moment, I see the shock on her face before it flickers through a myriad of emotions. *Guilt, maybe?* "Sh—ooot," she mutters, glancing around as if to apologize for her near slip-up in a church, color flooding her cheeks until they match her berry-colored sweater.

Something inside me softens—a blend of intrigue and an unexpected sense of protectiveness.

"I didn't know this was your church," she admits, the tension in her voice slightly less stubborn now. "I go to the coffeehouse every Sunday morning to stay out of Charlie and Hayes's hair. I just overheard a family mention it, saw it from the coffeehouse, and needed—" She trails off, and the silence settles thickly around us, gnawing at my conscience.

I watch her, noticing the way her fingers fidget at the edges of her sweater, her eyes darting away as if she's caught in an internal struggle.

She shakes her head and sighs. "I'll go."

The sudden panic that floods through me at the thought of

her leaving surprises me. "Wait," I blurt out, my voice louder than I intended. "Don't go." My hand reaches toward hers, hovering near it before I let it fall.

I try to offer a charming smile, but it comes off more like a grimace. Damn it, I'm terrible at this—at being warm and welcoming, especially around her.

"I'm sorry for being a jerk. It's not very Christian of me to kick someone out of church." I can't help but think of everything she must be dealing with, especially given the weight of her brother's problems. Hell, I feel that same burden myself.

She hesitates before sitting back down, but the silence stretches between us, heavy with the tension of unspoken words and unresolved issues.

"Odessa—" I say her name softer this time, a tentative bridge across the chasm of our uncertainty. Yet, I can still see her holding her breath, bracing herself for whatever comes next.

She refuses to look at me, and I wait, my gaze steady and unwavering, until she finally meets my eyes. This is it—my moment to extend the olive branch that I should have offered the first day she came back to be there for Everett and Isla.

"Don't let me stop you from coming here," I say, my voice low but firm. "My issues aren't your responsibility. If you need to be here, then be here."

Her vibrant blue eyes search mine, probing for any hint of dishonesty, any flicker of insincerity. When she sees only sincerity reflected back at her, it's as if I witness a small crack beginning to form in the wall she has erected around herself.

She nods slowly, that single, simple action feeling like the heartbeat of something monumental.

"Okay," she whispers, her voice barely above a breath before turning her attention back to the front of the church. That one word feels like a monumental bridge being built between us—one I'm not sure I'm ready for but can't help wanting to cross.

As the sermon begins, I struggle to focus. The words blend together at first, my mind solely fixated on the woman beside me. I attempt not to look at her, but it's a losing battle; her presence is magnetic.

Suddenly, a small snort escapes her, breaking through the tension. I snap my head to her, surprised to see she's genuinely enjoying what is being said. The curve of her lips and the faint twinkle in her eyes ignite a mix of curiosity and annoyance within me.

Tuning back in, I realize the sermon is about forgiveness, and I can't help but feel the irony prick at my chest. *Of course, he's choosing this subject—why wouldn't he serve my vulnerabilities on a silver platter to my biggest weakness?*

"Forgiveness is often misunderstood," he begins, the sincerity in his voice wrapping around me like a chain. "It doesn't mean we condone wrongdoing or forget what happened. It's an act of releasing our anger and desire for revenge."

The C.S. Lewis quote he says hits home: "To be a Christian means to forgive the inexcusable because God has forgiven the inexcusable in you." *Damn it, right to the chest.*

I glance sideways at Odessa, who seems drawn deeper into the sermon, her roiling emotions flickering across her features. My thoughts drift back to my own struggles with forgiveness— the mountains of anger I carry and the resentment that clings to me like a lingering shadow.

"Holding onto grudges can weigh heavily on our hearts," the sermon continues. "It can lead to bitterness and isolation. But when we choose to forgive, we free ourselves from that burden."

Bitterness—check. Isolation—check.

It's like he's peeling back the layers of my heart, forcing me to acknowledge truths I'm not ready to face. Yet, even as he speaks, I know I'm still too angry, too lost, and too hurt to let go of the pain that feels like a second skin.

As he wraps up his concluding remarks, signaling it's time to pass around the tithing box while he offers a prayer, I move mechanically, my mind barely engaged.

Before I step into my role to help, my hand moves instinctively, gently tapping the side of Odessa's thigh. "See you next week," I say, my tone coming out more like a demand than a question. I don't wait for her response; I recognize I'm being reckless, but something about her makes it difficult to stop myself.

I make my way down the aisle, pausing to help pass the box between the rows, the murmurs of soft conversations swirling around me. Each step feels heavier as I glance back at Odessa, searching for that fleeting connection, yearning to catch her eye one last time.

But by the time I return to my seat, she's already gone, leaving an ache I can't quite place. I'm not sure how to feel about that yet. It doesn't matter, though; I have a girlfriend, and there's no room for the disappointment blooming within me.

Chapter Four

Odessa

"Ouch! Motherfucker. Again?" Delta winced and examined his index finger like it had betrayed him. He's been on mail duty in the Cascadia Property Management office since everything has been in disarray for the last few weeks—taking a break from saving the world, or whatever the EFSC guys do—to help Olivia and Charlie.

Olivia, the main bitch in charge, is still off duty since the car accident in which *he*-who-shall-not-be-named slammed his car into hers, sending her into oncoming traffic where she was struck by another vehicle. Drew has been refusing to let her work more than a few hours a week since they found out she was expecting that night at the hospital. With her barely out of the first trimester, he's not taking any chances with her health. *Honestly, I think he's just projecting. But we are going to let him get away with it for a bit because we're all still feeling a little rocked too.*

Isla, Charlie and Olivia's assistant, was attacked by her ex-boyfriend shortly before he went after Olivia—the real asshole in this whole situation. That's why Everett shooting him was completely justified in my opinion. I can only hope the detective assigned to review the case, along with anyone else involved, feels the same way.

This leaves Charlie, who is now eight months pregnant, doing most of the work around the office. The guys on Hayes's team have stepped in to help, but to be honest, paperwork isn't their forte. I've heard Delta complain more about a paper cut than Olivia and Isla did the night they were both attacked by Jeff. For a super jacked guy covered in tattoos, he's a real wimp.

"You get blood on that notarized paper and I'll make sure Hayes kicks your ass," Charlie huffs at him.

"Pfft, not scared of him. Heard he's the most merciful of us all," he jokes, throwing a wink over his shoulder at her. When Isla's ex-boyfriend attacked her, she threatened him that if he went after Olivia, he better hope it was Hayes that found him and not Drew or Liam. Knowing Hayes my entire life, I'd say she was spot on. He's not a big softy, but he does have a tender heart. Drew, on the other hand, would've destroyed him without blinking, and Liam, Liam would've smiled the whole time he did it.

Liam chuckles from his seat at Olivia's desk, where he's immersed in updating client files. He's tall, towering even above my six foot frame, with a solid build that has him resembling the hulk. Today, he sports a skull beanie, a quirky reminder of a bet gone wrong that left him with a newly shaved head. It surprisingly suits him, adding a touch of character to his otherwise discreet demeanor.

Everett had warned me upon my return that Liam was reserved, but I hadn't fully grasped the depth of that statement. He's a constant presence around the group, his kindness radiating in subtle gestures—a door held open, picking up the tab—but his personality is as quiet as a soft breeze. He rarely speaks, and when he does, his words are carefully chosen, never straying into the territory of his own life.

Thinking about Luke feels the same, but he isn't nearly as tight-lipped around others. It's only been two days since I ran into him at the church, and I haven't stopped obsessing over it. It was the first time he actually spoke to me, and damn, it felt good. Just having a bit of his attention? Oof. I found myself letting my guard down, becoming more vulnerable. Usually, I'm the one who stands up for myself—perhaps a bit too "mouthy" and opinionated for my own good, or so I've been told. But with Luke, he practically pulled my vulnerability out of me.

Wack! My thoughts are abruptly interrupted as something squishy hits me in the head and bounces off. I glance up to see Charlie, a teasing grin on her face, having just thrown a stress ball my way.

"Hello! We are talking to you," she says, her tone playful yet pointed.

"Sorry," I mumble, not offering any excuses. There's no way I'm about to admit I was lost in thought about Luke. I haven't told anyone about my run in with him on Sunday and that I'm still dizzy from him actually speaking to me.

Charlie narrows her eyes slightly but lets it go. "Delta was asking what your plan is. Do you have to head back to New York soon, or are you sticking around a bit longer?"

I hesitate, feeling a familiar pang of guilt. The only person I've told about buying a house is Everett. I haven't shared anything with Charlie yet, and I can't pinpoint why. So much has changed between us over the years, and none of it is on her —it's all me, keeping everyone at arm's length.

A resigned sigh escapes me as I meet her gaze, acutely aware that I've been a less-than-stellar friend. Her strawberry-blonde hair shines in the light, looking more strawberry than blonde these days, and her face is just a bit rounder now that she's due next month. Simply looking at her smiling face reminds me of why I'm doing this—moving here.

"I'm staying. I bought a house and everything."

"What?!" she shrieks, her excitement palpable as she processes the news. Her eyes light up, and the smile on her face turns slightly wobbly. "You're staying? Like really, really staying?" In the blink of an eye, she starts crying.

She hugs me first, and then Delta pulls me into a hug next. "Congrats, Dess! Glad you're staying. Hey, uh, you need a roommate?"

"Uh, no."

"Come on, I can mow the lawn, take out the garbage—anything to get me out of living with four other guys."

Charlie ignores him, just as I do. "So whose house did you buy?"

When I give her a confused expression, she chuckles at herself. "Sorry! Once you live here long enough, you know everyone and where they live."

Hayes strides into the office, his dark brown hair slightly tousled, just a hint of troublemaker in his eyes. He's barely taller than me, but his assertive presence fills the room as he quickly makes his way to Charlie. Leaning down, he plants a kiss on her belly, a grin spreading across his face.

"What's all the yelling over here?" he asks, his voice playful, joy radiating from his affection for her.

Charlie shoos him away but beams at him. "Odessa bought a house! Here!"

Seeing her excitement adds to the guilt I already feel towards our friendship, but I smile back and nervously glance at Hayes.

At first, he looks skeptical, but then he shakes it off and his grin returns. "About damn time we have the gang together again living in one place."

"True. Now we need to get Mom to sell her house," I respond, trying to divert the attention from being all on me. I've been calling Hayes's mom "Mom" since seventh grade, the day she explained to me that starting my period wasn't the end of the world. She took me to the store, walked me through every product, and then treated me to a burger and a chocolate milkshake. I realized then that she was more of a mom to me than my own. When I mentioned it to my mother, she simply told the maid to add tampons to the shopping list.

"Guarantee once she holds the baby, she'll be calling her real estate agent," Charlie adds, looking at Hayes with a knowing smile.

The two of them are everything I didn't know I wanted. They've survived so much in such a short time together, and now they're expecting a baby. It feels like they've grown into the stable adults with careers they love, while I'm left starting over. What am I going to do if I'm not modeling? I won't deny it has drained the life out of me, but it also provided a paycheck—a reason to wake up and be productive. Now, I have more money than I could ever need, but I feel lost without a purpose.

Maybe that's why I'm so drawn to being here—hoping to establish what I've always wanted: roots.

Chapter Five

Luke

The phone buzzed wildly on my desk, snapping me out of the daydream I shouldn't have been having about a certain someone I can't seem to get my mind off of.

I answer before the second ring. "Sheriff Larkin," I greet, trying to shake off the lingering thoughts. Bradley Larkin is the newly appointed sheriff of our neighboring county, Deschutes. There aren't many who understand the challenges I face every day, but he's quickly becoming one of them. "How's it going?"

"That's a loaded question, and you know it. You get Woodyard's call yet?"

The mention of Woodyard has me sitting up in my chair, unease settling deep in my gut. Jordan Woodyard is one of our detectives assigned to the new Central Oregon Drug Enforcement team. With over twenty departments in our area and surrounding regions and drug trafficking on the rise, each department decided to allocate a member to form a specialized task force.

"Not yet," I respond with a sigh. "What's going on?"

"We've had our third bust in the last two weeks—same

packaging, same supplier, different colored Subaru," *Shit.* I'd heard about the last two busts from Jordan, and I'm glad we're on to something, but it's only a matter of time until we see the drugs hitting the streets.

"Big players in the game?" I question, trying to gauge what Larkin is thinking about the bust.

"Not really. Man named Freddy Rasbia," he continues. "Clearly just a courier, but he wouldn't give up the name of where he was going. Same story as the last two. We're looking at over 60,000 counterfeit Oxycodone pills, a few hundred grams of heroin and fentanyl, plus a substantial amount of cash."

"Anything out of the ordinary?" I lean back in my chair, rubbing my temples, trying to ease the tension that's been building all morning. Unfortunately, all of this has become all too common in this line of work. While that's still a large amount of drugs, it's not surprising given the current state of the world we live in.

"A couple dozen vials of something, but we aren't sure what they are yet." I can practically hear him shrug through the phone. Interesting, but not exactly unusual considering the other items found. It could be anything from experimental drugs to some new designer substances hitting the streets. There's always something new trying to break into the market, making our jobs even more challenging.

"Thanks for the update." I lean forward, already shifting my focus to the next steps, mentally preparing for the work ahead. I need to get a debrief out to the department—one that I know the team will take seriously but won't scare the residents of Three Sisters when they inevitably hear about it. It's a delicate balance, considering this town is full of busybodies who love to gossip.

With that thought in mind, I walk into the break room, only

to find Corbin and Ambrose, two of my deputies, engrossed in conversation over their lunches.

Corbin sits at the table, a picture of confidence. His neatly styled dark hair frames a defined face, accentuating his sharp jawline and bright blue eyes that always carry a hint of mischief. He has that classic charm, the kind that makes him instantly likable, always ready with an easy smile.

Across from him, Ambrose leans back in his chair, his tousled hair falling just right over a relaxed face that exudes a friendly, approachable vibe. His light brown eyes add to his boyish charm, making people feel instantly at ease.

For a moment, I look between the two of them and wonder when the hell the department got so soft. Maybe I'm just used to hanging out with Hayes and the guys on his team, who always have a scowl and an attitude, but my guys look like they work for the fire department and rescue kittens rather than catch bad guys.

Typically, I'd grab my coffee and head back to my desk, tuning out whatever chatter filled the air. But upon hearing the name of the woman who has been occupying my thoughts, I decide to linger a little longer—pretending to tidy the small area that is already spotless.

"You're telling me, Odessa—the hottest woman I have ever seen—just bought my pediatrician's house?" Corbin exclaims, disbelief evident in his voice, eyes wide as if he can't quite comprehend his luck.

The only pediatrician in town is Cecil Gravenstine, a well-respected doctor who recently retired. The Gravenstine family built a brand-new house in the neighborhood behind mine, with our properties bordering each other. After moving in, they decided to head to Arizona for a fresh start, leaving the house up for grabs.

The realization hits me—Odessa and I now share a fence;

our backyards could form one giant yard with the removal of some boards. I quickly admonish the thought; there's no reason for us to share anything, much less a yard. Even though she does have a pool and the thought of her in a bikini threatens to unravel me.

"Yep," Ambrose replies, nodding. "Delta was telling us last night at Ponderosa Pine."

As they continue to rattle on, oblivious to my inner turmoil, I can't help but feel a mix of excitement and dread at the thought of living so close to the woman who has captured my attention—and, by the way these idiots are talking, the attention of every other single man in the county.

Part of me wonders if that's for the best—if she's off the market and dating someone, then I can let go of any romantic notions and focus on being a good neighbor. *Romantic notions? No, just no.* But that devil on my shoulder wants me claim her as my own before any other man has the chance. I know I can't do that; *I won't do that.* It wouldn't be fair to Maddy and our situation, and even more so, it wouldn't be fair to Odessa.

Rather than listen any longer, I grab my coffee and storm back to my office. Focusing on my caseload feels safer—a balm against the turmoil of wanting something, or someone, that would only bring more complications. Thankfully, there's plenty to keep me occupied between Everett's case coming up for review soon, the CODE team working on the largest drug trafficking bust in Central Oregon, and managing an entire department.

Chapter Six

Odessa

Chasing the 'Bod Squad' all day left me gasping for breath, my muscles protesting in delightful agony as I rushed down the mountain after them. Healthy competition has never been my forte. Ruthless competition, however, is where I thrive. Still, I may be out of my league against these guys. Delta is a former Delta Operator, and Lincoln, Liam, Cooper, and Leo are former Navy SEALs. They have no self-preservation, no fear. It's exactly like it was when we went last week, although now I have a better understanding of their capabilities and can strategize accordingly—or at least, capitalize on their weaknesses. For instance, Delta tends to ride a little tighter on the right side when we reach a specific part of the mountain, which allows me to predict exactly where to crank a turn and blast him with snow, throwing him off balance. Cooper, well, Cooper has an affinity for showing off in front of anyone he deems may be a "hot chick," so he's easy to distract with a well-timed comment or gesture in the opposite direction.

By the end of the day, I can honestly say I held my own against them. Now all I want is a hot bath and to collapse into bed. Unfortunately, the guys have other plans—they want to have dinner at the lodge. And since I rode with Delta and Lincoln, I'm stuck.

I grump my way into the lodge, but as soon as the warm, rustic air envelops us, mingling with the scent of roasted meat and rich beer, I start to feel better. The hostess's eyes widen as if she's spotted a pack of wolves striding in, and I can't help but smirk at the scene. It takes her a moment too long to pick her jaw up off the floor when the five of them stop in front of her. It's comical to watch how women gawk over them and then glare at me, as if I'm the one blocking their path to the men. It's really foolish on their part because I'd gladly play the wing-woman for any of the guys. The easiest way to get into their pants would be to befriend me, but girls tend to be dumb and opt to hate on me instead. Whatever; it's nothing I'm not used to.

Our server, however, is great—completely immune to the guys' charm, even as they lay it on thick. She looks to be in her mid-thirties, with long, dark hair elegantly braided down her back. Her features are striking, with high cheekbones and warm brown eyes that exude both confidence and friendliness. She smiles politely as she takes our order, her demeanor effortlessly professional. Then, with innate grace, she navigates the room, balancing trays with ease and efficiently attending to the needs of other patrons—all while maintaining an air of calm composure.

"How much do you want to bet I can get her number before the end of the night?" Cooper grins confidently, revealing a cheeky smile beneath his well-groomed mustache. He has a rugged charm, with tousled hair and a strong jawline that he uses to full effect as he plots his next move.

"No!" I scold him. "Do not work any charm on her. If she

were batting her eyes at you, that'd be one thing. But she's clearly not interested."

Cooper gasps dramatically, as if I hurt his feelings.

With one arch of my eyebrow, he concedes, raising his hands in surrender. "Fine, fine. I'll behave... for now." I roll my eyes at his theatrics, knowing his resolve will likely crumble before the night is over—better yet, before my beer is gone.

The conversation shifts to Isla and Everett when Delta asks, "Where are you at with getting that asshole behind bars?" He's referring to Lincoln's probe into Isla's father and his partner, Cyrus.

"I've been sending whatever I find anonymously to Luke, but to be honest, there isn't much concrete evidence. Those fuckers sure know how to cover their tracks."

"You think they won't get charged with anything?" I ask, recalling our suspicions that Isla's dad was involved in murdering his coworker and passing it off as a logging accident. They were awful to Isla and Everett during the investigation, even dragging the media into it to slander them. Thankfully, that was shut down quickly, and Lincoln is a whiz on the computer.

"Honestly, no. Everything I look into leads to a dead end." I can tell it bothers him by the heavy sigh he lets out. Lincoln hates being one-upped when it comes to solving mysteries, especially when the protection of his friends is at stake. Not since Charlie's stalker had the best of them—he's hyper-vigilant now.

"Something will come up, I'm sure." I nudge Linc's elbow lightly. "If not, at least they're being run out of town." The Mitchells and the Waltons have dissolved their practice and listed their mansions for sale. Occasionally, one of us will spot them around town, but for the most part, they're keeping a low profile. I feel bad for Isla, but coming from shitty parents myself, I can honestly say that not having them in your life is much better.

Lincoln nods, but his gaze drifts away, and I can tell he's over the conversation.

"This place is pretty cool," Cooper chimes in from across the table, fingers combing through his mustache as he gives the room a proper once-over. To me, it looks like the standard ski-bum lodge, but what do I know?

"We should come here more often."

"Any place with a bar is cool to you," I reply pointedly.

He chuckles, raising his beer to emphasize his point. "Not wrong there."

Delta, seated beside me, shakes his head. "We should've gone to Ponderosa Pine tonight." Ponderosa Pine Tavern is the restaurant my friend Ethan opened after leaving the NFL—the best spot in Three Sisters, whether you want a night out or just a casual meal. The food is consistently top-notch, and the atmosphere is unbeatable.

Leo grumbles noncommittally, his baby face twisting into a scowl. Deep down, we all know he enjoys it there just as much as the rest of us; his annoyance stems from his crush on Maisie, who has a past with Ethan. Unfortunately for Leo, he and Ethan couldn't be more different—at least when it comes to looks. Leo's face is slightly rounder, with lighter hair, while Ethan sports longer dark locks and a stubbled beard. It's like comparing Armie Hammer to Joe Manganiello.

"So, Dess, the rumor is you're staying in Three Sisters—bought a house and didn't tell anyone," Cooper says, changing the subject.

"I did..." I reply, a hint of uncertainty creeping into my voice, clearly prompting Cooper to say more.

"Excellent. What's a guy gotta do to be your roommate?"

"Fuck off," Delta groans. "I called dibs and asked first."

"Ha! No. To both of you. The only way I'm having a room-mate is if I'm fu—" My voice trails off as a large hand clamps down on my shoulder. I go wide-eyed, noticing Cooper snick-ering across from me. Then I risk a glance at Delta, who has a huge grin. *Please, dear God, don't let it be Luke.*

When I finally turn to look up at the person touching me, I see shaggy dark hair and the scruff of a five o'clock shadow—Ethan. The biggest sigh of relief comes out of me which causes him to look at me sideways and raise an eyebrow.

Then with a smirk, he says, "Don't filter yourself on my account."

"If I'm *fucking* him," I shoot back without shame. Ethan knows I have the mouth of a sailor and the attitude to match.

He laughs. "There you go, men. Any of you planning to go against your bosses and start railing their sister so you all don't have to be roommates anymore?"

"I'd take a bullet for less," Cooper replies automatically. Delta taps his short beard as if contemplating it, but I throw my napkin at him.

"No! Absolutely not. Don't even think about it."

Even Liam cracks a smile at the thought, and I roll my eyes at all of them. "What do you want, Flacco?" I demand, narrowing my eyes at him.

"Just wanted to say hey on my way to the bar. Luke's taking a call." That's when my stomach drops and I turn to see Luke behind him. I've seen Luke in uniform, in casual clothes with wranglers and boots, and even dressed up for Christmas dinner. But Luke in snow pants and a long-sleeve compression shirt? *HOT.* Now I'm the one struggling to pick my jaw off the floor while mentally counting the ridges of his abs from here.

Luke notices us looking, his eyes bouncing around the table, and when they land on me, a ghost of a smile crosses his lips. *So maybe we're on good terms now? Is that really all it took—one awkward conversation in a church? Or is he feeling the push and pull between us, too?*

Ethan looks between us and then smirks like he's in on a secret no one else knows about. Personally, I want to smack it off him but before I can he excuses himself.

"*Anyway,* I'm going to grab a beer. Catch ya later."

Leo's shoulders visibly relax once Ethan walks away. Leo may have been a Navy SEAL, but I know for a fact that Ethan has kept up with his workouts since leaving the NFL, and he has at least thirty pounds and a couple inches on Leo. Not that I think Leo would ever stir up drama, but I can tell being around Ethan rubs him the wrong way.

It's Delta who speaks first once Ethan is out of earshot. "What the hell was that? Do you have a thing with Ethan?"

"No!" I exclaim, my voice a bit louder than intended, and I quickly lower it. "I've known Ethan since long before anyone even knew where Three Sisters was."

"When did you meet him?" Delta presses, clearly intrigued.

"We met at a dinner one night—our friends tried to set us up." This was back when he had just finished his rookie year with the Vikings, and I was still trying to find my footing in the modeling industry.

"Did you?" Cooper chimes in, punctuating his question with a ridiculous sexual gesture that makes everyone—but me —laugh.

"God, no. I was dating someone, but we weren't public about it. Even back then, I could tell he was wrapped up in someone." The moment Ethan started talking about his home-town, a wistful look settled on his face, revealing that he was thinking more about a person than a place. When I called him out on it, he clammed up at first. I'm good at prying, though, and eventually, he told me all about his best friend who suddenly stopped talking to him after they confessed some things to each other. I might be the only person in Three Sisters who knows the full story—his side of things, anyway—but I won't tell a soul. That's for them to figure out—and for me to maybe nudge in the right direction.

"And no one knows what that's about?" Leo prompts.

I sigh loudly and respond, "Nope," prompting everyone to drop the conversation.

I glance once more at Ethan, who is sitting at the bar. Luke has now joined him, and his body is angled toward our table. The optimistic part of me hopes it's because he wants to look at me, while the logical part knows he's just doing what all the other guys in our group do—keeping an eye on their surroundings to avoid surprises from behind.

I'm not surprised he didn't say anything to the group when his phone call ended, but I can't help but feel disappointed by that. The longer dinner goes on, the more confused I'm left feeling. Last week, he clearly said he wanted me to go to church tomorrow. But does he actually want that? Or was it just a pity invite because he felt bad for being kind of a dick at first?

Still, I swear I can feel him watching me as we finish our meal, even though I refuse to look.

I'm not sure where we'll go from here, but I refuse to make myself smaller around him anymore. If anything, I find myself wanting his attention on me now. That's why I smile a little more than usual and laugh a little louder at whatever dumb jokes the guys make, determined to make him think I'm having the time of my life and that he's not affecting me one bit.

Eat your heart out, Sheriff Hottie.

Chapter Seven

Odessa

It is crisp.

The tiniest pricks begin stinging my lungs as I hike around Smith Rock. It's a beautiful sunny day, with birds chirping and the sky bright and clear, but the cold is undeniable—like fingers stiff and aching, cheeks tingling, and a nose running kind of cold. Yet, I love it; it's a sharp slap in the face, reminding me that I'm alive and breathing. I add it to my mental gratitude list: the ability to endure this biting chill as I trek along the canyon, taking in the stunning views of the rock formations and the winding river below.

There are a few fellow hikers scattered along the trail, but for the most part, it's just me and the vast expanse of nature, a reminder of how small and insignificant I am in the grand scheme of things.

I pause to watch three climbers scaling the wall with what seems like just the tips of their fingers and a single toe. It's the real-life version of 'Free Solo' unfolding right before me, and I can't help but feel a mix of awe and fear. I like chasing adrenaline as much as the next girl raised by three older brothers trying to prove herself, but even that is too much for me—especially during the winter.

As I watch, my fingers flex inside my puffer coat, feeling the wind whip around me, carrying the sound of the climbers' laughter and shouts.

For a moment, I take in the breathtaking beauty of Central Oregon, savoring the evening light. I know it's getting dark, and I should start heading back, but the setting sun holds my gaze captive.

By the time I reach the parking lot, only a handful of vehicles remain, scattered like forgotten toys. My new car—a pristine white Cullinan—looks out of place here, its elegant lines and polished finish stark against the rugged landscape. It's something I hadn't considered when I asked Eddie for advice on a safe vehicle for snowy conditions. He suggested so many large SUVs that I ultimately chose the smallest option, not even glancing at the price tag, just relieved it wasn't a tank.

I hurry toward it, eager to escape the cold.

Just as I reach for the door, something catches my attention.

I pause, straining my ears to decipher a noise that suddenly punctuates the quiet.

Then I hear it again—a low whimper, almost a growl, coming from beyond the low wooden fence, deep in the sagebrush.

I've been warned about all the dangerous wildlife in Central Oregon by the guys and have read every cautionary sign posted at the trailhead. But something about that noise doesn't sound like a wild animal poised to attack; it sounds like an injured one.

For a brief moment, I consider walking away, but I can't shake the feeling that I should help. I reach into my pack—the one Everett insisted I bring, even though I swore I wouldn't need it—and grab the flashlight, cursing him for being right.

I shine it toward the sound, but no glimmering eyes reflect back at me.

With a resigned sigh, I feel for the pepper spray pistol that Everett insisted I bring. It's like bear spray, but designed for people, highly effective at getting them to do what I want. I hop over the fence and venture deeper into the underbrush, scolding myself the entire time as I listen for the noise—each step growing heavier as uncertainty gnaws at me.

Before I've gone more than twenty feet, I hear it again—off to my right, but farther out. I keep moving, hoping the sound will grow louder as I get closer.

As I continue to shine the flashlight in that direction, I also try to watch my footing in the dimming light. The ground is littered with rocks, pokey bushes, and random holes that I'm sure, given my luck, I'll trip over.

Finally, I see it. Not menacing eyes or a threatening snarl, just a black-and-tan shape lying on the hard, frozen ground beneath a tree. A big dog sprawled on its side, low whimpers escaping its mouth.

I approach slowly, then realize I should probably announce myself to avoid startling the injured animal.

"Uh, hi, Pupper?" I cautiously call out, hoping to ease its fear. Its tail wags weakly in response, but it doesn't lift its head.

"You're okay, honey. I'll help you." I reassure it, carefully picking my way through the rocks and brush. I have no idea how I'm going to get what looks like a hundred-pound dog back to my car, but I'm committed to finding a way.

As I get closer, I spot the rope tied around the tree and the collar. Suddenly, it hits me—someone left this poor dog out here.

I'm just a few feet away when a booming voice calls out from behind me.

"STOP!"

I spin on my heels, the flashlight beam landing on a figure approaching. All six foot three of Sheriff Hottie strides toward me, a stern look that causes all sorts of feelings to rise in me. The same feelings I've tried desperately to shove down at church the last three Sundays in a row.

"What the hell are you doing?" he demands, casting a glance at the dog and the rope tied to the tree. As he closes the distance, I can see anger in his eyes, mixed with a hint of concern—though I can't tell if it's for me or the dog.

"I was hiking," I explain, pointing toward the trail. "And when I got back to my car, I heard him whining."

"So you just walked out in the middle of nowhere by yourself? In the dark. With no protection. To rescue a dog?!"

My arms cross, chin tipping up naturally in defiance. "I couldn't just leave him out here *alone*. I had to help."

His expression hardens, as if I'm only escalating his irritation. *Great, just what I need.*

"Look, Sheriff, I'm not a damsel in distress. I have protection, a Pepper Ball pistol." I jut my hip out so he can see that I'm packing a non-lethal weapon—but a weapon nonetheless. "And I'm not an idiot. I wouldn't have approached if I didn't know for sure it was a dog and wasn't trying to attack me."

He raises an eyebrow, clearly skeptical, and the pause gives me a moment to rethink my approach.

"Wait, why are *you* here? You following me, darlin'?" I can't help but throw back the words he used on me the first time we crossed paths at church.

His head tips back slightly, giving me a nice view of the muscles along his jaw as they tighten. I swear I hear him mutter what sounds like a curse and then mention something about "Achilles," though I don't catch the reference—*or, maybe he just sneezed.*

When he looks back at me, the corner of his mouth tips up.

Not quite a smile, but the twinkle in his eyes tells me he's amused. "I'm not following you; besides, I was here first," he replies, his voice low and smooth.

I have to fight the twitch in my lips to keep from smiling. It's hard to stay mad at him when he looks at me like that.

The dog behind me whimpers again, and I spin back around. Up close, I can see how malnourished it is, its ribs poking out beneath its matted fur. My heart aches at the sight, but I can't look away from the poor creature.

"Why would anyone do this? Just leave it here to die?"

I can feel the heat radiating from Luke as he stands next to me, our shoulders nearly touching. He's only a few inches taller than I am, but he feels massive—in both presence and stature.

"People suck." He takes a few more steps closer and crouches down, still giving the dog some distance. He begins speaking in the same soothing tone I used, but the dog doesn't move. Not even a tail wag like it gave me.

I approach the same way he did and squat next to Luke.

"Hey, dog." At the sound of my voice, its head lifts, and it stares right at me like I'm the one it's been waiting for. In that moment, I immediately know I'll do whatever it takes to make sure this dog feels safe and loved. I can see the hope in its eyes, and I know I can't let it down.

Slowly, I extend my hand until my fingers are just a few inches from its snout. It tentatively sniffs before licking my hand. Taking that as a sign of trust, I gently run my nails through its coarse fur along the side of its face, trying to hold back my tears.

"Come on, dog. We're gonna get you out of here." It attempts to stand but doesn't get very far before it flops back down.

I look at Luke, and his expression of disappointment

mirrors my own—the weight of the world's monsters heavy on our shoulders.

Reaching around to my pack, I grab the knife from the side pocket. It isn't huge, just a standard pocket knife, but I know it'll be enough to cut the rope.

Luke's eyebrows raise, and the approval in his eyes makes my knees feel a little weak. *How lame am I?*

Before I can open the knife, he holds out his hand, silently demanding it from me. I hand it over willingly and return to petting the dog, this time around its ears.

He steps around me and the dog, expertly cutting the rope as close to the tree as possible. The dog doesn't move, even when Luke scoops him up and carries him back toward the parking lot.

It's officially dark now, and my little flashlight doesn't illuminate the path much, but I'm glad to have it.

"Open the bed of my truck," Luke commands rather than asks.

"You want him to ride back there?! He'll just slide around!"

"Do you have a better idea? My back seat is full of gear, and he's too big for the front."

"Put him in mine!" I say, scurrying toward my car.

Luke halts in his tracks, and I turn to see what's holding him up.

He looks between me and the car, then tilts his head in question. "You want this dirty, mangy mutt in the back of your Rolls Royce? It'll ruin the leather."

"So? They're just seats, Luke! I'll buy a new damn car if I have to." I don't care if that makes me sound like a privileged brat who doesn't care about costs. This dog is skin and bones and looks like it hasn't eaten in weeks. It deserves the luxury of Nappa leather and a comfortable ride to the nearest vet.

He doesn't move, just stares at me as if trying to solve a puzzle. Then, finally, he starts walking without another word.

I throw open the rear door, and he carefully sets the dog on the seat. Although it doesn't move much, I hear the soft rhythm of its tail patting against the leather.

"Follow me. The clinic I take Scotch to is on our way back to town. I'll call his vet and let her know we're coming."

I start to nod, then pause. "Scotch?" I ask.

A tiny smile graces his lips as he replies, "My horse." Then he climbs into his truck and slams the door.

I hurry to the driver's side of my car and back out, trailing behind the big black truck that reads 'SHERIFF' right on the side. I'm not sure how I missed the giant, glaring letters the first time I reached the parking lot, but I'd be lying if I said I wasn't happy they were there—*for more reasons than one.*

Chapter Eight

Luke

Odessa pulled in behind me at the vet clinic owned by my friend Jane, who recently returned from veterinary school to take over her grandfather's practice in the neighboring county. Normally, I would've chosen a vet closer to town for my horse, Scotch, but Jane's horse, Lucky, is boarded at the same facility, and she takes care of all the horses there. Plus, she's been a friend of mine for what feels like most of my life and we've always kept in touch.

As we parked, a knot of anxiety twisted in my stomach. That dog looked like it hadn't been getting enough food long before it was dumped out there to die. The image lingered in my mind as we hurried inside, where the smell of antiseptic mingled with faint hints of animal care.

As Jane and her technician entered the examination room, she exuded the calm authority I swear she's had since she was seven. Her shoulder-length blonde hair was neatly tucked behind her ears, and she wore a blue scrub top adorned with cutesy dog patterns. The technician, a young man with short-cropped black hair and a friendly smile, wore matching scrubs.

Together, they approached the frightened dog with a reassuring demeanor, getting right to work.

"Keep me updated on what you find," I said to Jane as she stepped out of the room next to me after gathering what she needed for the initial intake. "I'll reach out to Larkin. I want them to file a report, so someone should stop by soon to talk."

I'm going to do whatever I can to make sure they follow through with this case. The poor creature looked rough—matted fur, ribs protruding from starvation, and hollow eyes that spoke of a lifetime of fear and neglect.

"I will, too." She gestured toward her desk in the back room, and I followed her. "Want to tell me what else is going on?"

I shrugged, adopting an impassive expression, determined not to reveal anything.

"Don't even try, Lucas." Her use of my full name grated on me, evoking memories of a childhood I try to forget. I fought to keep my expression neutral as she continued. "Something to do with the beautiful blonde who hasn't taken her eyes off said dog?"

"The Cascadia County Sheriff Department treats animal cruelty cases very seriously."

"Yeah, okaaaay." She elongated the word with too much flourish before turning back to gather some paperwork.

"Fill this out for me so I can document it all—location, the dog's behavior, any supplies or food left near the dog, and any other pertinent information. And you owe me something from Maisie for staying open late." She handed me a pen, her warm brown eyes sparkling with curiosity—not about the dog, but about what I wasn't saying. I'd known her too long for her to buy any bullshit regarding Odessa, but I also knew she wouldn't push too hard. Most didn't, given Maddy; I seem to always get a free pass around any difficult situations.

When I returned after filling out the paperwork, they had already placed an IV in the dog, and he was starting to look a bit better. Odessa sat in a chair off to the side, her arms protectively covering her stomach as she watched the vet technician work on the dog, lost in thought. She didn't notice me coming in, or if she did, she didn't glance my way.

I took the seat next to her, and I could almost feel the tension ease from her shoulders at my presence. It was a stark contrast to the tension we had shared weeks ago at church, and it felt good—*dangerously good*. I had noticed the awkwardness slowly dissipating each service, even though we hadn't spoken a single word since that first day. Each time, I resolved to greet her, to say something—anything—but I chickened out, convincing myself it was for the best.

"You're such a good boy," the tech cooed, gently patting the dog's paw.

"He's going to be okay?" Odessa asked, her voice tense with hope as she looked at the tech with wide, shocked eyes, as if she were afraid to believe the good news. It hit me then—she thought he might not make it, yet she still chose to stay.

"He will be," the technician assured her. With every word, hope ignited in Odessa's wide eyes, but I noticed the tension in her shoulders. She sniffed and visibly shook before jumping up, excusing herself as she walked out.

I followed instantly, an invisible tether pulling me after her; my heart couldn't handle the thought of her falling apart alone. I caught up to her just as she reached the end of the hallway. My hands found her shoulders, and I turned her toward me, wrapping my arms around her in a tight embrace.

"Hey, it's okay. He's going to be okay," I whispered as she placed her head on my shoulder and sobbed. Her arms surrounded me like she was holding on for dear life, and I felt the weight of her pain in every tremor of her body.

One hand tangled in her hair, holding her closer to me, needing that connection more than I thought I would.

After a few minutes, her chest shook less, and she took smaller, steadier breaths, eventually pulling away slightly to look up at me with tear-stained eyes. "Thanks. I know he's going to be okay, but I just can't get over the fact that someone would leave him out there. They left him to die! How could they?"

"People suck."

"You said that." A small smile tugged at her mouth despite her tears.

"I know, but it's true. All day long, I'm reminded that people suck. Every single day." I used my thumb to swipe a stray tear from her face. "I'm so sorry you had to see it firsthand, though."

She nodded, looking up at me with the bluest eyes I'd ever seen. *Is it inappropriate to think about how pretty she looks crying? Yep. But, damn.*

Realizing I'm still holding her, I take a step back and clear my throat, trying to regain some assertiveness and put a little distance between us. *Fuck.* I should *not* be holding on to a woman like she's a fleeting dream threatening to slip away when I'm still beholden to someone else.

"I'm also pissed you ran off into the wilderness when it was dark. What if I hadn't seen you?"

The way she rolls her eyes so dramatically is both endearing and exasperating. "Spare me, Sheriff. I get enough grief from my brothers and Eddie."

"Who?" I asked, my curiosity more than piqued and laced with a hint of jealousy.

Her smirk at my obvious envy only fuels the fire in my chest. Finally, she says, "He's the head of my security. *Married* to one of my closest friends who manages the house in the

City." The more she shares, the more I feel my shoulders relax a bit, getting details I hadn't exactly earned.

I nod, feeling the brief sense of relief, but that calm disappears when she adds, "But like I've told them, I can take care of myself. I don't need anyone prying into what I'm doing."

"For fuck's sake, Achilles! You're going to get yourself seriously hurt one of these days if you keep acting like you're just any ordinary girl." A surge of protectiveness wells up inside me, despite her stubbornness. "You're one of the most recognizable faces *in the world!*"

"You called me that earlier, didn't you?" She replies, completely disregarding my concern and zeroing in on my slip-up.

"I did," I say, trying to sound stern but failing; a small smile tugs at the corners of my lips.

"Care to explain why?"

"Maybe someday," I shrug, stepping back further, not yet ready to admit the impact she's having on me.

"You're kind of an ass. You know that, right?"

That earns me a full grin and a light laugh. "I do."

Then, with a wink, I walk away from her and leave the clinic. The dog is going to be okay, and so will Odessa. The slip of calling her that nickname was just that—a slip.

But when I saw the curious mix with the blush on her cheeks, I knew it was fitting: my personal Achilles' heel. The weakness that may unravel me if I can't get my shit together—and with the way she looked tonight, I may be in more trouble than I thought.

Chapter Nine

Odessa

Giddy doesn't begin to describe how I feel as I whip into the parking spot at the front of the veterinary clinic. *Today's a monumental day; I can feel it in my bones.*

Not only did I close on a beautiful gemstone-blue house in Three Sisters, but yesterday, Jane called to let me know that Dog is available for adoption. I was able to visit him for a few hours yesterday, and I've fallen even more in love with him. It's only been a week, but he's already gained some weight and become more playful. He can walk on his own now, even running around, though he tires easily.

Jane estimates his age to be somewhere between two and four—not quite a puppy. She assured me that with a little love, care, and training, Dog will make a wonderful addition to my home. Yes—I've settled on naming him Dog. After everyone at the clinic, including myself, tried a few other names, he only perked up when we called him Dog. So, "Dog" it is—or "the best boy ever."

As I step into the clinic, I can't suppress my grin. The receptionist, a cheerful woman with bright red hair pulled back into a neat bun, beams when she sees me, her warm smile mirroring my own. She's dressed in a crisp white blouse and dark slacks, radiating professionalism with a friendly vibe. "Dog's ready for you!" she announces, her enthusiasm infectious.

"I'm ready for him!" I practically bounce on my toes, trying to match her energy. She retrieves a stack of paperwork from a drawer and hands it to me. Though it's standard adoption paperwork, I feel a rush of excitement as I sign my name at the bottom of each page.

"Were you able to get to the store? We have a few items we can send home..." She trails off, looking expectantly at me.

"Pretty sure I bought everything Dog could ever need, plus more," I reply, smiling as I hand her the collar and leash I picked out. After my visit yesterday, I couldn't wait and bought nearly everything in the pet section of the Country Store.

"Perfect! I'll go let Lori know you're here for him."

While I wait, the chimes above the door tinkle, and I turn to spot Luke strolling in, coffee in hand and a small bag from Maisie's dangling from his other hand. His uniform looks pristine, perfectly pressed, and his hair is neatly combed, giving him an air of effortless charm. *So freakin' hot.*

That familiar smirk plays on his stupidly hot face, making it hard to focus on anything else.

"You picking up Dog today?" he asks playfully.

I roll my eyes at him, but a flutter in my stomach accompanies the sight of his dimples. "Yep," is all I can manage before I turn away, fixing my gaze on the hall, eagerly awaiting Dog's appearance.

"Good, good." He taps on the counter and glances around. "Did you sign the papers for the Gravenstines' old place today?" My body goes on alert, and I narrow my eyes at him.

"You keeping tabs on me, or are you just that good at being sheriff?"

His chuckle sparks something alive in me that it shouldn't. "Both? I keep tabs on everyone in the county. It's not my fault the town busybodies love to track me down with gossip."

"Hmm." I respond noncommittally. Then it dawns on me—he not only knows about the house but also about Dog. He either keeps exceptional tabs on me, or Jane mentioned it. Sure, he talked about friends, but did I miss something major? My gaze flickers from the coffee to Maisie's bag, surely filled with her infamous treats. *Do I ask? Is there a way to do so without sounding jealous? I shouldn't.*

It's less than ten seconds before I cave, unable to stop myself. "How'd you hear about me getting Dog if this isn't even in our town?"

"I hadn't," he replies with a casual shrug. Then he holds up the bag and shakes it teasingly, as if he knows exactly what I'm asking. "Promised Jane I'd bring her something from Maisie for helping." The big jerk winks before walking toward the back, presumably to Jane's office. Something akin to jealousy takes root, but I quickly push it down. Luke is nothing to me. So what if I see him at church occasionally? We aren't even friends.

The receptionist steps out with who I assume is Lori; she's wearing scrubs, but my attention is riveted to Dog as he trots in beside her.

Dropping down, I scratch Dog's neck, and he noses my cheek like he's known me forever. His warm, slightly slobbery affection pulls a smile from me.

"We're really going to miss him, but we're so happy he found a loving home!" Lori says, her excitement genuine as she watches us.

"I promise I'll bring him back for all his check-ups and

vaccinations," I assure Lori, straightening up as I take the leash. Dog wags his tail, and I can't help but chuckle.

"Looks like you've finally found your partner in crime!" Lori teases, her eyes sparkling with delight.

"You have no idea," I reply, laughing as I picture the way Luke looked when he caught me attempting to rescue Dog in the first place.

I exchange one last glance with Lori, feeling a warmth in my chest as Dog prances toward the door, eager to go home.

But my gaze drifts once more to where Luke had gone, my heart pinching slightly. It's complicated. Luke and I aren't anything—barely friends. If he's seeing Jane, then good for him; she's beautiful, established in her career, and was amazing with Dog. She's about his age, early thirties, I assume. I hadn't heard he was seeing anyone, but if he only dated outside of Three Sisters, it makes sense.

I make a mental note to fish for info from Olivia tonight. She's known him forever and would probably be the only one he'd tell if he was dating.

"Let's go home, pup," I say, feeling a renewed sense of purpose as Dog barks happily, trotting beside me. "I think we're going to be just what each other needs." *Roots.*

My intentions to question Olivia, however, ground to a standstill.

I thought today would be monumental, but I had no idea just how monumental it would be. After picking up Dog, I went straight to my new house, where Everett met me. Midway through the tour, he casually dropped the bombshell that he was cleared of any wrongdoing in the shooting. The big idiot didn't even make a big deal out of it, but I insisted that we celebrate and go to the CPM/EFSC building where everyone should be working.

However, upon arrival, we were greeted by chaos: medical supplies were everywhere, and the office was in complete disarray. It turned out that just minutes before we arrived, Charlie went into labor a week early. Levi, Olivia's former brother-in-law and a paramedic, delivered a healthy baby boy right in the office. They were whisked away to the hospital for check-ups shortly after.

We all waited—patiently, or rather, not so patiently—for the text that would say we could visit.

"Knock, knock." I whisper as it's my turn to go into their room. Immediately, I douse my hands in the sanitizer by the door.

Charlie looks up and smiles from her hospital bed. "Look, August, it's Auntie Dessie." Tears well up in my eyes as I gaze at the beautiful baby boy in her arms.

"You're a mom!"

She laughs lightly. "Want to hold him?" I nod eagerly, and she gestures for me to take him from her.

Once I do, I settle down next to Hayes, who is perched on the couch beside Charlie's bed.

August is wrapped in a soft blue blanket that must have come from home; it's embroidered with 'A.R.C.'

"Congrats, Dad," I say, nudging Hayes with my elbow.

He grins proudly. "Can you believe we have a little office baby?"

"Considering he was probably conceived there—" I raise an eyebrow playfully at Charlie.

"Odessa Lynette!" Charlie scolds, her face flushing bright red. Hayes laughs loud enough to shake the couch. "I mean, she's not wrong," he chuckles, prompting Charlie to throw a chip she picked up from the side table at him.

Olivia has Ben and Ellie, who I already consider my niece and nephew, but they've long outgrown the baby stage, each now with their own established personalities and budding independence. August is the first of hopefully many that we'll get to see start from the very beginning, and it fills me with hope.

As I watch Charlie and Hayes revel in the joy of parenthood, a wistful thought crosses my mind: maybe someday it will be me that everyone is visiting here—a husband who adores me and a sweet little baby in my arms. I can't help but let my thoughts drift to Luke. I wonder if he ever wanted kids with Maddy; did he imagine holding his own little one, watching them grow and flourish? Was that a dream he had to set aside when she had the accident, or does he secretly still hope to experience fatherhood one day?

I shake off those thoughts when Charlie starts talking about how crazy it was to have Levi deliver August, redirecting the attention back to her, where it truly belongs. The laughter and chatter among friends envelop me, a welcome distraction from my earlier musings about dreams and possibilities. It's heartwarming to see Charlie in her element, filled with smiles and excitement as she shares her story.

But as the moment of celebration lingers, I know it's time for me to take my leave. Having soaked up all the baby snuggles I can, I say my "see ya-laters" and head toward the door. Just as I reach it, I inadvertently run face-first into Luke's chest. I'm not sure why I'm surprised to see him here; he's one of Hayes's best friends and has looked out for Charlie since she first ran away to Three Sisters. Even so, seeing him always catches me off guard.

His hands instinctively shoot out to steady me, his surprise mixing with a hint of sadness that lingers in his expression—something's clearly happened since I saw him this morning.

"You okay?" we both ask simultaneously. He nods, but the look in his eyes tells me it isn't true.

"Sorry to bump into you like that. I wasn't expecting anyone to be standing in the hallway."

Luke's eyes flicker with a hint of vulnerability before he quickly masks it with a smile. "No worries, I was just..." His smile falters as he struggles to finish the sentence.

"Just?" I prompt, hoping for more.

He runs a hand through his hair, a nervous gesture that only accentuates his broad chest. I have to consciously force myself to look away.

"Just trying to get my shit together," he finally admits, frustration and resignation lacing his voice. "I fucking hate hospitals." His eyes meet mine with a raw honesty that catches me off guard.

Without thinking, my arms go around him, surprising even myself with the gesture. He offered me the same comfort when I needed it at the vet clinic, so I'm taking a giant leap of faith and returning the favor. Thankfully, he hugs me back, his embrace tightening slightly more than I expected. I can feel the tension in his body gradually ease as we stand there, and then he releases me, giving a small, grateful smile.

"Thanks," he mouths softly before taking a deep breath and stepping around me into the room. I'm left standing there, unsure of what just transpired between us—a feeling that seems to be the norm when it comes to Luke.

Chapter Ten

Luke

It took me forty-five agonizing minutes to summon the courage to step into the hospital. During which, I sat in my truck, staring at the building as a flood of memories washed over me, reminding me of why I loathe this place—and for good reason. Within those sterile walls, I endured two of the most devastating losses of my life: Maddy's diagnosis of a traumatic brain injury and the heart-wrenching moment I lost my best friend—on the same damn day, no less.

Earlier that morning, I had parked outside Granny's Biscuits, waiting for Maddy. I was on the brink of ending a decade-long relationship—one that, deep down, I knew had run its course. I had felt it for a while, even before I found those messages, but I could never muster the courage to take that final step. Our lives were so intertwined that I couldn't bear to think about the aftermath of our separation. Yet, fate had other plans. As I anxiously checked the clock on my dashboard, wondering how late she would be, the universe was quietly setting its course.

I can still feel the way my body tensed at the exact moment

the radio crackled to life with urgent news of a nearly fatal car accident—a black Lexus traveling westbound on the highway at the Cascadia-Deschutes county line. Even before I heard the name of the victim, *I knew*: it was Maddy.

In that moment, I was on autopilot, my cruiser racing toward the scene with lights flashing and sirens wailing. I don't even remember leaving the parking lot, only that I arrived just as fire and rescue worked to pull her from the wreckage and began loading her into the ambulance. As they started closing the door in a flurry of chaos, I realized I needed to be in there with her.

I can still feel the ache in my chest, the pressure in my legs as I sprinted to get inside, but thankfully, Bill looked up just in time to see me. He's been a medic longer than I've been alive, and I trust him implicitly. I know he did everything in his power that day to ensure Maddy's survival; without him, I doubt she would have made it through the ambulance ride to Bend.

Once we arrived at the hospital, I found myself in a private waiting room designated for critical patients, anxiously awaiting Joe, Maddy's dad. Her mom was on her way from California, but it would take her a while to get there.

Deschutes County had sent two deputies to keep me company, but I couldn't focus on small talk. Instead, I paced the room, lost in my thoughts.

I can still feel my uneven breathing as I circulated the small room, my vision clouded by a haze of unknown and worry about Maddy. I may have been pissed she was cheating on me, but that didn't negate the decade of friendship we had before this happened.

And then, as if that wasn't enough for my mind to handle, I watched in horror as Levi, one of my close friends, desperately performed CPR on a patient being wheeled toward the emergency department.

I can still see him passing by in a blur, sweat dripping down his forehead and agony etched in his eyes as he pounded on the chest of the victim under him. I had seen Levi working in the field before, his concentration and attention to detail undeniable, but never had I witnessed him look so primal. Each thrust of his hands was fueled by desperation, an emotional fight against fate itself—as if he was channeling every ounce of his being into that moment, desperate to wrest life back from the jaws of death.

It wasn't until I caught sight of the lifeless form beneath Levi that I realized why he was so consumed by the need to save a life. Lying under him was the mirror image of Levi—his twin and my partner—Dan. *The best friend I've ever had.*

Every second dragged as they passed by, disappearing deeper into the emergency department. With each moment, the weight of the impossible crashed down on my chest.

Two senseless tragedies within the span of an hour—two devastating realities my mind refused to accept. Dan and Maddy were dying. Right here, right now.

My colleagues swarmed the area, but their voices felt distant and muffled. They tried to explain things, urging me to stop my restless pacing. Everything shifted, though, when Zeke stormed in—Sheriff of Cascadia County and Dan's dad. When I saw him crying, yanking his surviving son into his arms, I knew. I knew Dan was dead. I knew that my world would never be the same again.

The reality of the situation hit me so hard that I felt numb, devastated in a way I had never experienced before. I slumped into a chair, staring at a peeling piece of linoleum, bracing myself for the news that Maddy hadn't survived either.

Even Olivia's attempts to snap me out of it fell flat. I

knew how terrible a friend I was to her in that moment. She had just lost her husband, the father of her two young kids, and yet I couldn't muster the strength to offer her any support.

Hours dragged on, and at last, Doctor Beach entered the room. With a grave expression, she told me they were putting Maddy into an induced coma. She might survive, but she was barely hanging on. No one knew then that while her body would recover, her traumatic brain injury was too severe and that she would never regain her mental clarity.

But that was years ago, and I've been back to this hospital plenty since. It comes with the role I was thrust into only a few short months later—the town voting me in as sheriff in hopes it would boost my spirits, or at least give me something productive to focus on.

With a heavy sigh, a heavy heart, and heavy feet, I made my way through the front entrance of the family birthing center, heading toward the check-in area. I had visited the maternity ward before, each time my cousin Margie welcomed another baby into her ever-growing brood. Although she's a year older than I am, I've always felt closer to her sister Maisie, who is a few years younger—perhaps because Maisie has constantly supplied me with a never-ending stream of baked goods, dating back to when I lived with them off and on while growing up. The last time I was here was when Olivia and Dan were having Ellie, and a fresh wave of pain and sadness washed over me as I remembered how happy Dan looked cradling his new baby girl.

I do my best to shake off the anxious knot forming in my gut while I wait to give my information.

The security guard assigned to this ward is friendly, though he resembles a grandfather greeting visitors more than a serious security presence. The faint scent of antiseptic mingles with the subtle aroma of lavender air freshener, a familiar effort to mask the sterile environment of the hospital.

"Room 104," he says with a smile, handing me a tag that reads "Visitor 104." His reassuring demeanor contrasts sharply with the anxiety churning inside me.

I thank him and walk down the hall, the soft hum of fluorescent lights bathing the path in an almost unnatural glow. The walls are adorned with cheerful pastel-colored paintings of baby animals, their innocent expressions somehow deepening my sense of dread. The muffled sounds of cooing infants and the distant laughter of new parents drift through the air, mixing with the faint beeping of medical equipment.

Just as I'm about to enter the room, flashes of memories flood my mind of the "doomsday," as Olivia calls it. I hesitate, lingering outside the door, trying to let go of those thoughts. My hands tremble, and I look down, clenching and unclenching them. The cheerful atmosphere around me seems surreal in contrast to the fear and pain rising within me.

In the next moment, my favorite blonde crashes into me, and my shaking hands instinctively reach out to steady her. My worries begin to fade as her hair catches the light, almost appearing golden, and her eyes widen, sparkling with life. The warmth from her body seems to chase away the coldness within me. But in the distance, a machine beeps, the antiseptic begins to sting my nose, and visions of Odessa lying in the hospital swarm my mind—this time, instead of Levi working on Dan, it's Odessa in his place. Instead of Maddy on a gurney with a head dressing, it's Odessa. I forget all about why I'm here and focus only on her presence in this hospital. *Why is she here?*

"You okay?" we both ask in unison. I nod, but Odessa's head tilts slightly, as if she doesn't believe me. *Smart girl.*

My mind clears as I look into those electric eyes and remember I'm here for Hayes and Charlie. I loosen my grip on her biceps, letting my hands fall to my sides, aware that she's steady now and healthy.

"Sorry to bump into you like that. I wasn't expecting anyone in the hallway," she says, her voice warm. *Me either, but I'm a puss when it comes to hospitals.*

Instead of answering honestly, I try to mask my insecurity with a smile. "No worries, I was just..." The words escape me. *Taking a phone call? Standing here like a lunatic?*

"Just?" she prompts softly, encouraging me to open up in a way that most people haven't these last few years.

My hand drags through my hair as I wrestle with how honest I want to be.

"Just trying to get my shit together," I admit, letting her draw out my raw emotions. "I fucking hate hospitals." When our eyes meet, I see understanding and compassion reflected back at me in those uniquely blue depths.

Then she throws her arms around me, surprising me by yanking me into an embrace. But I let her, wrapping my own arms around her and sinking deeply into the hug. It's as if she takes all the pain I've felt over the last few years and wraps it up in that moment, offering me a reprieve that I don't believe I deserve.

Pulling back before I truly want to, I mouth a soft, "Thanks," and then step around her into the room. There's a large part of me that doesn't want to acknowledge how much I needed that hug, how much I needed her presence in that moment.

Leaving her standing there feels like abandoning a lifeline, but I know I need to see Charlie, Hayes, and their new baby—and she just gave me the courage to do it.

When I enter, Charlie and Hayes both look up and grin at me.

"Sorry to crash; mind if I stop in?" I ask.

"Not crashing at all! You're part of the family, Luke," Charlie beams, cradling the baby. She looks amazing for having just given birth—in an office—a few hours ago.

Hayes surprises me by slinging his arm around my shoulder, pulling me into a one-armed hug. "She's right. Whether you like it or not."

I nod, taking a better look at the new baby in Charlie's arms. His little face is exceptionally chunky, and I can't help but smile. I've always thought I'd have kids by now, and there were moments I imagined Maddy in this room. But that thought faded long ago, along with the hope of starting a family of my own.

Yet, as I gaze at the baby, I can't prevent the tiny piece of hope that has ignited somewhere deep within. A hope that I only feel when a certain person is around. It's like she's seeping through every lock I have around my heart, destroying every ounce of loyalty and integrity I have, and I'm finding it difficult to care.

It's time for me to acknowledge that I have feelings for Odessa, but I'll always be in a relationship with Maddy.

Can I become like the person I resent most in order to have a future with the person I truly desire?

Chapter Eleven

Odessa

I've always loved the Ponderosa Pine and what Ethan has transformed it into, but now that I live so close, it's become a regular hangout for me. I typically claim my spot along the bar, propping my elbows on the smooth, live-edge pine surface. I prefer arriving early—before the dinner rush and before the "Bod Squad" descends and starts causing chaos.

Having Everett, Drew, and Hayes as overprotective brothers was tough enough, but now I've got five more overbearing men in the mix who relish teasing me. Thankfully, I've developed thick skin because the banter can get pretty intense. But I thrive on it. After years of enduring backhanded compliments and worse—hearing things said behind my back—being around those who challenge my wit and keep me on my toes is exactly what I need.

"Hey, Dess!" I hear the cheerful voice of my favorite bartender, Callie—second only to Ethan—calling from across the room. She's one of those locals who radiate energy, despite her small stature, standing no taller than five feet. When I stand next to her, I feel like I'm towering over her. I'm used to being the tall girl; it's typical in the industry. But back in the real world, I feel like a Barbie among a sea of Polly Pockets.

As I turn to face her, I notice she's finishing up wiping down a table.

"Oh my God!" I pause mid-step, my jaw nearly dropping at her new look. "You got bangs!"

Self-consciously, she fluffs one side and adjusts the part. "What do you think?"

"Giiirl, grab a corset, and you're totally channeling Sab!"

"Sab?" she asks, clearly confused.

I wince at my lack of self-awareness. "Sorry, Sabrina Carpenter? She sings—"

"I know what she sings! You're friends with her?!"

I shrug, "Kinda? It's hard to tell who's a friend and who's a 'work friend.'" To put it nicely. Although I've never had a bad experience with her, trust doesn't come easily. I'm wary of anyone who might throw me under the bus for their own gain.

I can practically see stars in Callie's eyes as she stares at me. "That's so freakin' cool! I always forget you're, like, insanely famous. No offense—wait, is that offensive?" Genuine curiosity lights her face, devoid of malice.

"No offense taken. I try to forget I'm famous too..." *Which has been surprisingly easy here. Too easy, if I'm being honest.*

As I settle into my usual seat at the bar, I notice Ethan off to the side, chatting with someone I haven't seen around before.

He's not nearly as tall as Ethan—though not many men are—but his demeanor signals that he wants to blend into the background. His hands are shoved into the pockets of his hoodie, and a worn cap shields most of his face. Despite his reticence, he seems attentive to everything Ethan is saying, as if he's bracing himself for a quiz afterwards.

Something about him screams, "please don't look at me." I'm honestly surprised Ethan hired him to be a bartender.

Ethan spots me sitting and waves while saying, "Be right back." The guy looks up, his eyes barely visible beneath his hat. They widen for a moment before he quickly diverts his gaze back to Ethan.

Then, both of them disappear into the kitchen.

Callie quickly washes her hands while asking over her shoulder, "Usual? Or are you spicin' it up tonight?" My usual consists of a giant salad, a side of French fries, and a Diet Coke. I rarely indulge and opt for the biggest burger they have and a beer, but tonight, I don't feel like straying from my routine.

"The usual," I grumble. I crave the burger but don't want to think about the workout I'd need to offset it. For whatever reason, I'm not ready to break the strict routine I've maintained.

She nods and turns to place my order, filling my glass with ice and pouring my drink.

After a few minutes, Ethan returns from the kitchen, carrying a container, a cutting board, and a knife. It's crazy to think I met him long before Charlie ever stumbled upon this town, and we've been friends ever since. I never imagined I'd end up in the picturesque town he raved about on the first night we met.

"Hey," he says with a nod, positioning himself in front of me on the other side of the bar.

"How's it going, Flacco?"

His lip curls slightly as he pulls a lime from the container and starts slicing it. "Hate training the new people."

"Ahh," I respond, now that he's confirmed my suspicions. "New bartender? What's his story?"

"Not a bartender yet. C.J.'s a bar-back for now. I don't know much about him. His resume was spotty, but the background check came back clear, and I'm desperate for the help." *That makes more sense.*

My eyes drift back to the football game playing on the giant

TV behind Ethan. "You ever miss it?" I ask, gesturing toward the screen.

He glances back briefly, and I catch the hint of a sad smile. "Every day. But it's like missing the ease of high school. I wouldn't go back or change being home, but I do miss the camaraderie and the competition." Then, with a wink, he adds, "And the money."

"Oh right. Did you burn through that first-round draft pick on this swanky place?" He chuckles at my joke. Considering he was the highest-paid rookie and one of the youngest, we both know he could afford fifty of these restaurants and still have cash burning a hole in his pocket.

"Nope, it was the hookers and blow," Levi interjects, planting himself on the other side of me.

Ethan rolls his eyes, clearly choosing to ignore Levi's comment. "What's up, Vi?"

"Not much. Thought I'd check in, make sure our newest resident isn't getting into too much trouble," he grins at me, being his usual mischievous self. He reminds me so much of Everett it isn't even funny.

"You know me too well, especially around Ethan when he's paying for the party favors." I wink at Ethan, and that at least earns a laugh from him. Ethan hardly even drinks, and I think I've only ever seen him drunk at a party once.

Callie comes out with my food and blushes when she sees Levi. It takes every ounce of restraint I have not to roll my eyes at her. I can already predict she'll react the same way when the Bod Squad shows up. I know they're all good-looking guys, but none of them make my heart race like a certain sheriff does.

I sip the Diet Coke that Callie just refilled and pick at the french fries left on my plate, trying to pay attention to the game, but my mind keeps drifting to what I want to do next. I don't need money, but I do need to work. I need to focus on something and have goals and achievements that will make me feel fulfilled. But I have no idea where to start.

An elbow bumps into me, and I look over to see a guy now occupying the once empty seat. In fact, the rest of the bar on that side is filled; four more guys and one girl occupy the remaining spots. They're all still in snow pants and shirts, with a few sporting badges from the smaller ski resort outside of town.

The man next to me finally glances my way, flipping his shaggy hair out of his eyes with a head jerk. "Sorry 'bout that, babygirl." *Babygirl? Barf.*

He may be smiling, but the wicked glint in his eyes sends a shiver down my spine. Everything about him screams, "I'm going to charm you into danger." I can only imagine it's how I would feel if I ever met Ted Bundy—there's no way he's smooth-talking me into his Volkswagen. Although this guy looks more like a van driver than a Beetle owner.

Rather than respond, I offer a tight-lipped smile and turn my attention back to the bar, pretending to watch the game. I'm in no mood to be hit on by a potential creep with questionable taste in pickup lines.

Of course, he doesn't take my dismissal seriously. "You from around here?"

I don't acknowledge him, acting as if I don't even hear him. Most guys take the hint and go home to call me a bitch online—which, of course, I don't care about. I'm used to being loved in person and critiqued online.

"Hey," he bumps my elbow again, and now I'm starting to think the first time wasn't an accident. "You from around here?"

"Nope," I say, popping the "p" and redirecting my focus back to the game.

"Me either," he admits, turning his body to face me. *Great.*

I steal a quick glance toward the other side of the bar, hoping to spot some of the Bod Squad. The only one I see is Levi, sitting at a booth with a woman I recognize but don't know. He's not exactly the trained Navy SEAL I was hoping for. Not that he couldn't hold his own—especially against this guy—but I was really hoping for some scare-the-hell-out-of-you look vibes from Liam. Hell, even Cooper and his dumb mustache could intimidate this guy with a single glare. Unfortunately, it looks like I'm on my own for this one.

"We should explore a little together sometime. What's your name?"

"Sorry, I'm not really in the mood for company right now. Long day, ya know?"

"Yeah? Tell me about it." I feel my teeth clench as I stare at this guy who won't take a hint.

"Really, I'm just here to watch the game," I reply, injecting more sass and less patience into my tone. His right arm snakes out, and I watch over my shoulder as it slides around my chair.

My body stiffens when he leans in closer, his breath hot against my face. "Come on, don't be like that. Have a drink and chat with me."

"Look, I tried to be nice, but you're really starting to piss me off. Back the fuck up," I snarl.

His head recoils, a look of disgust flashing across his face before he mutters, "Bitch." *What-the-fuck-ever.*

I couldn't care less what this asshole thinks of me; I just want him to leave me alone.

I slide my drink closer to me, away from the invisible line between us. Part of me wants to change seats, but I don't want to give him the satisfaction of knowing he got to me.

Instead, I grab my drink, about to take a sip when someone shouts, "What the fuck?" from the back room. I glance at the screen to see the Vikings up by ten, but their quarterback just threw an interception. The thought of Ethan watching it in his office makes me chuckle. Poor guy misses it way more than he lets on.

Like I conjured him with thoughts alone, Ethan storms out from the kitchen and marches toward me, looking ready to tear someone apart. But instead of addressing me, he grabs the drink out of my hand.

In complete contrast to his fierce demeanor, he gently sets the glass down on the other side of the bar.

"What—"

His glare shifts from me to the guy behind me as his hand lands firmly on the guy's shoulder. "Don't even think about it, asshole."

I turn around to see the guy trying to leave. "Ethan, what is going on?" This can't really be because he was trying to talk to me, right?

"This fucker put something in your drink!" *Oh, shit.*

My heart races as I glance back at the Diet Coke, something akin to panic rising in my chest.

"You don't know shit, man. I didn't put anything in her drink."

"I saw it on the security footage. Then I replayed it to make sure. You're not going anywhere until a deputy gets here."

"Fuck off." He tries to shake Ethan's hand off his shoulder, but he must have missed the fact that Ethan is a big-ass guy with a strong grip. Ethan remains unfazed and unmoving.

The friends he came in with stare at us with wide eyes, and the girl looks downright terrified as she glances at her own drink.

My heartbeat begins to rise as I realize I might be on my way to incapacity. Everett is going to freak the fuck out. The guys will kill this loser, and Luke will have to arrest them. *Oh, fuck. Luke.* He's going to give me that same disappointed look he used to have.

My mouth gapes between Ethan and the guy who just tried to drug me—*did he actually drug me?*

My jaw hangs open when the front door slams against the wall.

Through the entrance strides none other than Luke himself, looking every bit the sheriff he is, with a wrathful expression on his face. My heart sinks a little more with each passing second, and I don't even know why. Technically, I've done nothing wrong here.

Another deputy follows him in. While he also looks serious, he doesn't carry the same intensity as Luke.

When Luke's eyes lock onto mine, I can see the disapproval written all over his face before he even utters a word.

"Ethan, what the hell's going on?" He looks between the three of us, his gaze lingering on the guy Ethan has in a vice.

"Fucker put something in Odessa's drink. I have the footage, and the rest of the drink is right there."

I don't even have time to look back at the creep before he suddenly twists out of Ethan's grip and lunges toward me. His body slams me against the bartop, knocking the wind out of me. His arms flail around me, but it doesn't feel like he's trying to hurt me—more like he's trying to get through me.

In the blink of an eye, an arm is thrust between us, pulling with such force that the guy has no choice but to fall back.

My gaze shifts from the arm that rescued me to the face of the person attached as I try to catch my breath. Once again, I feel like I can't breathe as I watch Luke slam the guy to the ground.

Intense. Hot. Swoon-worthy.

Chapter Twelve

Luke

When a call came over the radio about a patron who may have been drugged at Ponderosa Pine Tavern, I flipped on the lights and sirens and headed that way. Incidents like this are rare in our little town, but when they do occur, I make sure to show my face—especially since the CODE force is still trying to determine where those drugs were headed and who the ringleader is in Central Oregon. I don't want anyone thinking they can get away with that kind of activity in my jurisdiction.

Then, dispatch dropped the bombshell of all bombshells—Odessa Astor was the victim—and everything changed. Long forgotten was the calm sheriff known for his steady presence; now, a loose cannon with a thirst for blood.

My foot slammed down on the accelerator, my vision narrowed, and everything else faded away. Subconsciously, I must have been listening to the dispatcher because I arrived in one piece, but my mind only saw red the entire time. This is what they mean when they talk about being blindly consumed by a murderous rage.

When I entered, I was barely aware of Ethan looming over the asshole who had drugged her; my eyes felt glued to Odessa. The wide-eyed, doe-in-the-headlights look she shot my way both relieved and infuriated me, reinforcing the anger within me—an anger I hadn't allowed to surface in far too long. I welcomed the burn like an old friend as it spread through me.

I'm not even sure what I said to them, but it must have been the right thing, because Ethan began explaining the situation.

Then I felt the air shift, the hairs on my arms standing up, and sure enough, the bastard lunged at her. That same blinding rage took over again, and it took every ounce of restraint I had not to snap his neck right then and there—his only saving grace being the muscle memory embedded in me from years of training.

It was only the sound of my heart pounding in my ears and her shocked gasp that I heard as I yanked him off her, throwing him to the ground like the trash he was.

Then, fortune smiled on me when the dumb bastard decided to resist.

I let my body move without conscious thought as I scrambled to restrain him, welcoming the fight he tried to put up. Landing a few hits did nothing to quell the anger still boiling inside me, but before I knew it, I had my knee slammed into his back, driving him down toward the floor until I straddled him, using my free hand to wrench his left arm behind his back.

Deputy Corbin was right there with me, swiftly seizing the suspect's other arm and pulling it back. He secured one cuff on the arm I was controlling, doing so with practiced efficiency.

The guy screamed a string of profanities, but I turned a deaf ear, my focus fixed on getting him under control. Yanking him up off the ground, I forced him to his feet and maneuvered him toward the exit. Thankfully, it was still early enough in the evening that I hoped I hadn't traumatized the entire town. Still,

I knew the gossip mill would churn out the details faster than a speeding bullet.

"You're lying! You can't arrest me! This is bullshit!" He continued his ridiculous rant as we marched the walk of shame to Corbin's cruiser. Meanwhile, Corbin began reading him his Miranda rights.

Once Corbin finished, I felt the tension in my shoulders start to ease, the adrenaline ebbing away now that I wasn't staring into Odessa's terrified eyes.

"What's your name?" I demanded, leaning closer.

He glared up at me, his expression one of utter defiance. "I don't have to tell you shit. I know my rights!"

I swallowed back an eye roll, reminding myself that this idiot was clueless about the very rights he boasted about. Instead, I tightened my grip on his arm, forcing him to feel just how little power he truly had in this moment.

"Fine. We can do this the hard way—you can sit in a jail cell while I sort this out. Oh, wait," I say, grabbing the lanyard badge from around his neck. The photo shows his face clearly, name underneath it: "Zayden Thomas."

Deputy Corbin laughs, clearly enjoying the moment as he pulls on a pair of gloves. "Alright, Zayden. You got anything that could poke, stick, cut, or otherwise ruin my day?"

His grumbled response sounds like a reluctant "no," and Corbin starts rifling through his pockets, laying out his belongings on the hood of his SUV.

When Corbin pulls out a small bag containing a vial of liquid and a syringe, my anger flares back to life. It's probably for the best that Corbin is handling him now.

"What's this?" Corbin asks, holding up the clear bag.

"Nothing, man," Zayden mumbles.

"Oh really? So that drink isn't going to test positive for whatever's in there?"

Zayden smirks. "Might, but that girl asked for it. Said she wanted to try something fun."

The mention of Odessa snaps my resolve. In a swift motion, I twist him around to face me, and he nearly loses his balance. The only thing keeping him upright is my forearm pressed against his chest, pinning him against the side of the cruiser.

"You think this is funny?" I hiss, leaning in closer, my voice low, almost a growl. "I'm this close to smashing your face in if you don't stop talking."

"Fuck you, asshole! You can't do a damn thing!" he retorts, his bravado faltering just enough for me to catch a glimpse of the fear lurking beneath the surface.

"Oh, that's where you're dead wrong," I reply, each word dripping with menace. "In this town, no one would bat an eye if you just vanished. You'd be nothing but a ghost."

"I'm going to sue you!" He spits, the words laced with desperation, though the tremble in his voice betrays him. I can see the fear creeping into his eyes, his confidence crumbling.

I lean in closer, my grip tightening around his collar. "You won't get that chance. I know every rancher here, and I guarantee you, ninety percent of them owe me a favor. If I even catch sight of you in this county after you get released, I'll make sure you're buried so deep in a hayfield that not even God could dig you out."

He stutters, "Y—You can't say that! What's your badge number? I'm filing a complaint with the sheriff!"

I flash him the same mocking grin he had earlier, letting the humiliation wash over him. "I am the sheriff. Consider your complaint filed, fuckface."

The tension hangs thick in the air as Deputy Corbin swings open the back door of his cruiser, the faint sound of metal creaking to punctuate the moment. I can feel Zayden's pulse quicken, the reality of his situation settling in.

I catch a flicker of amusement in Corbin's eyes as I heft Zayden into the back of the cruiser and slam the door shut behind him. The sound echoes like a clap of thunder, and for a moment, I feel a rush of satisfaction.

But the moment doesn't last. "Luke," a small gasp pulls me back to reality, and I turn to see Odessa standing there with Ethan and Levi. My heart sinks when I notice her slightly swaying; Levi's hands instinctively move to her waist for support. A part of me wants to thank him for looking out for her, but another part burns with jealousy, wishing he would take his hands away.

I step toward her, resting my hands on her shoulders. "You okay, Achilles?"

She shakes her head, but her words betray her. "I'm fine! I barely had a sip."

Then she lifts her chin, her nose raised in a false show of confidence. "You idiot, you threatened him! What if this turns into another media storm?" The way she tries to deflect her vulnerability almost makes me smile, yet I can clearly see the worry etched into her features.

"I'll handle it," I assure her, trying to convey a sense of calm. "But you're getting checked out." I glance at Levi, who nods in agreement. "Already called it in. Bill's on shift and should be here soon." I exhale heavily—Bill's good, he's reliable, not to mention happily married.

Odessa pulls her phone from her pocket and begins calling someone. I assume it's Everett, and I take a moment to steal a glance at her beautiful face. I tell myself it's to ensure the drugs haven't taken too great a toll on her, but deep down, I just want to memorize every detail before chaos washes over us again.

She catches my gaze, a small crease forming between her brows. "Lincoln!"

My heart stutters, and my hands drop from her shoulders as

if she's burned me. The thought of her with Lincoln sends a wave of jealousy through me, despite him seeming like a decent guy. The caveman in me wants to scream that she needs to hang up, but the rational part of me knows I have no right to interfere in her personal life—not when my own is so fucked up that I could never commit to her fully.

But just as I'm stepping away, she turns to Ethan. "You care if Lincoln deletes it?"

Wait, what?

Ethan shakes his head. "Nope, just make sure it's only the audio," but I can't keep quiet.

"No."

I grab the phone from her hand and press it to my ear. "Lincoln, don't. It'll be fine. I said it; I'll stand by it."

On the other end, he chuckles. "Sorry, sheriff. I may be risking a night in the slammer, but I have to agree with Dess. We've had enough news crews snooping around."

I shoot a glance at Corbin, who shrugs, looking unfazed. "I was barely in my cruiser when we got the call. Didn't even have my body cam on yet."

I scan the rest of the parking lot, noting that it's nearly empty. Even if someone caught today's events on a cell phone camera, there wouldn't be any audio. It's a small comfort, but one I cling to as the weight of the situation presses down on me. I'm known for keeping my composure during tense situations, but something about Odessa Astor has me on edge, creating a weakness I hadn't known I had.

The ambulance pulls in and parks behind my truck. Bill steps out first, his bag slung over his shoulder. "How's it going, Odessa, right?" He greets her with a smile, as if it's just another routine call. I try to absorb his calm demeanor; I really need to pull myself together. There's protocol to follow, a scene to process, witnesses to interview, and reports to write.

I turn to Levi, keeping my voice steady. "Call Astor and Liv. Let them know what happened."

Ethan steps in beside Levi, his hand smacking my shoulder in a familiar gesture. "You good?"

I nod, and he arches an eyebrow, clearly not fully convinced but choosing not to press me.

"I'll have Deputy Corbin gather more details, but can you give me a quick rundown?" I ask, focusing on the task at hand.

"Sure. Odessa came in about forty-five minutes ago. She was just minding her own business when that guy and his friends sat next to her. I was in the office and saw him creeping on her. At first, he didn't say anything, but then he kept trying to talk to her even though she wasn't engaging. I noticed when she looked away, his hand slipped over her drink. Couldn't believe it—but I rewound the footage, and he definitely put something in it. As I was heading out, I passed Callie and told her to call it in."

"Fuck," I mutter under my breath, the anger simmering just beneath the surface. "You seen him before?"

"Maybe once or twice, but honestly, all those guys look the same," Ethan replies, sharing a knowing look of frustration.

"Thanks for looking out," I say, genuinely appreciative of his vigilance.

He smirks, lowering his voice conspiratorially. "That concern for Odessa specifically or the greater good in general?"

So far, he's the only one who's picked up on my fascination with her, and I'm hoping it stays that way. "Mind your business, Flacco." He just smirks at me before striding to the back of the rig to check on her.

I turn to Corbin, who is busy bagging the drugs and collecting Zayden's personal items while briefing Deputy Kade.

"I'll grab the security footage with Ethan," I inform them.

"Kade, you want to take care of interviewing the friends? Corbin can finish up here and take him in."

Kade nods, looking ready despite being a new deputy. "On it."

As I make my way toward the crew examining Odessa, I'm struck by the sound of laughter—her distinct giggle standing out from the others.

"All good here?" I ask, focusing on her. She seems fine, with no visible signs of the drugs in her system.

"Just dandy," she replies with a smile, though I catch a slight wobble in it. My fists clench at my sides, knowing I can't be the one to comfort her right now. From the outside looking in, we are barely even friends. But in my eyes, Zayden Thomas just solidified the fact that Odessa isn't a threat to unraveling me anymore—she already has.

And I think it's about time I tell her that.

Chapter Thirteen

Luke

Fighting off the cold, I stuff my hands into the pockets of my puffer jacket as I walk the short distance to Odessa's house. I can almost guarantee she has no idea that the backyard of the house she purchased borders mine. Sure, hers is in the sleek, brand-new neighborhood, while mine is in the older quarter with its creaky fences and overgrown gardens, but the layout is such that our properties are connected.

My breath fogs in the dim porch lights that illuminate my path, prompting a mental note to install new motion lights. It strikes me as odd that the guys haven't already set her house up like Fort Knox. Given everything that happened a few hours ago, I can only imagine they'll be here first thing in the morning to do just that.

I rap my knuckles against the front door in quick succession, the familiar nerves of seeing her bubbling up again like they always do.

A few moments later, the door opens partially, and Odessa peeks her head out, her eyes lacking the usual fire. "Sheriff," she says softly, "What can I do for you?"

Her body jerks forward abruptly as Dog tries to push his way past her.

"Dammit, Dog," she mutters before opening the door fully.

I can't help but smile as Dog shoves past Odessa to greet me, his tail wagging and tongue lolling out in excitement. "Looks like someone missed me," I chuckle, scratching behind his ears while Odessa watches, disbelief etched across her face.

"How? You barely met him!" she retorts, frustration punctuating her voice as she stomps her foot lightly, a mix of exasperation and jealousy.

Not exactly true; I visited him a few times while he was with Jane. Each time, I made sure he got plenty of scratches and treats, and when I learned Odessa was adopting him, I dropped by to give him strict orders to protect our girl—*his girl*. Over the last three weeks, I even threw treats over the fence, letting him sniff my hand through the slats, cementing our bond.

"Guess I'm just lovable," I reply, unable to suppress a wink. Her eye roll is endearing, and a warmth spreads through me as I notice the hint of a smile tugging at her lips, despite her annoyance. She steps back and gestures for me to enter. "Whatever, come in. It's cold outside."

Her invitation has me feeling uncharacteristically excited— much like Dog—ready to follow her anywhere.

"How's he doing? He seems to be gaining weight and looking healthier every time I see him," I ask as we step into the warmth of her home.

Odessa stops and turns to face me. "He's doing great. He's such a good boy." Her smile brightens, and I can see the affection radiating from her as she talks to him. "Huh? You're a good boy." Dog's tail wags enthusiastically as he nuzzles into her.

"Got a call from one of the animal welfare officers. They charged the guy who dumped him."

"You're kidding me! They found him?" Her jaw drops in disbelief.

"They said he couldn't afford him anymore and knew someone would find him. He left him the morning you found him."

"But he was in such bad shape!"

"I know," I reply, trying to suppress my own anger. "He was used to being tied up outside in the guy's backyard. Guess that explains why he wasn't barking."

"Fuck that guy. You're going to make sure he doesn't weasel his way out of it, right?"

I nod. "I promised to testify myself, if it comes to that."

"Thanks, Luke. I owe you one for doing that for him." Seeing the relief on her face is more than I could have imagined.

Seemingly overwhelmed by the moment, she steps back into the kitchen. "Drink? Beer? Liquor? Wait, do you drink? I have water!"

"I could use a beer." I glance around, admiring the inviting atmosphere of Odessa's home. The walls are decorated with large photos of different travel destinations, almost making me feel like I'm stepping into a travel magazine. A few framed photos sit on the kitchen counter: Ellie and Ben together, a young Everett, Drew, and Hayes, and one of Connie and Charlie on their wedding day. As I continue to look around, I notice there isn't a single photo of Odessa herself. Google her, and a thousand different images pop up, but here, not one is in sight.

"Thanks," she says, handing me the beer she pulled from the fridge. I take it without even glancing at the label; she could hand me anything, and I'd drink it.

"Are you here to let me know about Dog or to ask more questions about today?"

"Neither," I reply honestly. "Just wanted to check in and see if you're okay." For a brief moment, a little indent appears on her brow before she quickly schools her features.

"Oh, uhm, yeah." She sidesteps around me and settles on the couch, motioning for me to follow. "I'm good."

"No residual effects from earlier?" I ask, raising an eyebrow as I take a seat in the chair next to her.

She hesitates for a moment, then shakes her head. "Just a headache, probably from the stress of it all. Nothing major—I don't think I even consumed any of it."

"Surprised you didn't have SEAL Team Six out front guarding your door."

She groans, her shoulders sagging. "You just missed them. I had to threaten them to get them to leave."

"Yeah? What'd you threaten them with?" I can't picture them being scared of much, let alone anything Odessa could throw at them.

"That I'd personally make sure not another girl in this town looked their direction, let alone hooked up with them."

I pretend to shiver dramatically. "You threatened to cock-block? Evil, Achilles, pure evil..."

"Desperate times call for desperate measures!" She laughs loudly and unapologetically. "And that's *twice* today. Time to man up, Sheriff. What's with the nickname? You a secret nerd with a Greek mythology fetish? Because Odysseus and Achilles aren't exactly related. I googled it."

Chuckling, I sink deeper into the couch. "You're half right. I went through a phase in middle school, maybe even a little in high school." I wink at her, and she blushes. *Have I ever winked this much in my entire life? Probably not.*

"I loved reading about all the gods and heroes. Did you stumble across anything about Achilles in your Google searches?"

She shakes her head. "Not really."

"As the legend goes, Achilles was the son of Peleus, a mortal Greek king, and Thetis, a sea nymph." I wag my eyebrows at her, and she laughs. "When Thetis gave birth to him, she tried to make him immortal like herself by dipping him in the river that ran through the underworld—the Styx—said to be laced with achillea millefolium, or better known as yarrow. To do this, she had to hold him by his heel, the only part of his body left untouched by the water. His only point of weakness."

"And that relates to me?"

"Do you remember the first time we met?"

She nods and notes, "Charlie and Hayes's wedding."

"You remember what you were holding?"

She tips her head to the side, studying me for a moment. "I don't," she admits after a few seconds.

"Flowers."

"The bridesmaids' bouquets?" She asks, confusion knitting her brows.

"Yeah, it was like the moment I saw you, I felt the seams of my carefully constructed façade start to unravel. Sure, you looked like Maddy, which threw me off, but it was more than that. It felt like I somehow knew you were going to break down my walls—like you were my weakness."

She stays silent, the only sound coming from the gulp she takes as her expression remains unreadable.

"Then you caught me staring, but instead of looking away, you smiled—this big, beautiful smile. I had to look away, and the thing I fixated on was the flowers in your hands—overflowing with yarrow."

"And my first thought was, 'Fucking, Achilles.'"

"You think I'm your weakness?"

I pause for a moment, recalling the incident at Ponderosa Pine and the way it had shaken me to my core. Afterward, I called Zeke, and he offered to cover for me for a few weeks while I got my shit together. It was a generous offer, and one I knew I needed to take seriously.

I let out a puff of air that sounds like a laugh. "Know you are. I wanted to strangle that asshole today with my bare hands. Still do, actually. That's why I'm taking a vacation... Staycation? Is that what they call it?"

"Yeah, I mean, I think. I haven't taken too many of those myself in the last few years," she replies, a hint of regret in her voice.

"Well, how could you? Being one of the greatest angels of all time."

She rolls her eyes, but I catch a smile sneaking through. "Seems like you're the one who's been Googling too much."

I smirk, leaning back in my chair. "Nope, watched it live. Loved the red, by the way, but I could've done without the monstrosity of wings."

"Luke!" She throws the pillow she had been clutching at me. I catch it and hold it close, the warmth from her touch lingering on the fabric.

"So, you just show up here, pour your heart out on my loveseat, and then mock me?"

"Pretty much," I reply with a casual shrug, even though we both know it's a significant moment for us.

"What am I missing here?" she asks, narrowing her eyes. "You're not usually this chatty."

"Not missing anything. You asked about the nickname, and I answered. It just turned into a longer explanation."

"And you're the king of short versions."

"Says the queen of short versions herself..."

Chapter Fourteen

Odessa

Did Luke really knock on my door and confess his feelings for me? Maybe the drugs are messing with my head, but I don't feel loopy enough for this to be a hallucination.

He lounges on my couch, legs sprawled like he's claimed the spot, clutching my fluffy pillow—the comfort of it contrasting sharply with the tension in the air.

"Says the queen of short versions herself," he replies, that familiar teasing lilt in his voice.

"Not sure I've ever been accused of not saying enough," I tease back, forcing a smirk as my heart races with the banter. *This Luke, flirty Luke? I'm done for. Call Levi and immediately start CPR.*

He gives me a look that cuts right through my deflection.

"I have no doubt you say what's on your mind, but I think you also spend a lot of time watering down those answers."

"What makes you think that?" I shoot back.

"Game recognizes game." Instead of reacting, I toy with the tips of my hair, waiting for him to elaborate.

"You may not have noticed, but I've been paying attention

to what you've said over the last few months. You have a tendency to deflect or change the subject when things get too personal," he explains, his gaze unwavering.

"Yeah, right." I scoff. "People don't even ask you. It's like you have an entire county terrified to ask you anything." I refuse to back down. He's been paying attention? Well, so have I. No one dares press Sheriff Haynes about how he's really doing—either because they know he won't respond or they're too afraid to ask. There's a silent understanding that everyone has to tiptoe around him, terrified to push the Maddy button.

The corner of his mouth twitches with a reluctant smile.

"Yeah, but I have two trump cards," he quips, raising two fingers.

"Dead best friend. Girlfriend with a severe TBI." *Oh, fuck.*

I have to consciously relax and remind myself to breathe after that blow. Hearing him call Maddy his girlfriend hits me like a rusty butter knife to the soul. But seeing the pain in his eyes, those two fingers raised, is enough for me to muster my signature Astor "facade before feeling" and school my features.

It takes a millisecond but I manage to swallow the disappointment lodged in my throat before I respond, "I can see how that would earn you a pass."

"It does. But, like you said earlier, I'm feelin' chatty tonight. Ask away—whatever questions are burning in that beautiful brain of yours."

I feel the flush in my cheeks, but use this opportunity to distract me from the ache of hearing him refer to Maddy that way. It's a temporary relief, but at least it's something to focus on other than my own hurt feelings—*or him calling my brain beautiful.*

"How does that work with you and Maddy? When you see her I mean. Olivia told me the basics, but even she doesn't know much."

His head tips back, resting on the couch, eyes briefly closed as he lets out a deep breath, gearing up to lay it all out for me. "I visit her in the morning; we have breakfast and—"

"You go every day?" I interrupt, shocked.

"Yep." He nods, his frown deepening. "Usually, I have coffee while she eats. We talk, normally about the same things we discussed the day before the accident—work, family, the future." *The future?*

"I guess I don't understand. Does she not realize she's in a memory care facility?"

He sighs heavily, but it doesn't seem like he's shutting down; he's just trying to think of how to answer.

"It's day by day. The staff is great; they have protocols for communicating with patients. Her case is rare, but they know how to handle her bad or confused days. Some days, she fights them, thinks there's been a mistake and that she doesn't belong there. But most days, she's calm and content, living in her own reality."

"And you being there first thing helps, I'm assuming?" I ask, even though I'm afraid of the answer.

He runs a hand through his hair, a frequent gesture when he's thinking. "Yeah, I guess. I've just always done it—tried to make sure she's comfortable and okay."

"Does she have family, or is it just you?"

"Mainly her dad and me. No siblings. Her mom lives in California and visits occasionally. She tried to get her moved down there, but Joe and I thought she'd be better here. She still has friends that visit, and she was always closer to her dad."

I nod, even though that's something I can never truly understand. Both of my parents suck.

"How does it work with aging? Does she notice?"

He scoffs but can't hide his smile. "You trying to say I'm looking older?"

"Well, aren't you, like, 40 by now?"

"33. Miss 28." I knew that, but I can't help trying to lighten the mood. It gives me butterflies that he remembers such a trivial detail about me.

"But I don't know how that works with her. It's like she sees what she wants to see. She still acts like we were this happy couple, even though she was cheating on me."

My jaw nearly drops at the unexpected revelation. "Cheating on you?!"

He nods, his lips twisting to the side. "Yep. Haven't told a soul—actually, not a living soul. I told Dan when I found out, and then the next day he died."

"Wow. Holy shit."

His body tenses for a moment, fixing his gaze on me before he admits, "Maddy was only in that accident because I insisted she meet me at a diner to break up with her."

I can see it clearly now; he blames himself. "That's a lot of undeserved—"

He raises a hand to stop me. "I should have ended it the moment I saw the dirty texts on her phone. But instead, I went home and told Dan. He told me to sleep on it and meet her the next day. That next day, she was driving to meet me when she swerved into a truck."

"Luke—"

"That's not the worst of it."

My eyebrows raise, and he looks at me with such sadness that I feel it in my bones. "I was on my lunch break when Maddy's accident happened. I left to ride in the ambulance with her, abandoning my shift and my responsibilities—all because I thought I had to be there for her."

I stare, trying to process the weight of his words, but they tangle in my mind. I should be thankful when he fills in the details, but instead his words leave me broken.

"Which meant leaving my department down an officer—leaving Dan a sitting duck. I abandoned my position, he died, and then I ended up with the promotion he'd been vying for since he was a kid."

"That's— It's not— Luke, you don't truly believe that—" Even as I say it, I can see it on his face that he really does. We stare at each other for a long moment as I try to find the words to help him.

"I'm so sorry you hold on to that. I wish I knew the right thing to say here."

He gives me a sad smile. "Nothing really to say. I take full responsibility for that day."

"You're being unfair to yourself," I say with more force than I intended.

He nods. "Maybe. But either way, we still lost Dan, and I'm still stuck dating a woman I can't even really stand."

"What?" I ask, shocked, feeling like I'm seven steps behind wherever he's going.

"I can't break up with her! She just fucking forgets!" He shouts as he sits up, tossing the pillow aside, his cheeks flushed. His outburst leaves us staring at each other until an awkward chuckle escapes him, and soon we're both laughing.

"That's not funny," I say, laughing despite myself.

"Trust me, I know." The pause we take loses some of its earlier energy, and a silent understanding passes between us.

"So, is there any chance of recovery? Like, will her brain heal someday so that she'll remember what happened and learn new things?"

"Couldn't tell you. Joe has hope, prays a lot, but I don't think it's going to happen. The doctors were pretty clear about the severity of her condition."

"And that's it? You're off the market, stuck in a relationship with someone who cheated on you, and you're just going to accept that fate?" I question without malice, trying to understand his perspective.

He shrugs. "I don't know what else to do. It's complicated. If I move on, that makes me the asshole who abandons his girlfriend because she had an accident. Not like I can go around defending myself by saying she was fucking some guy."

"No," I agree, knowing it wouldn't be fair to Maddy for him to share that when she can't defend herself—though I acknowledge there's no real defense. "I don't think anyone expects you to stop your life, though. Couldn't there be a way to have both? Visit Maddy, be there for her as a friend, but also live your own life."

"Maybe." He fiddles with the texture of the pillow now sitting next to him. "I don't know who would be okay with a situation like that." When he looks up at me, I see vulnerability —and maybe, just maybe, a glimmer of hope.

"You'd be surprised at what people are capable of accepting and understanding when there's communication in a relationship. I'm not saying it would be easy, but wouldn't it be worth a try?"

I can see he isn't convinced, but he doesn't seem closed off to the idea either; it's clear he's wrestling with conflicting emotions as he stares at my coffee table.

Then, for the final shock of the night, he looks at me and asks, "Would you be willing to try with me? I can't guarantee I won't screw it up, but I'm willing to put in the effort if you are."

"Try?" I ask, my voice barely above a whisper.

He sits up, the pillow haphazardly falling off the couch. "Date. Be together and see how it goes."

"I—" I start, then pause, my heart racing as my mind struggles to catch up. "Do you think you're ready for that?"

"Full communication, right? If it gets too complicated or difficult, we talk about it." I can hear the excitement in his voice as he talks faster. "And if we promise to stay friends if it doesn't work out, then we can give it a shot."

Promise to stay friends. I repeat the words to myself, over and over again.

Can I do that? I've never stayed friends with an ex or even a fling. But I'd have to if I want to stay in Three Sisters; he's too entwined with our friend group. Is it worth the risk?

One look at him—seeing the way his eyes search mine, waiting for my response—and I know it is. Luke's worth it.

"Okay," is all I manage to say before he jumps off the couch and pulls me up from mine. He wraps his arms around me, hugging me tightly.

He grips my chin, tilting it up to meet his gaze. "Knew from the get-go you'd be my undoing, Achilles."

Then he kisses me, and I almost hope he's a terrible kisser so I could use that as an excuse to push him away. But he's not; he's damn near perfect—lush lips moving expertly against mine. I find myself melting into the kiss, forgetting everything else except the feeling of his lips on mine. It's a dangerous place to be, especially considering I still haven't wrapped my head around the fact that he called someone else his girlfriend just five minutes ago.

Chapter Fifteen

Odessa

"I don't... Luke, where did this come from?" I gasp as he parks a shiny vintage Bronco in my driveway. I couldn't tell you what year it is, but the meticulous restoration is obvious. The black paint glistens in the sunlight, and I can't help but admire the attention to detail in every inch of the vehicle.

"My garage," he replies with a smirk that's both stupid and panty-melting.

"Oh, you mean the garage that's NEXT DOOR to me?" He didn't come clean about being my neighbor until three days after we started hooking up—I mean, hanging out. It was only when I mentioned running out of sugar while baking that he casually told me he'd run home. Then he joked about putting a gate between our properties. Had I known, I would've been peeping through the slats trying to catch a glimpse since I moved in.

"Yep, that's the one!"

"This is yours? And you've been hiding it this whole time? Driving around in your big ole 'SHERIFF' truck, even on your days off?"

"Not hiding it. But it's not like you've been clamoring to spend time in my garage when my bedroom is—"

I smack his chest, rolling my eyes, which makes him laugh and pull me in for a kiss.

"It's beautiful! Where are we going?"

"Just a drive. Thought I'd take you and Dog out for a bit."

"Won't he ruin the leather?" I quip, using his own words against him.

"They're just seats, Achi! Don't talk about Dog like that." He opens the passenger door and adjusts the seat to help Dog in.

He then offers me his hand, and I take it, even though I'm tall enough to climb in on my own.

"Passenger princess? I could get used to this."

"Hope you do." He kisses my cheek and closes the door.

As soon as we hit the highway, a song comes on, and I sit up so quickly that I almost make myself dizzy.

"Don't sit in a shotgun seat,

Less I want to,

And you make me want to,

Hypnotized by the white lines—"

"What is this song?" I demand, and he looks at me like I'm crazy.

"Your hands ten and two on this heart of mine

Makes me feel at home

Yeah, boy, I'm right at home—"

"Luke! You know country music! What is this?!" When he doesn't answer fast enough, I fumble with my phone to look up the lyrics.

"Not so much the new stuff," he chuckles, tilting his head as if trying to figure it out. "But I'm going to guess it's Lainey Wilson."

"Oh, nothin' I love more,

90 to nothing but we in slow motion,
Up in the mountains or down by the ocean,
It's all the same to me,
Ain't nowhere I'd rather be
Than in a 4x4xU, babe."

I type in her name, and "4x4xU" is the first song that pops up.

"Yes!" I practically squeal. "It's our song!"

"Our song?" he asks with a grin, and I feel the heat spreading to my cheeks.

"Or—maybe I just mean I like it..." I say, suddenly questioning my outburst.

His warm hand grips my thigh, and he shakes his head. "Nope, our song."

The possessiveness in his words sends a small flutter in my stomach and I smile while settling back into my seat.

As he accelerates down the highway, the wind whips through the open windows, and the sun warms my skin. In this moment, I can set aside my worries about moving too quickly or falling too fast and embrace the feeling I've been chasing for so long. It's not the fame or the money I want; it's someone who makes me feel truly alive and connected. The music, the wind, his touch—it all feels like home. And for a girl who's desperate to feel at home, this moment is everything I've ever wanted.

Two weeks later—

The sun hung low in the vibrant sky, casting a warm golden hue over the expansive field that stretched before us. Early March in Central Oregon brings its surprises, and between Luke and the weather, I'm feeling more content and at peace than I have in a long time. How is that possible? I moved here feeling lost, worried about Everett, and doubting myself. Now, I have this big, brooding man next to me who gives long, slow smiles that melt my worries away.

Off in the distance, I spot Dog surging excitedly through the tall grass, his fur glistening in the sunlight as he chases a few startled rabbits that had been sunbathing. I can hear his excited barks as he races back toward us, paws kicking up little clouds of dust. I can't help but smile at his unbridled energy and enthusiasm. I've only been his owner for a month, but he's completely come to life. How anyone could abandon this beautiful creature is beyond me.

Luke's loud chuckle beside me makes my smile grow even brighter. He loves Dog's antics as much as I do, and the fact that he's spent every evening with us since his big declaration means a lot to me. Sharing this time together might seem trivial, but it's something I never realized I needed until Luke came along. I was busy in my life, and whoever I was dating was busy too—I just didn't care. But with Luke, he comes over after he's taken care of his obligations for the day; we have dinner together, whether I'm cooking or he's bringing takeout. It feels so domestic, yet it doesn't have me running for the hills. Instead, I look forward to it all day.

It's when he leaves first thing in the morning, before the sun has even risen, that I feel a pang of longing in my chest. I respect him immensely for continuing to see Maddy and being there for her, but I can't help but wonder how long this can last in the long term. Surely, if we were married and had kids, he wouldn't be kissing me, only to roll out of bed and... I quickly halt that train of thought. We've only been in this domesticated bliss for a couple weeks and that's it. None of our friends even know we're hooking up, and here I am, thinking about marriage and kids? *Nope, just no.* I need to rein it back in and focus on why I'm back in Three Sisters: repairing relationships with my family and setting roots. *But what if those roots grow with Luke?*

"Where'd ya go, Achi?" he asks, tossing a grape at me.

"Hmm?" I look up at him, a blush creeping onto my cheeks as I realize I've been caught staring off into space.

"Sorry, thinking about it all," I mumble, brushing a stray hair behind my ear.

He studies me with a knowing look, as if he can sense there's more. "What's that?"

"Living here. Being here." I gesture out toward the open field, my hand sweeping toward the Cascade Mountains in the background. "It's beautiful, but it's also a good place to settle and start the next chapter of my life. I know that sounds cheesy —" I glance down, feeling a bit awkward.

He shakes his head, a warm smile on his face. "I get it. For the first time, it feels like I *understand* that expression."

"Me too," I reply, meeting his gaze again.

"What are you dreaming of in this next chapter?"

We promised to communicate, so I give him the truth—or the closest to the truth I'm ready for: "Right now, getting back to the closeness I had with everyone before we all went our separate ways. Making new friends that are real."

"You had your share of fake ones?" He leans in slightly, his expression more serious, and I can't help but smile at his concern.

"Yeah..." I admit, shrugging my shoulders slightly. "Well, an employee I considered my best friend. Turns out, she was saying some pretty nasty things about me."

"Still your employee?" he asks, sitting up a little straighter, his brow raising in that delicious way.

"No, I fired her when I overheard what she was saying." I cross my arms, feeling the weight of it. "Well, I technically couldn't fire her because she's employed by the agency I'm signed with. I had her removed from my team, though."

"When did that happen? I didn't even know you had an assistant."

"'Bout a week before I got the call about Everett."

"I'm sorry. People suck." He leans back, shaking his head as if to dismiss the negativity.

I chuckle at his favorite expression, nodding in agreement. "That they do."

"What about long term? You plan on sticking around here, right?" The slight tinge of anxiety in his voice doesn't escape my notice.

"I do. I'm sure Everett and I will keep our grandparents' estate so I can still get my fix of the City every now and then, but for the most part, I want to be here."

"As for long term—hopefully marriage and maybe a kid or two."

He nods but looks away toward the mountains, lost in thought.

"Not sure how anyone could spend time with August and not want one of those little bundles." I tack on trying to add some lightness to the conversation.

"He is a cute one. Ben and Ellie were that cute, too," he agrees with a warm smile, his eyes reflecting a hint of nostalgia.

"Is it weird for you that Liv is pregnant again?" I ask softly, my voice gentle. We've talked about so much, but I always tread lightly around the topic of Dan.

"It's..." He pauses, his hand running through his hair as he considers his words, the muscles in his jaw tightening for a moment. "I want her to be happy. Dan and her—"

"Dan was the best at everything, except being a husband." He looks away for a brief moment, and I can see the pain flashing in his eyes. "It was hard to watch because I know he meant well. Then Drew and that whole situation was even harder to watch. It seems like they've turned a corner, though."

I nod, understanding. He may be understating it a bit based on what I've heard, though. I wasn't back yet, but Drew and Liv attempted a friends-with-benefits situation that turned into quite the ordeal.

"Drew's always been kind of an idiot when it comes to relationships," I laugh softly, shaking my head. "But yeah, I think he truly loves her. He'll be a good dad too." That I know for a fact. Charlie and he were raised by the best parents, and I'm thankful I was able to receive a few years of that unconditional love from them before they passed away.

"I hope so." He looks thoughtful, and I can see him grappling with his feelings. "He and I—" He stops, taking a deep breath, then continues after a brief pause. "Well, I wasn't his biggest fan, and we got into it pretty good. I should probably apologize for that at some point..." He trails off, his gaze distant as if he's reflecting on past conflicts.

"I have a feeling he's not holding on to it. Drew's not like that. He's fiercely protective, but he can also admit when he's wrong."

As our conversation drifted into silence, Dog plopped down beside us, panting happily. He nudged my hand with his wet nose, as if insisting it was time for me to pet him. I laughed, the sound bubbling freely between us, and reached down to scratch him behind the ears.

Luke watched us with a grin spreading across his face before he let out a low whistle.

When Dog heard him, he took off, abandoning me to lay beside Luke.

"Aww, I think he loves me more," Luke teased, his eyes twinkling with playful mischief.

"No way." I raised an eyebrow, feeling the warmth of competition stir in my veins.

"You ever see that trend where the couple takes off running in different directions and whoever the dog follows is the favorite?" He replied, laughing as he stood up and took a few steps backward.

"Fine!" I exclaimed, adrenaline surging as I stood up. "Dog." I lightly called, and he trotted over to sit between us.

Luke bends down and scratches the fur around Dog's collar, grinning at me the entire time.

"You ready?" Luke laughs, and I swear I see a hint of challenge spark in his eyes.

"Count of three—One, two, three!" I dart away from Luke, running in the opposite direction. When I turn, it's to see Dog sitting perfectly still where he was. Then I notice his nose twitching and his head leaning toward Luke, as if he desperately wants to go to him. *I wish I could say I didn't get it, but I do.*

"Dog!" I scold, and he immediately turns, running back to my side. As I bend down to give Dog a pat, I glance back at Luke, who is now watching me intently, his infectious smile warming the space between us.

I rise back up, crossing my arms playfully, triumph dancing in my expression. "See? He came back to me. Clearly, I'm the favorite."

Luke laughs, shaking his head in mock disappointment. "Alright, maybe you've managed to hold onto your title... for now." He moves closer, and I can feel the playful tension rising between us. "But don't think for one second that I'm letting this go without a fight. I'll just have to toss more treats over the fence."

"That's how you got him to like you when you came over a few weeks ago?! I thought he just naturally loved you."

"He did! And..." He pauses for comedic effect, his eyes sparkling with mischief. "I visited him at Jane's, took him on walks, and then when you moved in, I upped my game."

"In more ways than one," I say, raising an eyebrow as a teasing smile spreads across my face.

He steps closer, closing the distance between us, and the laughter fades into a warm, intimate gaze.

"Knew I had to win him over if I wanted to win you over," he whispers, his voice filled with sincerity. My heart flutters as I realize he was putting in effort before either of us even knew that we would give this a chance. It's those damn little things that catch me off guard, and Luke is an expert at subtly showing his dedication and affection. With a gentle touch on my cheek, he leans in and kisses me softly, leaving me breathless and wanting more.

Chapter Sixteen

Odessa

"We'll have to check Dog for cheatgrass when we get home," Luke mentions casually, tossing a sideways grin my way as we hike along the trail he picked for us today.

Curiosity piqued, I tilted my head, letting my hair cascade over my shoulder. "What's that?" I ask, leaning slightly closer to him, my eyebrows raised in question.

He gestures animatedly with his hand, pointing toward a patch of grass that sways in the wind. "The seed heads are pointy little bastards. They can get stuck in his fur, burrow in deeper, and cause a whole mess of problems," he explains.

My gaze shifts to the trail, now noticing that it is thick with overgrown plants.

"Should I be worried?" I ask, instinctively brushing my fingertips against my bare thighs, wishing I hadn't worn shorts.

"Nah," he reassures me, waving a hand dismissively. "He'd need to be glanced over anyway. Make sure he doesn't have ticks."

I stop in the middle of the trail abruptly, planting my hands on my hips. "Ticks? Luke!"

He laughs, a warm sound that bounces off the rocks surrounding us. "You wanted to hike, Achi!" He calls over his shoulder, then playfully adds, "Don't worry; I'll check you too."

"Didn't know I was signing up to be in a Brad Paisley song!" I respond, crossing my arms over my chest and feigning annoyance, but I quicken my pace to catch up to him.

Luke's expression shifts to mischief as he glances back at me over his shoulder, a roguish grin spreading across his face. "Hang out with me a little longer, and we'll be fishin' in the dark, too." The wink he sends my way is so unexpected that my knees wobble slightly, forcing me to quickly regain my balance.

When Luke knocked on my door with two coffees, a backpack, and a grin I couldn't resist, I hadn't truly grasped what an "easy hike" would entail with him. The trail itself might not be too demanding, but his presence is embedding something deeper—something I didn't even know I was ready to feel but suddenly can't imagine living without.

He had stayed the night but left early to go see Maddy—which I'm still not sure how I feel about. Cool girl Odessa wants to be okay with it, while anxious girl Odessa feels like she's not enough. I do my best to bury those insecure thoughts, reminding myself that this situation is unique, and we're all navigating uncharted waters.

The terrain continues its unpredictable dance as we hike on. One moment, we're right next to the river, trying to keep Dog from jumping in; the next, we're climbing a steep incline, the view plunging dramatically below us.

"I can't believe how many wildflowers are starting to bloom!" I exclaim, gesturing excitedly toward the vibrant colors emerging from the earth. "Isn't it too early? It's so cold!"

"It's been an unseasonably warm year," he replies, his gaze sweeping across the landscape. "I think yesterday broke the record; today's supposed to be just as nice."

The sky has been nothing but blue, with the sun shining brightly, birds chirping, and the sound of rushing water from the river filling the air.

Dog meanders nearby; while he still has a leash on, the lead is long enough for him to explore freely.

We've passed at least a dozen people, and Luke greets each of them with a friendly smile and a nod. I like seeing this relaxed version of Luke. His usual uptight energy has all but disappeared the further we got away from Three Sisters this morning. I make a mental note to get him out of there more often. Maybe we can even go on a real vacation. Mexico? Greece?

"Hey, have you ever done any traveling? Beyond Oregon, I mean?"

"Uh... hmm. I went fishing in Alaska, hunted a few times in Idaho and Washington, and I think I went to Disneyland when I was little."

"That's it? Not out of the country?"

"Nope. Never really thought about it until I saw all the photos in your house. Looks like some cool places."

"They were! I didn't get to sightsee much, but when I did, I made sure to document everything."

He stops, turning to look at me. "You took those? The ones that look like they belong on the cover of National Geographic?"

I beam at him, thrilled to be recognized for something apart from my job. "Yeah, not many people know that, though."

His eyes light up with curiosity as he asks, "Do you have any more photos to show me?"

I chuckle. "I have an entire finsta account devoted to my photography."

His mouth dramatically echoes "Finsta?" back at me.

"Fake Instagram. I didn't want anyone to know I'm the

photographer. I don't even control my own social media—only this."

"You're full of surprises, Achilles." He takes a step closer, leaning down to kiss me. "I kinda like it."

"Kinda?" I scoff, but he only kisses me again and smiles.

"Come on, I want to show you the caves."

We spent the next two hours hiking, peeking into the caves but not going inside. To be honest, no, thanks. I've read too many Catherine Cowles novels to want to venture into any Central Oregon cave, thank you very much.

By the time we begin our hike back, I feel a sense of contentment and peace that I haven't felt in a long time. The worries from this morning are long gone. Luke is easy to be around—easy to joke with, easy to talk to. I think I've revealed more about myself in the last few weeks than I have in my entire life.

"Back to those photos around your house..." he begins as we walk down a long slope toward the winding river.

"What about them?" I ask.

"For a model, I noticed there aren't any of you around."

"Feels kinda vain to put up pictures of myself around my house," I admit honestly. What does he think I'd do—post photos of myself from shoots? Or campaigns I was paid for?

"What if it was a gift? Would you put it up then?" He doesn't turn around, but I hear the lightness in his voice, making me want to give him whatever he wants.

"Probably. It's not that I have anything against photos of me..."

"Good. Let me take one of you and Dog," Luke says, his voice carrying a playful insistence.

"Of me and Dog?" I question, stopping on the trail.

"Yup. I'll get it framed and everything. I'm sure there's a holiday or something coming up."

A smile creeps onto my face at his pushed-out lower lip. "Fine, but I want it over there."

"On the rocks?" He raises an eyebrow at the section I'm eyeing, a cluster of stones beneath the flat rock wall of the canyon. It looks safe enough—flat and not too high—but is made up of tightly fitted stones.

"Yeah, it'll be such a pretty background with the canyon wall. Plus, if you stand over there," I point to a flat section off to the side, "you'll be able to catch the river behind us in the distance."

Before he can protest, I climb the slope of rock to reach the higher spot, calling Dog with a pat on my leg. As expected, he bounds up beside me with ease. He sniffs around the wide surface, as if searching for something, but I don't notice anything except a few cracks where two large boulders meet.

I leap to the other boulder, carefully avoiding a gap several inches wide. This spot is a bit flatter and should give Luke a better shot at capturing the view around the corner.

"Be careful," Luke calls, his concern tinged with teasing.

"I'm only about five feet off the ground. If you knew what I had to do to get some shots in the past..." My voice trails off as I step toward the edge and peek down. I'm really not that high up, but the drop still looks intimidating from this angle.

"Alright, Achilles. Let's get this over with before you give me a heart attack." I'm tempted to lean over the edge just to tease him, but when I look back, I catch him staring at me with an expression I didn't expect—something akin to reverence.

When his silence lingers, I can't help but laugh. "What are you staring at?"

"You're beautiful. I know you've probably heard that so many times that it doesn't mean much to you," he replies, a smile forming on his lips. "But, fuck, Achi. That carefree grin? It could bring any man to his knees."

"It does," I say softly, feeling a shyness creep into my demeanor. "Hearing you say it. It means a lot to me, actually. It's different."

I swallow hard, feeling the familiar rush of excitement as I shimmy my shoulders, putting on my game face.

"Okay, how do you want me?" My brows raise involuntarily at the gleam in his eyes, a smirk painting his face.

"Dammit, Luke. Not like that," I chuckle, feeling heat seep into my cheeks.

"Just smile, Achi. I don't want a photo of Odessa Astor, famous supermodel. I just want one of you and Dog."

"Sit," I command Dog, and he dutifully plops down next to me, staring at me with that adoring look, as if I'm the sun, moon, and stars all in one.

I pose for the photo, laughter bubbling up as Luke clicks away, capturing every angle of my smile. I swear my cheeks are getting more of a workout than my legs during this hike.

He pockets his phone and calls for Dog, who bounds down eagerly, joining him despite the rocky terrain.

"See? I think you're his second favorite person!" I announced, planting my hand on my hip, feeling playful and lighthearted.

"If you weren't so lovable, I'd be first!" He shoots back, adopting the same finger-pointing motion he used on Dog, gesturing for me to come down.

I roll my eyes but oblige, preparing to take the small leap toward the other boulder. But as I push off, my foot betrays me —slipping and sliding with terrifying speed. Time slows to a crawl, and I barely have time to process what's happening before it's too late. A sharp, searing pain blossoms in my kneecap as it collides violently with the unforgiving rock after my foot gets caught in that damn crack.

Chapter Seventeen

Luke

I look up just in time to see Odessa take a step, and her foot slide.

In the next second, a slew of curse words escapes her, and I can only see her from the waist up. Dog and I both scramble to her in sync, moving faster than I ever have in my life.

"Odessa!"

She fake laughs, but I don't miss the strain in her voice. "I'm okay! My leg is a little stuck, though. And maybe broken?"

When I reach the top, I see her left leg bent on the ground while her right leg is wedged between two boulders.

"Fucking hell. Okay, my ass," I grumble as I take a closer look.

"It's not stuck stuck. It feels more like I can't get leverage to pull myself out, and the edges are cutting me when I try."

"One second." I unbuckle the clip across my chest, preparing to throw my pack on the ground behind us when she suddenly says, "Do you hear that?"

Dog's low growl has me whipping around. But when I turn,

he's not growling at her; he's focused on the ground—more specifically, the crack where her leg is trapped.

Then I hear it: the buzzing of what sounds like a thousand pissed-off bees. *But I don't see any bees.*

"Fuck! Ow! What the hell?" she screams, flailing as her body contorts with pain.

"Stop moving!" I shout back, my adrenaline flaring to life.

She turns to me, wide blue eyes staring as she struggles to suppress her body's natural reaction to pain. "Do not fucking move your leg or foot until I tell you."

The sound grows louder, no longer resembling bees but the distinct rattle of rattlesnakes—and by the sound of it, a lot of them.

I yank my pistol from the holster on my back and hand it to her. "Why are you giving this to me?"

"Can you hold it for a second? Finger off the trigger. I'm going to pull you out of there. It's going to hurt like a bitch, but it needs to be done *now*."

Her mouth gapes open. "Arms around my neck." She does it instantly, but before I can wrap my arms around her waist, she screams in my ear.

I loop my arms under her butt and heave with everything I have. She slides out easily, but I lose my footing, and we fall backward with her on top of me. I quickly shift so that I can grab the gun from her hands, aiming it at the hole she came from. Part of me expects a rattlesnake to be attached to her leg, though I know that isn't how it works.

"What the fuck?!" she screams as she turns and stares at the puncture wounds on her leg.

When I don't see any vipers following, I lower my pistol and scoot us further away. Thankfully, Dog follows and sits next to us, his worried gaze darting between us and the hole.

"You're going to be okay. I've got you." My left hand pulls her in tighter, securing her to me.

Seeing the blood from her scratches and bites sets me in motion. I immediately grab my phone from my pocket to call for help. We are only about three miles from my truck, but I don't want to hike her out of here. Thankfully, I have service and quickly dial 911.

"Need a medevac to the Scout River Trail, 29-year-old female, multiple rattlesnake bites, possible broken leg."

"Sir, slow down. I can't dispatch a medevac until I have additional information."

"No. You listen to me. This is Luke Haynes, Sheriff of Cascadia County. You will dispatch it right fucking now!"

"Sir, I couldn't even if I wanted to. They're already on a call."

I hang up without another word, dialing Zeke as Odessa asks, "What's going on?"

Zeke answers on the first ring. "Can you get Everett to CC airfield? I need a transport to Riverbend *right fucking now*, and Deschutes is busy."

"Where are you? What happened?"

"East side of Scout River, about five hundred feet from where we went fishing. Odessa's leg slipped between some boulders into a fucking rattlesnake den. Multiple bites, possible broken leg."

"Dear God." I *don't need God right now, Zeke! I need fucking Everett!*

"There's a plateau around the river bend where I know he can land. Can you get her there?"

Before I can respond, I hear the words I'm desperate for: "Astor, you still at CC?"

I can't hear Everett's response, but I catch Zeke confirming the plan.

"Luke, you good?" Zeke asks when he returns to my call.

"I'll get her there."

I peer over the edge of the rock; it's a straight drop onto solid ground below, and there's no way for me to carry her down. I'm not risking even a step over that damn crack. "Get me where?" she asks.

"There's a clearing for Everett to land around the corner."

She nods, and I notice the tears streaking down her face. "I've got you. I'm going to jump down first, then help Dog, and then you."

I help her position herself so she's sitting with her feet dangling over the edge of the rock. Blood drips down, and I know I need to act quickly to elevate her leg until Everett arrives. I grab my pack and toss it over five feet down, then sit on the edge and jump. My feet hit the ground, and I turned to call Dog. He peers over the edge, and I've never been so thankful for my height in my entire life; the edge of the rock sits at my chest.

He hesitates, but I grab him by the collar and yank him over, supporting his belly and lightly tossing him when he's close to the ground. He lands on all fours, but I barely see it because I'm too focused on getting Odessa down.

I have to swallow the lump in my throat as I catch a glimpse of her leg. The marks cover her skin, and I know that if I stop to think about how much venom is pumping through her body right now, I'll lose my goddamn mind.

"Ready?" Before I can respond, she leaps off the edge and into my arms. I grunt at the surprise of her suddenly throwing herself at me, but I manage to keep my footing.

I set her down gently, her good leg going to support her as she props up the injured one.

"I think I can hobble," she says through clenched teeth. *Absolutely not.*

"One second." I throw my pack over my shoulder and scoop her up bridal style.

I carry her the entire way, trying to remember everything I know about rattlesnake bites. Every year, we train our department on how to handle these situations:

Calm the patient.

Clean the wound.

Splint and immobilize the leg at the level of the heart.

Monitor for signs of envenomation.

Evacuate.

Not only does she weigh less than most of the guys I normally train with, but the adrenaline surging in my bloodstream gives me a boost.

My breathing may be heavy, but I don't notice it as I set her down near the spot where I think Everett will land. It's going to be dusty as hell, and I don't want her getting blasted with dirt when he arrives.

I shrug off the pack and lay it down, propping her head on it as she reclines. Dog paces beside her, watching her every move. I can feel the worry rolling off him. *Same, bud, same.*

Does she look paler than normal?

I check her pulse, counting, and watch her chest rise and fall. Her leg twitches.

"It really hurts, Luke."

"I know. I'm so sorry, Achi. I promise you, you'll be okay. I'm so fucking sorry."

Not even 0.01% of snake bites result in death in North America. Everett is on his way. *She'll be fine. Stay calm. Splint and immobilize the leg at the level of the heart.* I pull my splint kit out of the pack and carefully strap it to her leg. *Monitor for signs of envenomation.* Running through the checklist for symptoms, I see she already has all of them: pain, swelling, and redness. *What's the other one? What am I missing?*

"Blurred vision!" I shout, and her eyes widen.

"What?"

Through a shaky breath, I ask, "Do you have any blurred vision?"

"Does from crying count?"

My chest constricts at her attempt to lighten the moment.

"No, blurred vision," she adds when she sees the despair on my face.

The sound of rotary blades whirling through the air makes my shoulders tense. The cavalry is here—her brother *is here*—but that doesn't mean I'm not still on edge.

I cover her body with mine, hoping to shield her from the dust.

The second the helicopter lands, I cradle her against my chest again and lift her up. Instead of wrapping her arms around me, though, her head lolls back. I stumble through the rocks and brush toward Dr. Peterson and the on-call SAR nurse, Claire.

"Leave it!" I shout as they start to slide the stretcher out. I'm already halfway there, and I'm not setting her down until she's on that helicopter. They can start working while Everett takes off.

Dog follows closely beside me, and I catch sight of him half-hopping and sniffing her hair as he runs. I've never seen a dog love its human as much as he loves her.

I shoulder past them and practically dive through the open door, setting her down on the stretcher.

"Luke, MOVE! Grab the dog and strap yourself in!" Claire demands, and I almost come unglued. If I hadn't known Claire since she was practically a baby, I might have lost it, but when I look at her, all I see is her determination to get through this. Crouching down, I slide behind her and reach for Dog, yanking him by the collar and hauling his heavy mass in.

I buckle into the seat furthest from them—the one behind Everett—so they can start working, pulling Dog into my lap.

I don't have a headset on, so I can't hear what Everett is asking, but I can tell the three of them are communicating.

The longest seven minutes of my life pass as I bury my hands into the fur on Dog's neck, both of us staring at Odessa while Peter and Claire work.

She's still conscious, but they must have given her some medication because I see the pain begin to melt away. Her eyes grow more tired. She answers their questions, her brows drawing together in confusion when she can't understand what they say because of the noise.

When she looks over and sees me staring, a small smile forms at the corner of her mouth. "You okay?"

The fact that she's concerned about me nearly guts me. It's my fault she's lying there with venom pumping through her blood, fighting for her life. I shouldn't have asked for the picture. Shouldn't have taken her for a hike. Shouldn't have mentioned trying for something more.

I wasn't even in love with Maddy when the accident occurred, and it still nearly broke me.

Continuing this with Odessa and then losing her? I'd never recover.

Chapter Eighteen

Luke

What seems like most of the Emergency Department staff meets us at the helipad. Doctor Lewis and Claire help guide the stretcher off the helicopter and toward the waiting medical team. The urgency in their movements is palpable as they rush into the hospital. My brain struggles to keep up with the medical jargon being thrown around, but I catch the doctors' nods and the rapid exchange of words. At some point, Claire turns back, heading toward where we came from—probably back to Everett. *Shit.* He should be here, not me. But I can't fly that helicopter, and I know he can't just leave it.

Someone in scrubs reaches out and grabs my arm. I try to pull away, but the grip tightens, and I look to find an older woman with a stern expression. Her short greying hair is neatly styled, and her eyes are sharp.

"You need to come with me. Let the doctors do their job," she says firmly, her grip unyielding as she leads me toward a waiting room. The air feels thick as we approach the door to a space—empty, completely private, and sealed off from the rest of the department. *The same room I was in the last time my world came crashing down.*

"You can wait here until we have more information," she adds before retreating the way we came.

This time, I can't even pace; my mind pulls me into the dark space I occupied when I saw Dan. I sit in the same chair as before, noticing they must have replaced the floors, as the linoleum is no longer peeling.

The uncertainty gnaws at me, making the sterile room feel even colder. Time slips away—could be a minute, maybe ten— and I get lost in my thoughts, replaying the scene over and over in my mind. Occasionally, a vision of Dan being wheeled by or the doctor telling me that Maddy was being placed into a coma intrudes. But mostly, it's Odessa's face—filled with shock and pain—that haunts me.

At some point, I hear Olivia's voice, but once again, I can't summon the strength to look at her. I don't want to. There are other voices too—Drew, Isla—low murmurs of male voices echoing in the hall.

Then a commotion arises—Everett shouting—but even that doesn't pull me out of my spiral. I don't want to look at them; the guilt is too busy eating away at me.

"We saw you fly by the house," Isla announces to the room. "Drew picked me up, and we had just gotten back to their place when you went by."

"Why was Drew picking you up?" Everett asks, and if I could focus, I'm sure I'd be able to pinpoint whatever tone he's using. I don't hear Isla's reply, but then I catch the jealousy in Everett's voice when he says, "Why didn't you call me?"

I feel my lip curl at the trivial comment. His sister is fighting for her life, and he's jealous of his best friend. I *never* would have worried about Dan and Odessa. A sob threatens to rise at that thought. Dan would have loved her—loved her for me. He always politely told me I needed someone with a little more fire in them; someone who wasn't afraid to say what they meant for fear of not being liked.

Everett's sharp intake of breath grabs my attention.

"You don't think—?" he says, incredulity lacing his tone.

Olivia, sitting on my other side, asks, "Think what?"

Isla starts talking so softly that I barely catch what she's saying—something about "a ghost?"

Olivia gasps. "You're not joking?!"

I try to replay the conversation, making sure they're not talking about Odessa, but I feel like I'm missing key pieces.

"You think it's DAN!" Olivia shouts next to me, and just hearing his name nearly sends me into a panic attack. *I miss the hell out of that guy.* It's almost been three years since someone shot him—three years of missing my best friend, wishing I could ask him for advice, and feeling guilt knowing it's my fault his kids are being raised without their dad.

"The doctor? Or a nurse?" My panic begins to subside as those words register. It's like my hearing is coming back, but I'm still frozen in place. I focus on my breathing, counting as I inhale.

"Dog." *Dammit, Dog.* I need to make sure he's okay. He looked as helpless as I felt on that helicopter.

"Wait, who was she dating?" *Me.*

"Casually seeing. Not dating." *Casual.* I almost snort. Nothing Casual about what we've been doing.

"What does that mean? She's hooking up with someone?" *Hooking up? What is this high school?*

"She's fucking some random guy?" *Random? Little bit.*

"Who?" *ME.*

"One of the guys from the team?" *No.*

"Wasn't there a thing at Ponderosa Pine? I know Ethan freaked out." *Oh, there was a thing. Where I almost lost my job and killed someone.*

"Could it be Ethan?" *Hell no.*

"No way. Delta? They're the most comfortable together."

"She's sleeping with Delta?!"

"No!" This time my internal monologue lost, and I all but shouted.

"No, what?!" Everett demands, looking murderous and confused at the same time.

"We're—it's—" I stumble over my words, my chest heaving as I try to figure out how to explain what Odessa and I are.

"Complicated."

Everett's face morphs into shock. "When the hell did that happen?"

I lean forward, resting my forearms on my thighs as I struggle to catch my breath, glancing around the room at the expectant faces of everyone who loves Odessa. Finally, I settle on a small portion of the truth.

"At the beginning of January, we ran into each other at the church I go to. We... became friends. For the last few weeks, we've been hanging out and hiking together. She said she wanted to see Central Oregon, and I didn't want her to go alone."

"So you were hiking? That's how she got bit?" Olivia asks.

"She climbed onto some boulders so I could get a photo of her and Dog. Her leg slipped into a fucking den of rattlesnakes. I got her out—" I choke on my words. "But it was too late. A few of them bit her."

"Holy shit," I hear Charlie comment from where she stands by Hayes. "A *den*? Only Odessa!"

I nod, swallowing the emotion lodged in my throat.

"How close to where Everett picked you up?" Drew asks as I glance in his direction.

"Little south of where the river bends, up against the wall."

Drew nods and glances at Hayes, who returns the nod. "Why?" I ask, immediately regretting it.

One of Drew's eyebrows raises, his face remaining emotionless. "You don't want the answer to that." The sheriff in me absolutely doesn't want to know. The part of me that's in love with Odessa hopes explosives are involved.

Just then, Doctor Lewis steps into the waiting room, and we all stand.

"How is she?" Everett and I asked at the same time.

"She's okay. Fully awake and talking—probably a little too much with all the painkillers. But I wanted to lead with the fact that she's okay. When her foot slipped through the crack, she fractured her kneecap on one of the rocks. It must have been a den because we counted eight puncture wounds from four snakes. That doesn't mean all the snakes injected venom, but time is on our side if they did."

He looks at me briefly. "You did a good job, Lucas. The splint, calling in Everett, and keeping her calm all helped get her here in time."

Then he looks back at Everett. "For now, they'll monitor her closely for signs of coagulopathy and tissue necrosis. Ortho wants to wait on her knee; he doesn't think it should require surgery and doesn't want to do anything unnecessary."

"Thanks," Everett says, extending his hand to shake the doctor's. "I'll take this explanation over critical individual presenting with a polytraumatic condition resulting from envenomations."

Doctor Lewis chuckles at that. "Sorry about that. Zeke and I weren't sure how to handle this. It was my suggestion to keep it vague until we knew more."

Graciously, Everett nods. "Understood."

"Can we see her?" Connie asks from behind him.

"One at a time for now. There are a lot of moving parts right now. She asked for Everett and then Luke."

It takes everything in me not to claw my way into that room, but I know Everett takes priority.

Chapter Nineteen

Luke

Everett walked back into the waiting room, and I shot past him, my heart racing. I was already focused on the clock on the wall, each tick a countdown to when I could go into her room and kick his ass out. Do I deserve to be in there? Not at all —but another minute and my heart would explode.

He shouted directions over his shoulder, and subconsciously, I must have absorbed them because I found her room without a hitch.

As I stepped inside, my breath caught. Odessa lay there, her eyes closed, her skin so pale she looked nearly dead. Her leg and foot are swollen so large that they're nearly double the size of her other leg.

My knees almost gave out at the sight. If it weren't for the gentle rise and fall of her chest and the steady beeping of the monitors, I would have thought she was gone. She was already in a gown, hooked up to so many wires and tubes that I nearly passed out. Maybe it was a blessing that Everett had taken his time; I shuddered at the thought of what I might have missed during the frantic moments of her treatment. Now, the doctor was absent, leaving only a nurse to monitor her vitals.

"Luke," the nurse greeted me softly, her familiarity disarming. I couldn't tear my gaze from Odessa to see who she was; surely, she recognized me from when Maddy had been here.

"How is she?" I managed to ask, though my voice came out more garbled than I'd intended.

"Vitals are good. They gave her the initial ten vials. The antivenin is working as it should, but the doctor has already ordered more and is having additional vials brought in."

"Have a seat, honey. She just fell asleep, but she was trying to kick her brother out for the last thirty minutes so she could see you. I know she'll be happy to see you when she wakes up."

She shouldn't be; I'm the one who caused this.

I sit on the hard chair next to her bed, staring at the ink marks on her calf. It looks like they placed a Sharpie around the red area from when we first arrived. With each passing hour, they must add a new circle to track how far it's spreading, marking the time and measurements like a timeline. *I should have done that in the field! I carry a fucking sharpie in my pack for situations like this...*

She receives another dose of antivenin, and I watch in a disassociated state. I'm present in the room but feel checked out. When Odessa wakes up a little later, she smiles at me as if it's not a big deal that she's lying here fighting for her life because of me. I can't recall what I say in response, but I find myself gripping her free hand like it's a lifeline.

The only reason I'm aware of Charlie entering the room is because Odessa waves with her other hand. Whatever Charlie says brings smiles and jokes back from Odessa, and for a moment, I'm almost reassured.

Charlie squeezes my shoulder, snapping me back to reality. I'm about to say, "I'm not leaving," when she says, "They're allowing another visitor as well. I'm only here for a minute. Connie wants to stay the night, and then we'll take turns in the morning. You don't have to go." Her reassurance softens my shoulders, but I see in her eyes that she understands. She knows the depth of my pain—she witnessed me firsthand when Dan died; *she knows*.

Everyone I love ends up in this hospital through no fault of their own—just mine. I'm the underlying cause of all these accidents.

I can't escape my thoughts. The longer I sit here, the more I torture myself with ways I could have prevented this.

It all started with that day I went to her house a few weeks ago, telling her I wanted to try. Falling for her so completely.

Then taking her on that hike. Not being cautious of our surroundings. Asking for the picture.

I should have insisted she not go onto those rocks. I should have asked more questions about the surface. I should have paid closer attention to Dog when he was clearly trying to alert us to something up there.

I ignored all the signs. For what? A picture of her and Dog because I wanted it.

I know I'll never forgive myself for this.

The real question is, will she forgive me for what I'm about to do?

Chapter Twenty

Odessa

The first thing I notice when I wake up is that my eyes are itchy, dry, and irritated. My leg isn't in as much pain, but there's a dull throb that serves as a reminder that I'm still in the hospital. I think it's day two. No, wait—day three, since I've slept here two nights.

Upon my arrival, the Emergency Department doctors swooped in and pulled me from the helicopter. I wasn't able to talk to Everett, but I at least made eye contact and tried to mouth that I was okay and that I loved him. Luke was nearby for a moment, but they soon sent him off to wait somewhere else.

Then there were what felt like a hundred different faces in and out of my room, all trying to decide what to do. They needed to confirm that I had indeed been envenomated and not just bitten without injection—apparently, rattlesnakes don't always deliver venom, and it's very rare, even for a hospital this size, to deal with envenomations at all.

After that, they discovered I had a fractured kneecap, which sparked a big debate about whether I even needed

surgery and how long they should wait before making a decision. Thankfully, I was finally given a proper dose of pain
meds, and they started administering the antivenin vials. Lucky
for me, I felt like I was higher than a kite, essentially sitting
back to enjoy the show.

They fitted me with a proper immobilizing brace, which
wasn't any more comfortable than the one Luke pulled out of
his bag. Who *even* carries that sort of thing on a small hike?
Luke.

Once they moved me into the ICU, it felt like a never-
ending cycle of labs, antivenin vials, and constant monitoring of
my vitals. Everett was able to come back after a few hours, but I
was mostly out of it, so I don't remember much. Then Luke
came in and hasn't left since.

He hasn't budged from his spot in the chair by my bed.
Honestly, he looks like he hasn't moved at all. Someone must
have brought him a clean pair of clothes because he's not
wearing what he had on while hiking. He's so lost in thought,
staring at my leg, that he doesn't even notice I'm awake.

I reach for the water next to my bed, and it startles him out
of his trance. He looks up at me with a mix of relief and
concern, but what nearly crushes me is the guilt etched all over
his face. This poor guy— I can't imagine what he's thinking.
After everything he went through with Maddy and now this,
it's clear he's beating himself up about it.

"Luke—" I begin, but he cuts me off.

"Here, let me help," he offers, reaching for the water and
positioning the straw right in front of my mouth. I take a sip,
feeling the cool liquid soothe my dry throat. Luke's eyes never
leave mine, filled with what can only be described as a deep
sense of remorse. It sends a shiver down my spine, like I'm
experiencing déjà vu from the way he used to look at me.

"Thanks," I say as I watch him retreat back to his seat. He

didn't even touch me, and now that I think about it, I don't believe he has since we left the trail. *He's already checked out; I can feel it in my soul.*

Instead of looking at me, he keeps his gaze fixed on my unmoving leg.

"Are you okay?" I ask. He stares at me as if I've grown a second head, concern not just etched on his features but practically ingrained. "Being here?" I continue. "It can't be easy with your history."

"I'm fine," he replies curtly, darting his eyes away from mine.

"You look like shit, Luke."

The only reply I get is a noncommittal grunt.

"Why don't you go home? Shower, eat some real food? I'll call Ev or Connie, and they can keep watch."

"All good here," he says, but his face is permanently frowning.

"You're not good! You won't even look at me!"

When he doesn't respond, it only fuels my anger. Somewhere deep inside, I know I shouldn't push him right now. He's clearly struggling and shutting down, but I need some reassurance—anything, really.

"Luke, talk to me. Please?"

"Now's not the time or place."

"What does that mean?"

"You're in the hospital, Odessa. You need to focus on getting better. Everything else can wait." *It feels like a damn snakebite to the heart.* Has he ever called me Odessa? It's always Achilles when he's frustrated with me, Achi when he's being loving. Odessa? Only that first day at the church.

"I'd rather not wait." I muster up whatever confidence I have. I feel my nose tip up, my chin rising on its own. "It'll only make me worry and stress until the conversation happens."

This time when he looks at me, he seems taken aback—like maybe I'm right.

"Say it, Luke," I demand through gritted teeth, my voice firm and unwavering. I refuse to let my emotions get the best of me in this moment. It's time for us to address the elephant in the room and have an honest conversation about our relationship.

His eyes harden, but I can see the concern lurking beneath as he squares his shoulders.

"Seeing you here, in the hospital, has put a lot of things in perspective. I never should have agreed to a 'seeing where things go' relationship with you—" For a brief second, my heart stutters; this could go either way, but there's still a tiny bit of hope in me that he's about to say he wants to be with me.

"—when I haven't begun to heal from my past. To be honest, I don't know if I'll ever be able to recover from the trauma I've played a part in," he finishes, his voice heavy with regret. *And just like that, the hope is smashed into a million pieces.*

"What does that mean? Trauma you've played a part in?"

He sighs through his nose. "This—You. Maddy. Dan. All of those things had a common denominator—me."

"What?" I ask, shocked. Other than the fact that we all knew him, I'm struggling to see the comparisons.

He looks down, avoiding my gaze. "I'm sorry," he adds softly. "I think it's best for both of us if we only remain friends." The finality of his words hits me like a ton of bricks, leaving me powerless and heartbroken.

"You should go."

He runs his hand down his face and groans. "Don't. Don't be like this, please..."

When he meets my eyes again, I see the pain reflected back

at me. "You promised we would still be friends if it didn't work out. You told me there'd be no hard feelings."

"I guess we both lied then," I shoot back matter-of-factly. "You lied when you said you'd give us a real chance, and I lied when I said I could handle just being friends with you. But the truth is, I can't. It hurts too much to pretend like everything's okay when it's not."

"Achi—"

"No! You don't get to call me that anymore." I take a deep breath and, more calmly than I feel, say, "It's done. We're done. You can go."

The nurse chooses that moment to shuffle in, clearly over-hearing our disagreement. "Everything okay in here?" She looks between the two of us, but I don't respond. Instead, I turn away from him and focus on the nurse. "Yes, everything's fine. Sheriff Haynes was just leaving. Thanks," I say with a forced smile, trying to conceal the pain in my eyes.

She nods and begins to check my vitals, clearly waiting to ensure Luke follows through.

Out of the corner of my eye, I see his shoulders slump before he stands up and walks toward the door.

Before he exits, he rests his hand on the doorframe and pauses. "I'll be back in the morning to check on you and give you a ride home." His index finger taps three times before he walks out without another word.

"Need anything else, sweetheart?" the nurse asks gently.

I shake my head as the first tear falls, quickly looking away so she doesn't see it.

The only thing I want to do is cry alone and then do what-ever I can to get out of the hospital before he arrives tomorrow.

Chapter Twenty-One

Luke

Warm, dry air hits me as soon as I step out of the hospital, but instead of heading to my truck, I take a seat on one of the benches outside. I haven't been outside since Odessa was admitted, and I don't even want to leave now. *Three days.* Even when Maddy was in the hospital after her accident, I left. I told everyone it was to check on Olivia and the kids—Zeke and Levi. But looking back, it was really just to escape the hospital. Each day, I went home, slept, showered, checked in with everyone, and then returned.

With Odessa in there? Only God himself could have dragged me away. *Or I guess, her kicking me out.* I wasn't ready to tell her we should end things; I wanted to handle it the right way. I needed to explain my reasoning.

Instead, she knew. She read me like a book.

Only I can't leave—not until I know someone is there to stay with her. Even then, while I may have exited her room, I'm not sure I can truly leave.

My phone has been clenched in my hand for so long that my fingers are stiff.

As I stare at the black screen, about to call Everett, someone sits down next to me.

Hayes.

"What'd ya do to get kicked out?"

Rather than answer right away, I scrub at my eyes with my fingers and lean back, tilting my face toward the sky.

"What'd you hear?"

"Nothin'," he chuckles low. "But I saw you up there. That look in your eye. No way you'd leave willingly."

My head bobs in confirmation, but I don't respond.

"Charlie and Ev got her for now. Olivia and Drew have August for the afternoon." We sit in silence for a while longer, watching people mill around, going in and out of the entrance.

"Come on. I'm playing chauffeur," he says, patting my shoulder before standing up.

"My truck's here somewhere. Will dropped it off."

"Wasn't a question. You're not driving," he replies, looking down at me. "Drowsy, distracted, drugged, or drunk—you preach those four D's at every opportunity. You're not above 'em. Let's go."

I follow him, knowing he's right, even though I don't want to drive anywhere. I'd rather stay here and sleep on that bench.

Neither of us speaks during the thirty-minute drive. I expect him to turn toward my house, but instead, he goes the opposite way. He drives for a few more minutes, heading out of town, and I realize where he's taking me. The problem is, I don't know why—and I'm too tired to protest.

He turns down a paved road lined with white fences and lush green grass, under the arches of Three Sisters Cemetery.

It's a beautiful cemetery, well cared for. Unfortunately, I've been here far too often; I know it like the back of my hand. It's the final resting place for most of Three Sisters, and I've lived here for too long.

Hayes shifts into park and steps out, and again I follow, weaving our way toward the large headstone bearing the Cascadia County Sheriff badge—the one I still wear every day and can't look at without thinking of him. *My best friend.*

We both stand in silence, staring at the portrait of him in his uniform. The camaraderie, the shared jokes, and the memories come flooding back of the day that photo was taken; we had to line up like it was elementary school. I think it took the photographer just as long to get us to focus as it would for kids.

If Hayes notices the tears spilling down my face he doesn't say anything.

"Why'd you bring me here?" I finally ask, my voice raspy and barely above a whisper.

Hayes looks at me with understanding in his eyes. "Three reasons come to mind, but the main one is that Olivia mentioned something when we dropped off August."

"What's that?" I ask after clearing my throat.

"She said she's worried you're going to blame Odessa getting hurt on yourself, like you do with Maddy and Dan."

I don't respond.

"That true? You holding on to guilt that doesn't belong to you?" Hayes asks gently, his voice filled with concern. I look away, not ready to answer that question truthfully just yet.

"Human nature, right?"

"Sure, but that doesn't mean it's healthy—especially if it keeps you from moving forward," Hayes replies, rocking on his heels.

"You didn't shoot him, Luke. Hell, you weren't even the owner of the grocery store that stopped carrying the damn gluten-free bread."

"No, but I should've been there. I shouldn't have been taking a lunch to talk to Maddy only for her not to show up. I shouldn't have been in a hospital waiting room because she was hit on her way to meet me."

"You're grasping, bud. Trying to make sense of a senseless situation by placing the blame somewhere. You think shouldering it all will make it easier to bear when, in reality, you only played a minuscule part in that day. There are a million different things that could have changed the outcome—light turning red, phone call taken, a hunter shooting that fucking deer the prior season. We make decisions all damn day without realizing the potential consequences they may have. It's not your fault that the deer ran out in front of Maddy; it's not your fault a lunatic shot Dan; it's not your fault Odessa's leg slipped into a rattlesnake den."

Accepting that feels like I'm shirking responsibility, like it lessens the impact of their tragedies.

On some level, I know what he's saying is true. It's what most of the sermons at church were about: forgiving ourselves, laying it down at the feet of God, and trusting Him to carry the burden.

"I don't know where to go from here. I don't know how to let it go. I thought I would be able to move forward. But seeing Odessa..." I pause, unsure of how much I want to reveal.

"I get it. Falling in love ain't for the weak of heart."

"It's only been a few weeks..." I say trying to downplay it.

"You can lie to yourself all you want, but not to us," he says, gesturing toward Dan's picture. "One of the other reasons I brought you here? Sometimes you just need to talk to your best friend about the girl you can't stop thinking about."

My shoulders sag under the weight of grief. Hayes, Ethan, Levi, Zeke, Everett—the list goes on—have all been damn good friends over the years, but nothing compares to the first true best friend you ever had.

"I'll give you some time alone," he says before turning to walk away.

"Wait, what's the third reason?"

He lets out a light laugh. "Has more to do with me than you. You know my dad was a SEAL, too? He said the only place a man is allowed to cry is at a funeral or during the birth of his child. Not that I believe that, but you looked like you could use a good cry—seeing as you've been celibate until recently, I figured this would be close enough to a funeral."

"That's fucked up," I reply with a shaky laugh, feeling a little of the weight lift off my shoulders.

"Yeah. Charlie and Drew got fucking cheeseburgers and milkshakes, while I was told to 'man up.'"

"How'd you end up so soft if your dad was such a hardass?" I joke as he walks away. When he throws his middle finger up in the air, I can't help but laugh.

Then I sway on my feet, sobering up when I look back at the picture of Dan.

"Really fucking miss you, man. Nothing's been the same since you've been gone. Olivia and the kids... You'd be so proud of them. Ben's still smart as hell—probably smarter than both of us combined at his age. Ellie's got the personality of a mini-you, always cracking jokes and making everyone laugh. And Olivia... She's been holding everything together like a rock. The way life throws shit her way and she just keeps going is incredible."

I gently kick at the grass, staring down at my boots. "Her strength is unmatched. I'm not even close to how strong she is. Get this—I couldn't even look at Odessa for weeks because it hurt too much. Then somehow, she was everywhere I looked, and I couldn't stop staring. Felt like I was cheating on Maddy, but at some point, I stopped caring." We've only been trying to see where things go for a few weeks, but I already feel like I'm in too deep.

Birds soar through the sky somewhere in the distance, calling out to each other but everything else is quiet.

"That morning I picked her up before we went hiking, I couldn't get over how happy I was. How amazing Odessa is—funny, beautiful, confident." If there was a checklist for my dream girl, she would check every box.

"Then hearing those rattles and her scream..." It was a nightmare I couldn't wake up from. I still feel the worry that she wouldn't make it to my core.

"I'm not strong enough. I don't think I could handle losing another person I love. I'm *barely* surviving now, ya know?"

After laying it all out there, I remain quiet for a few minutes, letting my confession sink into the dirt and disappear into the silence.

"Rest easy, friend." I let my knuckles knock three times on his headstone before heading back to the truck where Hayes is waiting.

I'm not sure this pit stop accomplished what he thought it would, but I do feel lighter. Like speaking my thoughts out loud somehow lifted the burden.

When I get in the truck, I thank Hayes, and he nods, giving me a sad smile before starting the engine and driving me toward my house.

The short drive is quiet, only the music filling the air, which is fine by me. The exhaustion of not sleeping the last few days begins to weigh heavily on me, even though it's not even close to dinner time.

When he pulls onto my street, he starts talking. "Everett offered to drive your truck home so you have it in the morning."

"Sounds good. Tell him thanks." At least that saves me the money I was planning to spend on a taxi.

"Listen, Luke..." I sit up straighter, inhaling deeply, mentally preparing for the "big brother" speech.

"You've been a good friend to me over the last few years. Not just to me—Charlie, Liv and the kids, Isla, Ev. The entire town has nothing but respect and gratitude for you. I just..." I'm still waiting for the "but," yet it doesn't come.

"I needed you to know how much you mean to us. Our lives are better with you in them."

"Damn, Hayes," I choke out, my voice brimming with emotion as I attempt to conceal my feelings and crack a joke. "You really did turn out soft."

"Oh, fuck off. You're in a shit place, man. Mentally, emotionally, physically. Don't forget I was there when Maddy went to the hospital and when we lost Dan. Odessa has you in a chokehold, and you know it."

"I know, I know," I mutter, feeling a lump form in my throat. "But I can't go there. My head is too fucked." I open the door abruptly, ready to leave the conversation there.

"Yeah, yeah. Get your ass to bed. The problems of today will still be there in the morning, and the only way you'll solve them is with a clear head."

"Thanks for the ride," I say and slam the door.

He's not wrong; the problems will still be there in the morning. Exhaustion hits me in full force as I crash onto my bed, not even caring that I haven't eaten or showered in days.

Chapter Twenty-Two

Luke

My body naturally wakes me up at 0430, which means I miraculously slept over twelve hours.

The memories of the last few days come crashing in and I search for my phone, only to find it on my bedside table. At least I had the common sense to plug it in.

Seventy new messages sit unread, but most are from the town and the gossip—trying to get information or do their due diligence and inform me Odessa's in the hospital.

A handful are from the care facility Maddy is at, updating me on her. When I told them I wouldn't be able to come in for a few days they were understanding and assured me they would take good care of her. The anxiety I would have felt a week ago over missing a day is gone; it evaporated like it was never there to begin with.

Nothing new from the group chat that Isla started when Odessa was still in the ICU. Only one text from Everett letting me know he left my truck keys under the planter on the porch.

Rather than dwell on not hearing about Odessa, I focus on

what I need to do so that I'm back at the hospital as soon as I can be.

First, shower, then food.

When all of that's done, I decide to try to spend some time checking through work emails and responding to what I can from the text messages I missed. I technically still have another week off, but I've been trying to keep up on the day-to-day things as much as possible. Considering we still haven't caught the drug trafficker that is living somewhere in Central Oregon. The couriers that have been arrested haven't rolled yet, but considering each of their charges could result in up to a decade in prison, hopefully they'll start talking.

Even knowing that doesn't keep my attention on work though, my gaze keeps going to my backyard and Odessa's house beyond the fence.

By seven, I'm pulling out of my driveway and heading to Maisie's to get Odessa her favorite coffee before I go to the hospital.

Three cars are in front of me, both lanes already filled with eager customers. Maisie's is always like this, she makes the best pastries and coffee in Central Oregon. I may be biased because she's my cousin but her loyal customer base speaks for itself.

As I finally make it to the drive-thru window, Maisie greets me with a smile that quickly falters when she realizes it's me.

"Hey, Luke." She regains her smile but it's clearly fake. "What can I get for you?"

I can't stop my eyebrow from arching at her strange behavior. She's never blown me off before; usually she won't stop talking.

"Uh, my usual black and whatever you think Odessa would like. I'm heading to the hospital."

"Oh, uhm. Well, I'll get started on yours. But—" she trails off and starts busying herself with the coffee pot.

"But, what?"

"Didn't you see the group chat?"

I shake my head and grab my phone, no new messages. "What?"

"Odessa got out last night, ignored doctors orders and insisted on leaving."

I scan through the group message but the last one I have is from before Hayes got to the hospital and gave me a ride.

Is it suddenly hot or is my blood just boiling with anger? How could she be so reckless with her health? How could her family just let her leave?

She pulls out her phone and scrolls and then her eyes go wide.

"What?"

When she clears her throat and looks back she says, "Uhm, Charlie started a new one? Per Odessa's request. It's much smaller—she must not have wanted everyone to know what's going on."

Yeah, because she knows I'd lose my shit.

"She's at home?" I ask, my heart pounding with worry.

"No, I think she's with Everett and Isla." That at least removes some of the immediate panic, but I can't shake the feeling that something isn't right.

"Guess I'll take her coffee there then," I say pointedly.

"Luke..." her shoulders sag like she knows more but doesn't want to say it.

"Maisie. Not once have I questioned your estranged relationship with Ethan, even though he's one of my best friends and once upon a time was yours also. I haven't meddled, interfered, or even brought it up because I respect your privacy and autonomy."

I can see on her face that she's weighing her options, but ultimately she nods and starts making a coffee.

"Be careful with her." She says while handing me the coffee she made for Odessa. "I don't know what's going on, but I have a feeling the reason she bailed from the hospital has something to do with your sudden departure from the hospital after refusing to leave."

"I'm trying to be a good friend. That's it."

She looks at me skeptically and I almost laugh. All of a sudden she looks just like her mom did when we got caught sneaking cookies before dinner.

"She may not want to be your friend. Not if she finally admitted she had feelings for you and you ripped that chance away from her."

"You speaking from experience?" I level her back.

With a sigh, she hands me two brown bags full of pastries. "There's some things you can't go back from, is all I'm saying. If she fell in love with you, there's no going back to being friends."

"Appreciate the unsolicited advice." I say while handing her a twenty. She rolls her eyes and turns around, never letting me pay. Of course, I always stuff into the tip jar.

By the time I get to Everett and Isla's, I'm a ball of nerves. Maisie's words are echoing in my head, making me question every decision I've made regarding Odessa. She's right though; how do I let go of the feelings I have when she's all I can think about.

I shouldn't have told her I could handle more.

When I turn into the driveway, I have to roll my window down and hit the button so Everett can unlock the gate.

Only the longer I wait, the more frustrated I get. After a minute, I hit the button again, and look toward the house. The lights are all on, Everett's 4runner in the driveway, only no one answers.

By the third time I hit, I'm well and pissed off.

My phone dings from the dash holder and I look to see a text from Everett.

> "Sorry, boss. Girls say I can't open the gate. Dess doesn't want any visitors."

I snap a picture of the coffee and treats and send it off.

> "Shit. Feels like a sin to turn away Maisie's but orders are orders and right now you technically aren't my boss."

Instead of texting back, I call him. He can't hide behind his phone for long.

"Hey..." He says somberly.

"What's the deal, Astor? You let her leave the hospital and don't tell me. Now you won't let me in?"

"Not up to me. I'm letting Dess call the shots right now. When she's ready for visitors, I'll let you know. She didn't even want Charlie and Hayes to come by today, though, so don't take it personally."

How could I not?

Chapter Twenty-Three

Odessa

Three of the longest weeks of my life were spent holed up at Everett and Isla's place. During the first week, I refused any company except for my hosts and Connie. I wasn't allowed to put any weight on my injured leg, so I spent most of my time in bed, feeling helpless and frustrated. I couldn't even have Dog with me because I couldn't get out of bed without help. Thankfully, Connie temporarily moved into the other guest room to assist me with using the bathroom and showering. Everett and I are close, but not that close.

By the second week, I limited my interactions to brief visits with Charlie and Olivia. Not even Hayes or Drew were allowed over, which really pissed them off, but I didn't care. I was fully embracing my T. Swift Vigilante era—something only Charlie would understand. No man was safe—not even Everett. By then, he was used to my moods and glares and didn't even blink at my icy demeanor anymore. It felt like a shield I had put up to protect myself from getting hurt again, and honestly, I wasn't sure if I'd ever take it down.

By the third week, thankfully, I was able to use crutches

and get around more independently. After some bribing, complaining, and a lot of convincing, Everett finally agreed to let me go home—on the condition that Connie stay with me, I take it easy, and Dog stay another week with Olivia and the kids. Begrudgingly, I agreed, even though I missed Dog the most. I couldn't bear to spend another day with those two love-birds. I was happy for them, but I needed space to heal and process everything that had happened—and Connie must have felt the same because she jumped at the chance to stay with me before I could even get the words out.

However, her moving in came with its own issues, like the way she side-eyes me anytime a call or text from Luke comes in —which is multiple times a day—and I choose to ignore it. Right now, my phone lights up on the coffee table with the picture I took of him throwing the ball to Dog in the meadow. I need to change it, delete it, remove it from my life, yet I can't bring myself to open the photo app and do just that. Instead, I stare at the picture the entire time it rings, pretending it doesn't kill me to see it.

"Dess," Connie starts, and when I look at her, I see the turmoil on her face, framed by her salt and pepper hair that falls softly to her shoulders. I know she wants to talk to me about it, ask questions that I don't have the answer to, and every fiber of my being what's to shut her out. I know I shouldn't, though. I may not be able to give her all the details, but I can give a little.

"I'm mad at him. I know, *I know*, how immature it seems to hold on to anger against someone who is obviously trying so hard to be friends, but *I can't*."

"You can't what?" she asks, her voice gentle yet probing, her eyes searching mine for clarity.

"I can't be his friend."

"What happ—?" I watch as Connie's brows knit together,

the concern deepening the lines of her forehead, and I have to cut her off.

"I'm not ready to talk about it yet," I say, and the look she gives me is full of understanding.

I'm still too raw, too sad, and too in love for that conversation. So, I shove those feelings down, burying them like Luke said he'd do to that guy who tried to drug me. Instead, I focus solely on anger because if I let myself feel anything else, the hurt and sadness will drown me.

I've never fallen for someone so quickly and deeply, only to have them rip the rug out from under me. It doesn't help that I felt safe with him when everything happened. The moment we both realized what was under the rock—pure terror and heartbreak—will forever be etched in my memory. That terror was quickly replaced with his resolution and courage, but I still feel the weight of both. One comforted me, knowing he cared so deeply; the other reassured me he'd do anything to save me. I was being attacked by a pit of vipers, yet Luke stood ready to protect me.

He got me out of there and into his arms in what felt like seconds, his steady voice assuring me that everything would be okay. At that moment, with him holding me close, one arm wrapped around me and his gun trained on the hole I had fallen into, I couldn't deny that I had fallen in love with him any longer. As excruciating pain coursed through me, all I could think about was how grateful I felt to have Luke by my side. That feeling never left—not when he carried me to safety or confronted Dr. Lewis and Claire about their care for me. It didn't fade when I saw the worry on his face in the helicopter or the way he clung to Dog like he was his anchor.

No, I didn't feel anything but relief until the day he told me he didn't want to be with me. The previous two days, I'd been too doped up to notice he was checking out. Maybe I could have prevented it—said something to reassure him that I was okay and that we'd be okay. But by the time I realized it, it was too late. He'd already made his decision: he couldn't be with me —couldn't put his heart on the line again.

I get it. Right now, I feel that same heartbreak. I don't know how I could ever give my heart away again, knowing this could be the outcome. His heart was already broken beyond repair, and the band-aids I offered weren't enough to heal those wounds. It's a painful realization: love isn't always enough to fix what's been broken—and neither is friendship. I can't be friends with him; I can't even look at him. When I see his pathetically sad face, all I want to do is cave and take the scraps he offers.

Instead, I focus on how mad I am. It's been years since Maddy's accident and Dan died, and he hasn't gone to therapy. I'm angry that I have to deal with the brunt of his emotional baggage. And yeah, I obviously knew he had it, but I didn't think he would completely bail on it after a couple of weeks. So I'm mad at myself, too. I knew better. I shouldn't have put myself in a position where I could be hurt.

"Hey," Connie says, breaking into my thoughts as she stands in the doorway. "I'm headin' to visit August for a few hours, just to let ya have some time alone. Call me if ya need anythin', alright?"

I nod, grateful for her support but also wishing I didn't need so much of it.

"You know I'll be just a phone call away," she adds, her voice gentle with concern. "Take this time for yourself. You deserve it."

"Yeah, I will. Thanks, Connie," I reply, forcing a small smile.

My plan is to lounge on my couch all day, watching trash TV and napping on and off. I don't know if I've ever allowed myself this much time to be lazy, but maybe the injury was the setback I needed.

Plus, this couch is spectacular. Its leather is buttery, and the enormous fluffy blanket draped over it only adds to the comfort. I've found solace in this temporary escape from the world outside. As Connie leaves, I sink deeper into the cushions, ready to lose myself in mindless distraction. Maybe just a few hours of forgetting could help me breathe again.

That is, until thirty minutes later, when my phone dings, and I hear the hum of an engine starting up.

It only takes one glance at the small photo icon to see it's Luke. And he's mowing my lawn.

That motherfucker.

I noticed it was getting a little longer than the HOA would like, but I was already planning on calling a landscaping company to take care of it for the next few weeks. Seeing Luke out there, taking care of it without even asking me first, ignites a fire within me I didn't know existed.

Reaching for my crutches, I maneuver my good leg so that I'm able to stand and hobble toward the door—faster than I've moved in weeks, if I'm being honest.

When I fling the door open, Luke and the lawn mower are facing me, and his head snaps up, startled. His shocked expression doesn't leave his face as I narrow my eyes and tip my chin up. If there's one thing my evil mother taught me, it's how to look down on someone.

In what seems like less than a second, he abandons the mower and marches toward me. He's on my front step before I even realize the engine has shut off, and the only sound between us is the quiet hum of the surrounding neighborhood.

"What the hell are you doing here?" His voice is low and tense, carrying an edge of urgency that hints at his frustration.

It's my turn for shock. "It's my house. I live here. What the hell are you doing here?"

"Who's here with you? Helping? I swear to God if you say you're alone—" He entirely ignores my question, his tone sharp and demanding as he storms past me into the house.

"Luke!" I shout after him, but he doesn't stop. He quickly walks through each room, his voice echoing with rising anger. "You're here alone?!" he shouts while storming through the kitchen. "What, did your brother just dump you off and tell you to fend for yourself?"

I snort a sarcastic laugh at that, the tension hanging in the air thickening as I stood rooted in my spot in the entryway. When he makes it back to the entryway, he looks like he's ready to explode.

"Didn't know you were such a hothead," I throw out with a hint of sass.

"Me either," he replies, his jaw clenched so tightly it comes out sounding more like a growl.

"Not that I should have to explain this to you, but my doctor cleared me. I can get to and from the kitchen, the bath-room, and my bedroom by myself. I'm not taking anything stronger than ibuprofen right now. I have my phone, and I promised to send him check-ins. AND Connie is staying here— she just left to visit August so I could have some space." I can tell I'm walking a fine line between being a brat and setting the boundaries I need to, but I can't stop myself.

"You promise she's staying here and you're still sending updates?"

"Yep." That's the only response I can give without cursing him out.

He runs a hand through his hair, looking away for a moment. Finally, his shoulders sag as he looks back at me, sadness etched into his expression that makes my gut clench.

"I'm sorry. I shouldn't have gotten so riled up. I'm worried about you. It was terrifying—"

Rather than let him express his feelings, I cut him off, bypassing brat and going straight for bitch. "I'm sure a therapist can help you with that. But I'm not one, and I'm not your friend."

You'd think I slapped him with the way he recoils at my words. Guilt eats at me, but I stand my ground, knowing that setting boundaries is necessary for me to survive this. *Two drowning people can't save each other.*

"Now, please leave and take your lawn mower with you."

His chin lifts as if he's trying to mirror my own defiance. In an instant, the hurt vanishes from his face, replaced by a look of stubbornness.

Then he walks by me and calls over his shoulder, "Sure. Shouldn't take much longer to finish up."

"Don't bother! I hired someone to take care of it!" I shout, even though I haven't actually done that yet.

"Fire them! I've got it until you're able to."

"No!" I want to stomp my foot in frustration, but I can't because of the stupid brace.

He starts the engine again and smirks when he sees me still staring. In a fit of irritation, I slam the door with my free hand and head in search of my phone.

I'm hiring someone right now and praying they can come next week before Luke shows up again.

Chapter Twenty-Four

Luke

Week Three—

I left Odessa's house and promptly called every landscaping company in Cascadia County, kindly asking them not to accept any business from her. Thankfully, they all obliged, and only a few probed for details. The next day, I realized that the fleeting glimpse I had caught of her wasn't enough. Determined to see her, I knocked on her door, offering one of her favorite snacks—sour cream and onion Pringles. She didn't answer or even peek through the blinds, but I expected as much, so I left them on her doorstep.

The following day, I returned with her favorite drink—Diet Coke—once again placing it carefully on her step. Soon after, I brought her a vanilla cupcake from Maisie's, knowing how much she adored them.

Each morning and night, I texted her a simple "Good morning" and "Goodnight," hoping she felt my presence, even from afar. Lunchtime calls became my routine—a gentle reminder that I was still here, waiting. Yet, not a word came back.

So why was I so disappointed when she didn't show up to church on Sunday? I knew she hadn't been cleared to drive, and yet, I still half-expected her to be there when I arrived.

Week Four—

The lawn became my canvas as I mowed it with care, then I pruned the bushes and shaped them gently, all the while praying for her to come out and yell at me. I made my usual delivery of her favorite things, one item a day, placing them carefully at her doorstep. As always, I texted her "Good morning" and "Goodnight," and once again made the lunchtime call to check in. This time, when Saturday night rolled around, I texted her to ask if she'd like a ride to church the next morning.

Once again, there was no response.

And the only person to blame was myself.

Week Five—

Mowing her lawn had become almost meditative at this point. I checked her sprinkler system this time, ensuring everything was spruced up and ready for the season. My texts continued— "Good morning" and "Goodnight." Each lunchtime call was met with the same silence, a void that echoed louder than any reply.

But, I refuse to give up. Not when I still can't get her out of mind.

Week Six—

I mowed her lawn again, the grass swaying under the weight of my sentiment, and cleaned the gutters that probably didn't need my attention. My deliveries were made, my texts sent, and calls placed, but I fell further into a depression of regret, wondering why I seemed to fuck everything up.

Week Seven—

In a burst of inspiration, I switched up my tactics and started delivering expensive relaxation essentials—candles, bath bombs, and face masks—recommended by the woman at the counter who clearly understood the value of self-care and a clueless man. I texted my usual greetings, hoping they might somehow reach her, and continued my daily call around lunchtime.

Still, no answer.

Week Eight—

To be determined... At this point, my routine feels like second nature. As I pray for a glimpse of her throughout the day, I find myself spending every evening watching from my dining room table, peering out the back window for just a moment when our paths might cross again. Occasionally, they do; I see her driving by or playing outside with Dog, but she always looks the other way upon seeing me. Although I've fallen mostly into stalker mode, she hasn't asked me to stop. I'm not hunting her down or forcing her to talk; I'm merely making sure she's okay and showing her that no matter what, I will always be a friend to her. *Friend. Ha ha. What a fucking joke.*

Chapter Twenty-Five

Odessa

I pull into Maisie's and park my car next to her silver RAV4. I assume it's hers anyway; it's the only car that's here every day, pretty much all day.

She texted this morning and told me she had some free time if I wanted to stretch my legs and go for a walk now that I'm officially rid of my boot and cleared for light exercise.

As I walk up to the window where cars usually line up, I'm surprised to find it empty, though the window is open. I've always appreciated my height, but now I especially do—I can see everything inside. Maisie is helping a customer on the other side and hasn't noticed me yet.

"We should go there! I've been a few times with the girls, and the mechanical bull is so fun. How long are you here for again?"

The woman on the other side laughs. "Yes! I'm not really sure how much longer I'll be here, but I'd love to."

Her voice almost sounds familiar, and I quickly try to get a better look. The black floppy hat covers most of her face, but I can tell she's very blonde, very beautiful, and very overdone—

like every wannabe famous person I've ever seen. I can't quite place where I know her from, but maybe it's just from around here. Maisie seems to be friends with her, so rather than dwell, I let it go.

Maisie hands her an iced coffee and takes the card she extended. "Thanks for stopping by!"

"I'll text you," the woman responds, and once again I'm hit with the feeling I know her.

When she leaves, I crane my neck, trying to see inside her Jeep, but I can't make anything out.

"Who was that?" I ask, and Maisie spins around, grabbing her chest.

"You scared me!"

"Sorry!" I chuckle. "But also, you're lucky I'm not a murderer!"

Her college-aged employee walks up from the back and smiles at me. "Go! I've got it from here, promise." Then she looks at me. "Don't let her come back for at least an hour. She needs a break. A real break."

"You got it," I say with a mock salute and wait for Maisie to come out through the back door.

"I feel so honored that you're actually out with me!" I say to Maisie as we walk toward the path that leads along the river. As soon as I was able to drive, I started stopping in every day to get a coffee from her and our friendship really blossomed.

"As you should," she replies with a smile. "I don't usually have time to get out, but now that I have a full staff taking care of things, I can finally enjoy some free time."

"If anyone deserves it, it's you!" I say sincerely. Maisie is always at the coffee hut helping out, and if she's not there, she's usually running errands or baking for the next day.

"How's everything going with the new staff?"

"It's been good! They're not all completely new; some have

returned for summer break, which makes it easier. I only had to train one new girl, and she's been great."

She turns to me, asking, "How are you? I can't believe you don't have crutches or a cane anymore. It's been, what, two months? And you're already healed?"

Just hearing that reminds me of the tenderness in my knee. "Eight weeks, yeah. It was a pretty minimal fracture—more of a nuisance than anything. I'm almost cleared to go back to full activity, but my PT still has me at 75% of what I'm used to."

"Which I guarantee is more than most people's 100%," she laughs. "I swear, you all showing up in town really lit a fire under us—especially the bod squad," she adds, fanning her face.

A brief cringe washes over me at her reference to the guys. Not because I don't want her to be happy, but because I know how much Ethan still cares for her. I'm skating on thin ice, caught between his side and hers.

"What?" she says, misinterpreting my silence. "You don't think any of them would be into me? They're always stopping by—"

"Are you kidding?! They think you pee rainbows and unicorns," I interject, trying to lighten the mood. "Any of them would jump at the chance to date you—especially Leo. That man is crushing hard. It's... Ethan."

Her shoulders go rigid, but she quickly recovers, forcing a smile. "I really wish everyone would just stop speculating about what happened between Ethan and me. It's no one's business!" Her smile slips as frustration tinges her voice.

"Whoa, whoa, whoa! No speculating here. I, um, actually know the story."

Her feet falter, and she comes to a stop next to me. "What?" I see tears gathering in her eyes.

Stepping toward her, I set my hand on her shoulder.

"Did you know that I knew Ethan before Charlie ever came here?"

"I—No?" She looks away, confused, then her eyes widen when she looks back at me. "Did you—?"

"God—No!" I make a disgusted face and fake gag. "Ethan and I never. We met because a friend of mine was dating one of his friends. Our friends were getting wasted, and neither of us was drinking, so we just chilled and talked."

She nods, but I can tell she's still processing the information. "It really breaks a lot of friend code to tell you this, so I'm going to keep it vague."

I glance around and notice a bench. "Actually, can we sit? My knee is a little achy." The second I say it, memories of Luke calling me that flash through my mind, causing a surge of sadness. I quickly push the thought away and focus on finding a place to sit with my friend.

"Okay, so. It was his rookie year; they'd just come off a high from playing that season and doing so well. But he was so young, like barely—"

She grins with pride. "Barely twenty-one! One of the youngest to ever be drafted to the NFL and nearly the highest-paid rookie contract!" Then she winces, as if she shouldn't have reacted that way.

For that brief moment when her mask dropped, I felt confirmed in my decision to share this with her. "Yeah, he didn't mention that. But I definitely Googled him afterward. Anyway, he went on and on about Three Sisters and his beautiful best friend that he did everything with."

Her shoulders tighten slightly as she gazes into the distance toward the pine trees.

"His best friend stopped talking to him the night of graduation and hasn't said a word since. He swears he has no idea what he did to her—other than maybe revealing some feelings. But we both agreed that didn't seem to be the issue."

Her eyebrows knit together, a slight furrow deepening across her forehead. A sense of wariness radiates from her, as if she isn't sure how to respond.

"He doesn't know... and I'd like to keep it that way."

"Why?" I ask, my breath hitching with a sorrowful exhale.

The honey colored depths of her eyes gloss over with unspoken memories, revealing a fracture beneath the surface that I hadn't noticed before. "I can't—I'm sorry. I just can't go there."

In that moment, it dawns on me: whatever happened that night had everything to do with Maisie and most likely nothing to do with Ethan.

"Okay, I'm here if that ever changes," I manage to say, pouring every ounce of sentiment into my words. "But I don't think anyone will stop pressing you about it until they know that chapter is closed."

"It's been twelve years... He has Jake! The chapter is closed," she shoots back, her voice sharp with frustration, a wave of emotion tightening her shoulders.

"Is it?" I ask cautiously. "Because he still looks at you all moon-eyed while you're avoiding him."

She looks at me deadpan. "Sounds like someone else I know... maybe a certain cousin of mine." *Fucking small towns.* I know she's aware of the doorstep deliveries. Just yesterday, he left a blueberry muffin topped with a crumble made from pure sin that I know came from her.

"Luke and I are... different. The history isn't there, and there's no confusion about how it ended." I add, "All I'm saying is, you need to talk to Ethan if you truly want to move on. Everyone around here thinks you're still tied up in him and are afraid to cross any lines."

"You think that's why I don't get asked out by anyone here?"

"Uh, yeah! Have you seen Ethan? Not only is he huge, but he owns the best bar in town. No one wants to risk getting their ass kicked and banned from the best bar for asking you out."

"He wouldn't do that." She pauses, contemplating. "But I think maybe you're right. If I want to move on, I need to let go of some stuff. It's just hard."

"I get it... Holding onto the past feels safe because it's the hurt we know. Letting it go means opening yourself up to new vulnerabilities."

She nods. "Is that how you feel about Luke?"

"Won't let that go, huh?" I groan.

"Nope. You meddled in my love life. What's the deal, Dess? I've never seen him so lost—not even with Maddy." That shouldn't make me feel good; it shouldn't be a competition. But it does. I want him to be as lost without me as I am without him. It's a twisted kind of validation, but it's all I have left.

"I fell for him. Before the accident." I clarify. "It started out slow—I thought he hated me—but we were always running into each other." The more I talk, the better it feels to get this off my chest. "When that guy put something in my drink, something snapped in him. He came over that night and confessed he was feeling the same but was scared to start a relationship."

She nods but remains quiet, so I add, "We agreed to just try, and if it didn't work out, we could be friends. It was the best couple of weeks—a crazy whirlwind romance. Then everything changed in the hospital; he ended it."

"But you fell in love and couldn't go back to being friends."

"Yep."

"I thought as much... I'm sorry. I wish you could have known the Luke before Maddy. Not just after her accident, but before they started dating. He was so different—full of life, joking all the time, charming." *I do know that Luke.* At least I got glimpses of him.

"She really did a number on him? Even before the accident?"

She scoffs. "You have no idea. Levi couldn't be around them half the time because she was always trying to make him jealous. She did that with a lot of guys, but it never worked—even despite their history."

"Wait, Levi and Maddy?!"

"Once, way before her and Luke. But she always wanted to get a rise out of Luke. It never worked, though. He was the same even-tempered guy, never took the bait."

I nod, absorbing the information. "Sounds like quite the drama."

"That's why I was so surprised when I heard about him punching that guy for you."

"It didn't exactly go down like that, but yeah, he lost his cool for sure."

"I think he's in love with you, and you nearly dying scared the hell out of him. I don't know if he'll ever move on from that day, but I hope he does. And when he does, I hope you'll give him another chance."

Would I? Right now, the answer is no. I'm keeping the anger I feel wrapped around my heart like a protective shield, and I don't know if I'll ever be able to let that go.

Chapter Twenty-Six

Luke

Every Sunday for the last two and a half months, I've gone to church and still felt let down when she hasn't shown up. Three months of having her by my side and the pain I felt coming nearly disappeared. I could almost look at the pity glances from everyone around and not feel immense guilt—or maybe those looks had transformed into something else all together and I hadn't realized it. All I know is that the looks are back.

"Good morning!" The familiar pastoral loud voice booms, a wide grin on his wrinkled face, that should bring me comfort but instead weighs heavily on me. "Today's you're lucky day, you won't be listening to my boring voice all service. Our guest speaker is Aaron Bocker. He's home from a recent mission trip in Uganda and would love to share his experiences with you. Because of this, I ask that you give your tithing at the end while you leave. We will have volunteers in the hall to collect them. Thank you. Without further ado, Mister Bocker."

I barely glanced at the missionary, only enough to notice he's close to my age and looks like a fresh faced kid. Even though he has young kids and a wife. To be honest, I'm only really coming here in hopes Odessa decides to return. My faith still hasn't returned, despite how convincing the sermons may be. My priorities shifted from coming here because I owed it to Maddy to coming here to see Odessa, and I should probably be ashamed of that, but I'm just not.

A hand settles on my shoulder, and I already know it's going to be Joe before I look up.

"Mind if I sit by you, today?" He asks.

I nod and slide down so that he has the spot I'm in and I'm sitting where Odessa normally sits. Something about that thought clenches my heart. Damn if I don't miss her. After Maddy's accident, I expected to feel this. The normal conversation, seeing her at church, but never came. I know it's different, I still saw her and talked to her so maybe that's why but I never necessarily cared that I don't get to create new memories with her. I've always only felt stuck. Stuck on that day like she is. *Until Odessa.*

I'm so lost in my thoughts about Odessa that I don't even notice the sermon ending and the last prayer. It isn't until everyone is standing to leave.

I look to the side to tell him goodbye, and instead he hits me with, "Sit with me a minute?" Nerves settle in my stomach like a deadweight.

"Everything okay?"

"You tell me. I haven't seen you look this withdrawn in a long time. Maybe ever." The look he gives me is all knowing. Considering he's know me since I was a gangly teenager, I'd say that isn't a good sign.

"It's been a hard few months." I answer honestly.

"Does this have anything to do with the woman who is no longer present at this service with you?"

The guilt of his acknowledgement eats at me and I wince.

192

It's not that I was hiding it or flaunting it, but your exes dad calling you out on seeing a new woman isn't exactly easy conversation.

"What happened? Things looked good from where I was standing up there," he says, pointing toward the front of the now mostly empty room. The smile on his face throws me for a loop.

"You're not upset with me?" I ask, bewildered and trying to wrap my head around the fact that he could feel anything but.

"For what?" He looks at me with the same confusion.

"Moving on." Then, with raw vulnerability, I admit, "It feels like I'm cheating on Maddy."

Sympathy fills his eyes, a look of understanding. "Maddy was... flawed. But in her own way, she loved you." *Not really making me feel better here.* "She wouldn't have wanted you to stop your life because of her accident."

I attempt to let his words resonate with me, but they feel like they only bounce off my chest. He has no idea I'm the reason she was in the accident that day, that the only reason she was driving to Three Sisters was so I could end things.

He takes my silence as a cue to continue. "What happened with Maddy was a tragedy, but it's not on your shoulders."

I have to look away at the now empty church, the final service of the day complete. The lump in my throat feels enormous, but I finally push out the words that have been eating at me. The only other person who knows is Odessa, and while she may feel sorry for me, it doesn't affect her the way it will telling Maddy's dad. I brace myself for the recoil of my confession, knowing the hurt it will bring him. "She was coming to see me the day of the accident..."

"I know," he says casually, like it doesn't rock me to my core. "She called that morning to let me know she was ending things with you, but she wanted to make sure I understood that it wasn't anything you had done. She didn't give me details on what had transpired."

My whole body recoils at his admission, as if he just hit me. I feel like I've been holding on to the secret that we were about to end things for so long that it physically hurts to hear it spoken so casually. He knew all along that she was coming to see me and that we were breaking up. Hell, she told him she was ending things with me. I don't know what else she told him about the reasons, but I still don't feel right sharing the texts I saw the morning before; some things a dad doesn't need to hear about his daughter.

"We weren't in a good place," I finally manage to say. "Hadn't been for a very long time."

"I remember. I think part of that is on me. You were the dream son-in-law—took care of her, kept her grounded, and I never once doubted you would put her first. But she'd always been the type to need more than what she had. I pushed her a lot to stay with you, and for that, I'm sorry."

My throat only gets thicker with emotion, and all I can do is nod. He was a huge part of why we stayed together; neither of us wanted to disappoint him.

"Her accident was a tragedy, but it's not something anyone could have prevented. God's got a plan for all of us, and while we may not like it or understand it, it's not up for debate. We just have to trust that everything happens for a reason and try to find peace in knowing he will always be watching over us."

"That's it?" I choke out. "That's what we're supposed to believe?" My voice cracks as tears sting the back of my eyes.

"Having faith during the hard times can be incredibly difficult, but it's what helps us get through the darkest moments. We have to believe there's a greater purpose behind our suffering, even if we can't see it right now."

"I'm not sure I'm there yet," I admit honestly.

He nods. "I've got enough faith for the both of us until you do. I just hope it isn't too late for you and your new woman."

"Me too," I agree solemnly. "But unfortunately, I think that ship with Odessa has sailed."

"I wouldn't be so sure. Something tells me the reason she's still attending services here isn't because of my charming sermons."

"What do you mean, still attending?" My shoulders tense up as I ask, going ramrod straight.

"You do know we have more than one service on Sundays, right?" He smiles knowingly.

I do—three, actually: seven-thirty, nine-thirty, and eleven-thirty. I always come to the last service to see Maddy before.

"She's coming to the first service?"

"Think it's time you change your priorities, son. Maddy's not going anywhere, and while I appreciate that you've stepped up and helped with her, I think it's time to let go. The staff and nurses are great; they can handle you not visiting as much." The relief washes over me instantly, though it's coupled with a guilt I know I shouldn't feel but find hard to shake. Still having his approval means everything to me, even if it means letting go a little.

"As hard as that'll be, I think you're right."

I leave church feeling more broken and confused, yet I also have a new sense of hope. Odessa hasn't completely slammed the door shut—there's a small crack that I can blow wide open if she gives me the chance. And I have a week to prepare for it.

Chapter Twenty-Seven

Odessa

I've been showing up to the early service for a while now and so far haven't had any sign of Luke. I'm always on guard, searching the parking lot for his truck before I enter a few minutes after the start time.

I let out a deep breath every time he's not here, yet, feel a sadness in my chest for his absence.

The crisp morning air hits me as I climb out of my car, and make my way into the church. I still haven't figured out why I keep coming back, to the place I thought of as ours, but here I am. Sunday after Sunday, tormenting myself.

The choir is almost finished singing, and I'm starting to recognize the songs now, humming along to the tune as I sit in the pew I've always sat in.

I'm mostly ignored except for a few friendly smiles; everything is as usual, but something in my gut feels off. Especially when Pastor Joseph catches my eye and smiles. He's done it before, but something in his smile today feels different, almost knowing.

Before I can even really begin to wonder what that was

about, someone is sliding into the place Luke used to sit. I don't want to look, already knowing who it is. The electricity shifted in the air and directly into my body, like it always does when Luke is around. *A live wire.*

When the song has ended, Pastor Joseph approaches the stage and begins prayer. I'm thankful for the few moments of reprieve where I can close my eyes and pretend I'm not here. Only I can feel the bench move as Luke scoots toward me.

I peek through one eye to see he's now next to me and staring at me with the big, sad eyes that I knew would crumple and resolve I had.

We stare at each other for a beat before he mouths "Hi," and I look away so he doesn't see the tears threatening to spill over. *It's been months*; he shouldn't still have this effect on me.

Pastor Joseph begins his sermon, but for the first thirty minutes, all I can think about is that Luke's here and figured it out. How good it feels just to be near him, the comfort I feel even though I shouldn't. He's the one who got away, the one I can't seem to shake off, no matter how hard I try. The ache in my chest grows stronger as I realize how much I still care for him, despite everything that has happened between us. I wanted so badly to be the one he chose, the one that he couldn't live without, the one who "fixed him." I even told myself I'd be okay with him still loving Maddy and visiting her every day.

Quietly he says, "Pretty smart, switching up the service to avoid me."

I don't respond, but I swear the entire congregation could hear me swallow.

"Last week, Joe filled me in. Gave me a pretty good reality check, too."

"Joe?" I question, unsure of who he's talking about.

"Pastor Joseph," he says, nodding toward the front. I hadn't realized they were close, but I guess if he's been coming here for so long, it makes sense.

"What does that have to do with me?"

"He said some things I hadn't realized I needed to hear—about Maddy."

That catches my attention. *Why would Pastor Joseph, Joe, be talking to him about Maddy and me?*

"She called him before the accident and said she wanted to end things with me. I had no idea he knew any of what happened that day. I was worried he'd hate me for leaving her, for ending things."

"Why would he hate you?" As soon as the question leaves my mouth, everything starts to click into place: the times he mentioned her dad being around a lot and the memory of Luke saying her dad's name was Joe.

"Pastor Joseph is her dad?"

He nods, his eyes reflecting confusion, as if I should have known that.

"This is her dad's church? You two used to come here?"

He nods again but must see the panic starting to form on my face because his expression turns softer. *The one thing I thought was ours—the one sanctuary that belonged solely to me and him—was actually theirs first.*

"Achi—it's not like that."

I turn toward the front and try to push the rising feelings of betrayal out of my mind. I know I stumbled upon this place and that he didn't bring me here, but that doesn't negate the fact that our special spot wasn't as exclusive as I had believed. It was theirs. Everything around here, around him, revolves around Maddy. There isn't a place where I come first.

There's a sob building in my chest, threatening to escape, and I have no idea how I'll make it through another few minutes.

Thankfully, I hear the most blessed words: "Before we begin our tithing," and I know I'll have my escape—the same one I took the first day I attended service. I can feel Luke's gaze on me before he quietly says, "Please, don't leave. There's more I'd like to say."

Like hell am I staying.

I don't move an inch, keeping my chin up and my face as composed as possible. I can feel the tension in the air, but I refuse to let it break me. Luke may want to say more, but I've had enough for one day.

As soon as he reaches the middle section, standing at the end of the pew, waiting, I bail.

I swear I can feel his disappointment in my bones as I practically ran out of the building, but I wasn't stopping.

When my feet hit the concrete in front of the building, I sprint to my car, keys in hand. *Thank God this car is fast.*

I wouldn't put it past Luke to try to follow me out of here. The look in his eyes said he's ready to talk, and that's the last thing I want right now—maybe ever.

Sure enough, I can't resist looking in my rear view mirror as I pull away and there he is. Standing in front of the door I just escaped, looking every bit as hurt as I feel.

My fingers move on their own accord, hitting the call button before I even realize who I'm calling.

My manager, Londyn. The woman I've politely avoided and told not to book any jobs from. She understood and surprisingly, was cool with me taking the time away.

She answers on the first ring. "My favorite client."

"Hi," I say, knowing she can hear the sadness in my voice.

"Who am I killing?"

That earns a small chuckle. All five foot nothing of my manager couldn't do much physical damage, but there's a reason she's gotten to where she is.

"No one, I just need..." *To talk? To vent? What do I need?*

After a moment, I settle on, "A job. Now. Anything. Just get me out of here for a few days."

"Dess—"

"No, please. No questions. I'm okay."

"Alright," she sighs. "Let me check to see if they still need someone." I hear typing on her end as she remains quiet.

"Can you be back in the City by tomorrow morning?"

"Yes!" For the first time in a long while, I feel a weight lifted off my shoulders.

I hang up and immediately call Isla. Normally, I'd call Everett, but I already know he wouldn't believe a word of my bullshit. Isla, though, despite everything she's been through, is still too trusting.

"Hey girlie," I say with more enthusiasm than I feel, "I need a favor."

Isla listens patiently as I explain that Londyn is calling in a favor and needs me to fly to NYC for a few days to help her.

"That's so fun! Jetting off at a moment's notice! What do you need us to do?" she asks with genuine enthusiasm, and I almost feel guilty for lying.

"Could you watch Dog for about a week? I think the competition is about five days, but I may stay in the city a few days longer."

"Of course! We'd love to have him! Maybe I'll be able to convince Ev that we need a pup too."

Good luck with that. Everett is a lot of things; a dog person isn't really one of them.

"Thank you, thank you!"

"Need a ride to the airport? Do you have a flight?"

"I'd hate to trouble you more..."

"Nonsense! What time do you leave?"

"Five tonight. Londyn got me a flight to Portland and then

a red-eye." I should've chartered a plane, but since it's so last minute, I didn't want to stress Londyn out any more.

"Okay, want me to pick you up around two thirty?"

"How about I come to your place? That way, Ev can have fun with my car while I'm gone." And Luke will know I'm not here. *Not that I care.*

"Way to sweeten the deal," she says with a giggle.

Chapter Twenty-Eight

Luke

I watched Odessa leave, the familiar ache settling deep in my chest. Everything I had planned to win her back—the speech I'd rehearsed day and night—went out the window. I fumbled it all worse than when the New York Jets lost in 2012 because Sanchez collided with Moore's butt, losing the ball, only for Gregory to scoop it up and run it back for a touchdown.

I forgot everything the moment I sat down next to her and breathed her in.

Then there was the look on her face when she connected my calling Pastor Joseph, Joe. The betrayal written so clearly across her features, even though I never meant it that way. I thought she would have understood when I mentioned I'd been going there for over a decade, the times I spoke about Joe while discussing Maddy.

And of course, just when I finally commit to getting her back, I screw it all up even more. I'm not sure where to go from here, but I know I can't give up.

I walked to my truck and sat in the cab for a while,

watching the other churchgoers say their goodbyes. My stomach twisted with the heaviness settling on me like a weighted blanket of misery.

What the hell do I do? Chase her down and beg her to listen? Based on past history, she'll ignore me if I show up on her doorstep.

I could wait until tonight when I know she'll be home and calmed down, but that won't be until late. She always goes to Sunday night dinner at the Carrington's, and while I've been invited before, I've never gone.

Maybe that changes tonight. The invite has always been open-ended, but I still called Hayes.

"S'up, Luke?" he drawls, his southern accent slipping through, a rarity that only happens when he's relaxed or had a few drinks.

"Hey, man. I, uh—" I fumble through my words until I hear the laughter of his friends in the background. Definitely been drinking. *Right, Hayes and Drew had invited me golfing today.*

"You finally calling for advice on how to win Dess back?" He chastises in good nature, his smirk practically audible.

"Yup," I confirm, "and to make sure I'm still invited to Sunday night dinner."

"You're always invited." He makes a tsk noise as if contemplating my predicament. "As for Odessa, well, that's a bit more complicated."

"All ears," I say quickly, desperation laced in my voice.

"She's guarded, man. Fort Knox could take lessons. She keeps everyone at arm's length, even Charlie and Ev."

He continues, "I don't know how you did it, but you managed to break in once. I'm sure you can do it again."

"That's zero help. Absolutely zero."

He laughs. "Sorry, shoulda called Charlie." He's probably

not wrong, but Charlie would also rip me a new one, and I'm already feeling bad enough.

"Next time. See ya tonight."

After I hang up, I replay our conversation during the drive home, trying to remember what I did the first time. Other than being honest and direct—not pussyfooting around—I can't recall much else.

Then it hits me: maybe that was it. I didn't offer pretty words or false promises; I just spoke my truth and let her see the real me.

I spend the afternoon with a long workout, trying to devise another plan. Because the first one went to shit in a matter of seconds, and I'm not sure I'll get a second chance—or maybe a sixth, at this point.

Tonight, I'm winning her back.

I pulled into the Carrington driveway and nearly forgot the entire plan when I saw her car parked there. *Damn witchy woman.*

I parked next to it and stared at it for a moment too long, hoping to remember what I was going to say.

Finally, I mustered whatever courage I had and knocked on the large wooden door of the Carrington's log home.

Everett opened it, surprise crossing his face. "What's up, Boss?"

Just then, Dog came bounding from the kitchen, nearly barreling into my leg. I reached down to pet him with my free hand. It's amazing how healthy he looks now, filled out and happy.

I held out the container of treats I had picked up from Maisie earlier. "Here for dinner."

"No shit!" Everett exclaimed, just as I heard someone cough dramatically and say, "Bullshit!"

Hayes's deep laugh followed, and I looked past Everett to see Drew and Hayes both grinning like idiots.

Everett turned to them, clearly missing the joke. "What?"

Drew's grin widened. "I've been waiting *so long* for this!" Then he mockingly imitated Everett's voice, "Don't act like you don't know!"

"Know what?" Everett asked, eyebrows raised as he looked at me.

Instead of answering, Drew again imitated Everett. "You naive SOB. Luke's been in love with Dess since what? Christmas?"

Everett looked confused, but I remained standing in the doorway. I might not get the joke, but Drew wasn't wrong.

"Wait, you're in love with Odessa?" Everett gasped.

I nodded, and he let out the loudest cackle. After a few wheezing breaths, he said, "Damn. Good luck, man."

Not the reaction I expected, but I'd take it.

"Where is she?" I asked quietly.

"New York," Hayes answered, a grin stretching across his face.

"What?!"

"Sorry, sprung it on us last minute. Didn't know she was going until after you called." *Motherfucking-fuck.*

"For how long?"

"'Bout a week. Which is good, actually. You're going to need all the help you can get if you plan on winning her back," Charlie said as she emerged from the kitchen.

The rest of the evening was filled with our friends giving me a hard time, but they also offered some great advice on how to win her back. Hayes pulled me aside at one point, his tone serious as he recommended I see a therapist. "Been where you are. A lot of fucked-up things going on your head, making you believe things that aren't true. Guilt will eat you from the inside out." Then he gave me the name and number of his therapist, and I agreed to call him the next day. Something I'd never considered, but if it helps me work through my shit, I'd give anything a shot.

Drew, surprisingly, chimed in next with a pep talk that felt like the boost I needed. "Take it from someone who knows how it feels to keep messing up with the dream girl—it's never too late to apologize and do better. You just have to plead your case. Offer yourself up like a sacrificial lamb and show her you're not taking this situation lightly."

Charlie glanced at me with understanding in her eyes. "I know what it's like to run away from your problems. I love her to death, but that's what she's doing. What you're both doing. I'm glad you've decided to stop running away from her and to start chasing her."

Even Everett, typically the jokester, offered some insight into Odessa's psyche. "She's always been stubborn, hard-headed, and independent. But that doesn't mean she doesn't want to be loved and fought for. Show her that you're willing to do both."

As the laughter and camaraderie swirled around me, I felt a renewed sense of purpose. My friends' support and advice sparked a determination within me—this was my chance to change things. I may not have the exact plan yet, but I know one thing for sure: I wasn't going to let this opportunity pass me by.

Chapter Twenty-Nine

Odessa

"Ladies and gentlemen, this is your captain speaking from the flight deck. We have just touched down at Newark Liberty International Airport, and the local time is 7:00 am. We appreciate you flying with United this morning and hope you had a pleasant journey with us from Portland. The weather here in Newark is mostly cloudy with a high of 53°F. As we taxi to the gate—"

I begin to tune out the rest of the spiel and close my eyes again. I barely got a catnap in on the red-eye, but I at least slept a few hours. Londyn was able to send me the contract for the "guest-judge" gig, and I skimmed through it during my layover in Portland.

I signed it without really comprehending it, but I know I'll be here for at least five days and will be working on set for a spin-off of Project Runway. I get to hang with the upcoming models, meet designers, and give my opinion on their creations. It's something I've done a hundred times before, and I was hopeful I'd never have to do again. I lost the excitement for it a long time ago, but the reprieve from Three Sisters, *cough*

Luke *cough*, was too good to pass up. Plus I'll get to see Eddie and Monica and fill them in on everything that's been going on.

Oh shit. Eddie. It hit me like a freight train that I hadn't even told Eddie I was coming back to the city. He would've been here waiting already, probably with the rest of the team, to escort me through security and safely to the car. He makes the Bod Squad look like mall police when it comes to my safety

My phone nearly falls from my lap as I reach for it to send him a text. With any luck, Monica and he are sleeping in, and he's actually enjoying "trial-run retirement," like I told him to.

> Landed. Heading to GUM!

> Sorry I forgot to text you! Will be home for about a week. Helping out Londyn and guest-judging with a new show.

> Hope it doesn't interfere with any plans you and Monica have!

> I'll call Brandon and see if he's able to cover the week and I'll book a suite close to the studio so that I'm not in the way at the house.

Technically it's still my house, but that doesn't mean I want to interrupt their routine.

My phone rings and a photo of Eddie and Monica lounging by the pool pops up. It's my favorite photo of them because it's the first time I've seen Eddie ever relaxed. Their anniversary fell during a week I was shooting for a fragrance ad campaign in the South of France. I dragged Monica along as well as two other guys Eddie hired to the private villa I rented for the week. I knew Eddie wouldn't let himself relax without extra help.

I answer on the third ring, bracing for the inevitable lecture I'm about to receive. For the past decade, Eddie's treated me like a daughter, and he still isn't thrilled I've been in Three Sisters without my usual team.

"Hi!" I answer with perhaps a bit too much excitement.

"Odessa Lynette Astor!" His tone cuts through my enthusiasm, and I immediately regret my chipper greeting. "What do you mean you just landed?" His concern seeps through his stern words.

"Uhm, well—"

"I swear to God if you get in a cab or one of those damn ride-share apps, I will personally handcuff you to myself or someone on the team for the next ten years!" His voice rises, a touch dramatic, but I can hear the genuine worry behind it.

"I'm sorry! I promise all of this was so last minute that it completely slipped my mind to call." I'm not even exaggerating. I've been so focused on the little bomb Luke dropped in my lap at church that I hadn't thought about anything other than running.

"Slipped your mind?! Like you being in the hospital for three days slipped your mind?" His shout makes me wince as a car door slams in the distance, the tension palpable. He's clearly still furious about me keeping the snake attack a secret. But why worry him and Monica when they're all the way across the country?

"This really did! Come on, it hasn't even been twenty-four hours since I left. We're still taxiing, waiting for our gate!" I shoot back, hoping to defend myself.

"*You* flew commercial?" Eddie's tone shifts to one of disbelief, as if it's totally unheard of for me to travel by anything other than private jet.

"Yeah, yeah, I did. And I'm sorry for not calling sooner, but I swear I'll make it up to you," I plead, trying to convey the whirlwind of circumstances that led to my oversight.

"I'm already on my way," he replies, his tone softening just a bit. "Traffic is light too, so I should be there before you even get out."

With that reassurance, I hang up and start heading through Newark Airport. I keep my head down, hoping to avoid any eyes. But it doesn't do much; people recognize me left and right, pulling out their phones and snapping photos as I walk by. A knot twists in my stomach at the realization—I'd almost forgotten how recognizable I am, even after just a few months away from the city.

As I walk out, I spot Eddie pulling his blacked-out Escalade to the curb. He's out of the driver's side before I even take a step. Although he may be in his late sixties, nothing about his appearance suggests it. His thick, light-colored hair, styled in a high fade, is turning grey on the sides, giving him a distinguished look rather than an aged one. When he does smile—rarely—there's a noticeable dimple that adds character. His smooth forehead remains wrinkle-free—thanks to some pampering I've encouraged him to try while I receive my own Botox—but there are faint lines that etch the corners of his piercing blue eyes. I've warned him too many times about the negative effects of leading a life filled with cautious observation and squinting, but he doesn't pay attention. Even his thick eyebrows frame his narrowed eyes, obscuring their blue hue while reinforcing an impression of vigilance.

Today, he's dressed in one of his custom designer suits, a striking all-black ensemble that effortlessly conceals hidden weapons and a bulletproof vest. I should be surprised he's wearing it, considering he had not a minute of warning about my return, but it's all too typical of him to be prepared for anything. Knowing him, he probably sleeps in it, ready to spring into action at a moment's notice. The thought of him "superman-ing" across the country, even in casual moments, isn't far-fetched. His polished look reminds me that I need to update the guys' suits—even if they despise getting fitted—so they have something for occasions that call for more than tactical gear. I briefly consider getting a suit for Luke but quickly dismiss the thought, reminding myself to stay mad at him. At least Eddie's a constant. Everett too, but right now Eddie's the one who deserves the recognition for always being reliable.

As I approach him, the urge to hug Eddie surges within me, but I stifle it, respecting the boundaries of professionalism— His, not mine— and get into the passenger seat. Especially when he doesn't return my smile; he simply rushes to my side and escorts me the rest of the way. He may not fully realize it due to his businesslike demeanor, but he's one of my best friends.

When he slides into the driver's seat, he does one cursory scan of me with his still narrowed eyes.

"Well, what did he do now?" he asks, his tone serious and probing.

I can't help the loud groan that escapes my lips before I can stop it. I should've known Eddie wouldn't let me off the hook easily. He's been my mostly silent confidant for years—offering fatherly advice or sending me to Monica for girl talk if he was in over his head.

"You know the whole straw and camel thing?"

He nods once but doesn't say anything.

"This was that. I'm the camel, and my back is broke."

This time all he does is blink at me, spurring me to go on.

"Just start driving; people are already staring." I grumble out, and the sound of a car honking emphasizes my point.

He sighs, but his hand moves to shift into gear as the SUV hums to life.

"So, remember that church I started going to? The one where I ran into him?"

He grunts and shifts lanes. When Eddie and Monica called in a near panic after Everett spilled the beans about me being in the hospital, I gave them a very watered-down truth—one could even say a bald-faced lie. In my defense, they were scrambling to book the next flight out, and I just couldn't deal with that. So, I gave them a half-truth: I ran into Luke at a random church, we made peace, and he took me hiking once. It was more than I shared with anyone else, but still not the full truth.

"Well, I liked the sermon, so I kept going back after everything that happened and I could drive again," I add, trying to infuse some levity into the moment. His quick glance says it all —a clear 'that's bullshit' look.

"I did! Pastor Joseph has a way with words," I defend, crossing my arms as if shielding myself from his incredulity.

"Alright, go on," he exhales, still focused on the road as we merge into the stream of bustling traffic heading toward Brooklyn.

"Well, apparently, Pastor Joseph is also Joe—Maddy's dad. And it was 'their' church long before it was ever 'our' church." I watch as he flinches in the seat next to me, looking overly sheepish.

"You knew!" I accuse, my voice rising with both surprise and frustration.

"I did. Well, I inferred," he replies, a hint of defensiveness creeping into his tone.

"What? How?!" My confusion hangs in the air, intertwining with the scent of leather and the subtle hum of car engines around us.

"From the beginning—when you first mentioned you ran into 'that damn sheriff,' I ran the standard report—background check, familial connections, the whole nine yards. It's my job to know everything about everyone, remember?" He glances at me, his expression a mix of seriousness and warmth.

I nod, caught between embarrassment for not making the connection and admiration that he cared enough to check. It may be his job, but technically, he didn't have to go that extra mile for me when he's on "practice retirement."

"Could've told me," I say, pretending to be more betrayed than I actually am.

"I assumed you'd already made the connection. You told me he'd been going there for most of his adult life." His eyes don't leave the road as we hit a red light, but I can sense the calm authority he always exudes.

"Shit," I mutter under my breath; even I can't believe I hadn't thought of that sooner. "Fine. You're right. The red flags were all there, and I had on love-tinted glasses," I admit, letting out a heavy sigh.

"Is that a red flag?" He challenges back. "His ex-girlfriend's dad is the pastor of a church you enjoyed going to, and you hadn't realized said ex and he attended that church?" Eddie asks, a teasing note creeping back into his voice, but I can see the concern still lurking in his eyes as he maneuvers through the afternoon rush hour traffic, the skyline of Brooklyn growing closer with every passing moment.

My chin tilts upward on its own accord, defiance bubbling to the surface at being questioned like this. A red flag? Maybe not. Arguably, it's not Luke's fault that I had a major oversight, but there's something about the omission that feels like the final nail in the coffin of my denial. I had wanted something with Luke that was ours, untouched by the shadows of his past or the specters of old relationships.

"I guess not," I finally concede, feeling the weight of the admission hang in the air.

"The situation still hurt your feelings, though," he acknowledges, his tone softening as we merge onto the busy highway.

It doesn't feel that simple, but maybe it is. Maybe all of

this really does stem from my feelings being hurt. He didn't pick me, and that sting cuts deeper than I want to admit. Luke's been an honorable guy, despite the rocky history of his previous relationship, and I threw a big fit over it. Then, because I'm immature and petty, I couldn't even be his friend.

Eddie remains quiet, giving me the space to unravel my thoughts as we glide past the tall, familiar buildings that line the route to Brooklyn. The skyline looms closer, a reminder of the world I'm headed back to. I hate it, though. A city I used to love, but looking at now, doesn't bring anything but anxiety and loneliness. If I hadn't had Eddie and Monica, I never would've lasted living here.

"I let him in. You know how hard that is for me." I glance down at my hands resting in my lap, feeling vulnerable and exposed. "I let him in, and he didn't pick me." Groaning, I cover my face with my hands, the frustration bubbling to the surface. "Oh my god! Does that make me a 'pick-me girl?'"

"What the hell is that?" Eddie asks, his brows furrowing in genuine confusion as he accelerates slightly to merge with faster traffic.

"You know, 'Pick me. Choose me. Love me!'" I say dramatically, channeling my inner Meredith Grey as I shift in my seat. "It's what you tell someone when you want them to choose you over everything else."

"That a bad thing?" he says gruffly, his hands steady on the wheel.

"Well, it's supposed to be, yeah," I reply, my voice tinged with uncertainty.

"Why? That's the foundation of a good relationship—choosing your partner over everything else." He glances at me, and I can see that he's genuinely trying to understand.

I shrug, unsure of how to articulate the layers of the term

'pick-me girl' to him. "I guess it's more about being desperate for validation rather than genuine love and respect."

"Were you desperate for validation because you put yourself out there, took a risk on a potential relationship, and it didn't work out?" He probes, keeping his eyes on the road.

"No," I respond, shaking my head firmly. "I was desperate for him to love me back, though."

Eddie nods slowly, as if digesting each word as we pass the city limits, the landscape shifting from highway to the bustling neighborhoods of Brooklyn.

"We're all desperate for someone to love us back," he reflects, a reminiscent smile creeping onto his face. "I was a mess when I met Monica—jealous, insecure, and constantly seeking reassurance. I don't think I formed a rational thought until she married me."

"That's sweet," I say sincerely, touched by his vulnerability.

"My point is," he continues, his voice steadying with conviction, "we're all a little 'pick-me girl' when we find someone we truly care about. It's just human nature to want to be loved in return."

As Eddie searches for a place to park, I feel the weight of his words settle into my chest. I was hurt that Luke didn't want me, and I let that insecurity consume me. It's time for me to let that go, to focus on getting through this week and moving on from Luke. I think the only way to do that is to release the anger and try to be his friend—a distant friend, at that. But I think I can handle that. Hopefully, it will help him let go a little too.

With that resolve forming, Eddie finally finds a spot and pulls into it, turning off the engine. I take a deep breath, steeling myself for the next phase of this emotional journey. "Alright, let's go," I murmur, summoning the strength I need.

Once we step out of the car, the vibrant sounds of Brooklyn

fill the air—the distant laughter of kids, the chatter of friends gathering on street corners, the rhythmic beat of music spilling from nearby cafes. It's the confirmation of life moving forward that I needed, a stark contrast to the cloud of uncertainty I've been carrying.

With a nod from Eddie, we start our walk toward the studio, my thoughts shifting to the tasks at hand. I slip back into the mindset of the badass model I used to be, ready to tackle the whirlwind of work ahead. Thankfully, the agency wanted to finish the shoot as quickly as possible, meaning I'll be working fourteen-hour days. I'll be able to immerse myself with the other models and the fresh faces of new designers, allowing myself to let go of the drama that's been bringing me down. Funny how one of the things that had me running to Three Sisters is now the very thing that's helping me escape it.

Chapter Thirty

Odessa

The last day in the studio is supposed to be the longest of all—final photo shots, six interviews, as well as four outfit changes. To top it all off, it ends with a fashion show to showcase what the designers created, me as well as the panel of judges critiquing each model and outfit, and then a party to celebrate the winner and all the hard work put in throughout the competition. I hadn't realized I'd be the guest judge for the last week to choose the winner, but by the end of it, I'm glad I was able to.

I was able to meet some incredibly talented new designers and give advice to models that are still early in their careers.

It isn't until the afterparty that things began to get complicated. The guest judges from the previous weeks were all invited back as well—everyone from the top designers, models, and A-list celebrities. One of whom is Lily Moss, a friend of mine, who's one of the top plus-size models in the industry.

"Lily!" I shout to get her attention; it's been less than a year since I saw her last at the VS fashion show. She has a different manager, but we both work for the same agency, so it doesn't surprise me seeing her here. What does surprise me is the five-foot-nothing, try-hard standing next to her. My former assistant, Jessica Wilthers, with the same fake smile plastered on her face that she used to wear when she was still working for me.

"Oh my God!" Lily looks genuinely shocked to see me here while she gives me a hug. Her face then grows concerned, and she whispers, "Are you okay?" Genuine concern rolls from her.

Taken aback, I'm trying to figure out what she's talking about. My mind instantly goes to Luke. Maybe the Everett thing? But that was so long ago.

When it's clear I don't know what she's talking about, her gaze shifts ever so slightly toward Jess. Then delicately she says, "I heard you checked into some type of inpatient center after everything that happened with one of your brothers and the pressure of everything."

My head rears back, but then it dawns on me—that's what Jess told her. Not that I fired her a week before the news about Everett's work incident even hit the tabloids. Or that it was because I overheard her saying terrible things about me. No, she tried to say that I left for rehab because I couldn't handle the stress of fake news at the height of my career.

I can feel the weight of her gaze on me, waiting for a response, but I can guarantee it's not what she's expecting.

My eyes flicker to Jess briefly, showing my annoyance. "No. I bought a house in Three Sisters to be closer to my family."

"Three Sisters?" she says with a head tilt like she's trying to place the name. "Wait, you mentioned that town! At the show, right?"

I nod, "Yep, that's the place!" I had already told Londyn I was cutting back by then, that I was planning at least a year break to spend some time with everyone. It just happened to be moved up because of what happened with Everett and then turned into permanent.

"I totally forgot about that," she admits and flips her long brown pony behind her shoulders. "Shoot! You even mentioned you were lessening your work load."

"I don't know why I ever thought.." Her head does the same head tilt it had just done, like she's once again pondering something.

When her eyes land on Jess they immediately flick back to me, and she puts on a fake smile. Without looking at her she says, "Hey, Jess. Could you grab me a glass of champagne? Oh, and get me a little plate of snacks?"

Jess awkwardly looks between us, then lightly touches her arm and turns so that her back is facing me. Quietly I hear her whisper, "Are you sure? You've already hit your calor—"

"Right," Lily quickly interjects, looking ashamed. "Just a water then."

Jess nods, a triumphant smile on her face as she walks away.

"Lil, please tell me you don't let her talk to you like that all the time."

She shrugs, "Audrey insisted she's one of the best." Just her name alone has my lip curling. Audrey has always been Londyn's lesser in my eyes, constantly trying to one-up her when it comes to clients and gigs. It's not surprising she hired Jess as soon as she could, thinking she had found a way to get ahead.

"She's not." I say giving her a sincere look. "I fired her because of the way she was speaking to me and about me. I know it's a dog-eat-dog world around here, but trust me, Londyn would never encourage someone to speak to me that way. Have you thought about changing agents?"

She shakes her head quickly, "We have a two-year contract."

"Call Londyn as soon as it's up. In the mean time, stand up for yourself. Trust me, you want to play the long game? Don't get walked all over by tiny women in stilettos."

"I'll think about it," She concedes, "I'm glad you're here. Does this mean you're back?"

"No, I was only filling in because Marc dropped out last minute. I missed the city too, had to make sure Eddie wasn't having too much fun without me." I add with a wink over my shoulder to the man who hasn't left my side all week.

"Ugh." she groans, "Well maybe I can come visit you and see this town you settled in. You mentioned your brothers had started some business hiring all the military guys, right?"

With that I let a real laugh, "Hayes and Drew did, yeah. The 'Bod Squad' as the girls and I like to call them.

The clacking of Jess's shoes alerts me that she's back with the bottle of water, and I can't help but roll my eyes.

A server carrying a full tray of champagne glasses greets us before she gets to us, though.

"Champagne?" He asks, extending a gloved hand adorned with flutes.

"May I?" I ask, gesturing to the tray he's holding. He nods, but I'm already reaching for another glass.

I quickly hand both glasses to Lily. "Do you mind holding these?"

Her jaw drops in surprise, but she takes them without question.

I grab another two glasses and wink at the server. "You, sir, may be my new favorite person. Mind sending someone with food toward us? We're going to need to soak up all the champs we'll be stealing from you."

He nods quickly and leaves to track down the other server.

Jess looks utterly murderous at me and the glasses, but I only smile innocently in return. Lily raises an eyebrow at me, clearly amused by my antics.

"Is that really necessary?" Jess snaps, irritation sparking in her voice.

"Absolutely necessary," I reply with a mischievous grin. "We can't let all this champagne go to waste, can we?"

"What I actually meant was, is it necessary to send the server off like that? It's getting increasingly obvious that someone is growing dependent on the universe serving her," she smirks, the challenge still lingering in her tone.

I arch an eyebrow at her, feeling the heat of her accusation. "And what's wrong with politely asking for what we want? Besides, a little charm never hurt anyone," I retort, trying to diffuse the tension with a playful smile.

Jess scoffs, crossing her arms. "A little charm or manipulating others into fetching you things? There's a fine line, you know."

"Oh please, Jess, it's just a couple of glasses of champagne. Don't get your knickers in a twist."

"You would think that, wouldn't you? All those small 'favors' you ask for always seem to add up," she replies.

"What? You're saying that because I politely ask someone to do something for me, I'm manipulating them? That's a bit of a stretch, don't you think?" I respond, feeling defensive.

Jess shakes her head, her expression unyielding. "Not really!"

"Did I do something to offend you?" I cannot laugh her off anymore. "Because the last time we spoke was when I fired you for spreading lies about me and trying to sabotage my career. So, forgive me if I don't take your opinion on charm or manipulation too seriously."

Jess's eyes widen in surprise at my direct response and then quickly turn icy as she narrows her gaze.

"You're delusional! You couldn't even order takeout without my help. I was practically your little bitch for years, doing everything you asked. Don't forget, I was the one who made you look good all those years." Jess's voice drips with venom as she spits out her words, revealing the true extent of her resentment towards me.

"What are you talking about?" I ask, genuinely confused by her sudden outburst. "You were my assistant! Paid an astronomical amount of money and treated with respect. I never manipulated you into doing anything. You barely worked eight hours a day, had paid vacation and sick days, and never once complained about your job. That's unheard of in this industry, but I always respected your time. So what's your problem now?"

"You're my problem!" She shrieks, and it's at the point I realize we've gained an audience. "You think you're so perfect because you're outgoing and outspoken. Well, newsflash, you're not. You're just a selfish, overbearing bitch who doesn't care about anyone but herself." I had overheard her say the mild version of all these things, but having it shouted at a work event takes it to a new level of humiliation.

Eddie takes a step in front of me when she continues to yell, attempting to shield me from her wrath. But I can still hear her loud and clear, every word cutting through me like a knife. "It's no wonder you can't keep a decent relationship in your life, and your family keeps their distance from you. No one can handle your obnoxious attitude for long."

Woah. Her words cut deep, and I struggle to find a response as the weight of her accusations sinks in. It's something I've heard my entire life. "You're too much, too loud, too opinionated." But this time, it stings more than usual coming from someone I once considered a friend.

"Hey, back off," Eddie says in a stern voice.

"Whatever. Lily! Let's go." She tries to stomp off, expecting her boss to follow. Only Lily doesn't move.

Slowly, she turns to look at Jess. Calmly she says, "You're off my team. Not one of the things you said was true, and to speak to a colleague of mine like that is simply inexcusable."

I remain hidden behind Eddie, listening through the tension in the air. It's kind of Lily to stand up for me, but ultimately the final blow to my self-esteem has already been dealt. Luke left me teetering on the edge of self-doubt, worrying about my personality, and now Jess's harsh words have pushed me over the edge. I feel defeated and unsure of myself as I watch Lily handle the situation with grace and strength.

Eddie's hand reaches behind him, and he pulls me forward, guiding me out of the building. Despite the onlookers around trying to get me to stay, I leave with my head hanging down and tears threatening to spill from my eyes.

Paparazzi takes photos, but Eddie made sure our driver was already waiting and had Steven and Bridger waiting to help escort me the short distance.

They open the door, and I'm shuffled in, ignoring everyone shouting my name.

Eddie takes the seat next to me "Buckle, Dess."

On autopilot, I buckle and the first tear slides down my cheek.

"Hey, what the hell was that?" he asks, clearly frustrated.

I don't respond, only gaze out at the passing city.

"Odessa Lynette Astor."

"That's twice," I say with a sniffle.

"Twice, what?"

"Twice you've used my full name in the last week. You only do that when you're really mad."

The streetlights flash by, giving me a brief glimpse of his face, which softens slightly.

"Yeah, well, you've had a way of pissing me off this week. Why on earth did you let her go on about you like that?"

I shrug and look away again, feeling the weight of his words.

"Fine, we'll let Monica have a talk with you." I know what that means: an hour-long lecture about my value and how I should never let anyone disrespect me like that.

"Tomorrow. We'll talk tomorrow before I leave."

He must be able to tell I'm at my breaking point tonight because he sighs but nods. "She's making brunch and wants to take you to the airport with me."

"Okay. That'll be nice." I smile softly at the thought. I've only been able to see her for a few minutes here and there over the last week, so it gives me something to look forward to before I leave. Maybe a little warmth and wisdom from her will help me navigate all of this. Plus, it might just be the break I need, a moment to recharge before diving back into the chaos waiting for me back home.

Chapter Thirty-One

Odessa

The next morning, I wake up close to eleven, my head pounding relentlessly. I wish I could blame it on the one glass of champagne I sipped before that verbal sparring match with Jess. No, it's more likely the result of tossing and turning all night.

As I stumble out of bed, the sun sneaks through the heavy drapes, casting light on the warm, rich tones of the brownstone home. There's something wonderfully comforting about waking up in a place steeped in memories. The elegant moldings and intricate woodwork seem to whisper stories of days gone by, even as I've enlisted Monica's help in modernizing the place over the last few years.

We tried to preserve the French Gothic grandeur, but it needed desperate updates—the gym was one area I outsourced to Eddie. Everything else, though, has been a labor of love from Monica and me. I wanted them to feel this place was as much theirs as it is mine, so we created private spaces on the upper floors, all seven stories of cozy, welcoming rooms.

Everett has his own suite too, considering he's also an

owner; I thought it was only appropriate. Though he visits so rarely that it mostly sits unused, a ghost of happier times with Grandma and Grandpa. It was the room he always chose whenever we came to stay with them, so it seemed only fitting that it remain his.

I make my way to my ensuite bathroom, my feet padding softly against the cool hardwood floor as the smell of fresh coffee wafts up from below. Guilt pricks at me like an angry bee, and I forgo the shower I was planning when I remember Monica was organizing a brunch for us—though Eddie never bothered to give me a time.

I take the stairs two at a time, skipping the elevator for the three floors down to the parlor. There are two kitchens; the garden floor boasts a full-service culinary kitchen where my grandparents once had servants bustle about. But when I invited Eddie and Monica to move in, I insisted we add a new kitchen on the parlor floor so that it features a large island, perfect for gatherings, where we can sit and laugh while preparing meals together. Not that I've been able to experience much of that since I've been gone so often, but I know Eddie and Monica will while I'm in Three Sisters.

As I slide into the kitchen in my socks, I see Monica lounging at the table, a cup of coffee cradled in her hands. Her eyes widen, then she bursts into laughter, the sound bright against the muted early morning. Her copper hair gleamed with blonde highlights, flowing perfectly as if she just emerged from a salon, though I know she likely did it herself.

"Where's the fire?" she teases, arching an eyebrow.

"Eddie mentioned something about brunch, but now it's practically lunch." I manage a sheepish smile, feeling the flush creep up my cheeks.

"Pfft, don't sweat it," she says, waving her hand dismissively as she gestures for me to take a seat. "He filled me in on last night's drama."

"Oh," I say, cringing at the memory.

"Sit. I'll whip you up an Americano while you explain," she insists, turning to make the coffee with brisk, confident movements. "From the top, and don't skip any details. Especially about this Luke guy."

As the aroma of brewing coffee fills the air, a wave of nostalgia washes over me, tugging at my heart. The house looks completely different from what I remember growing up, yet it holds a treasure trove of wonderful memories since the remodel. I may have dreaded modeling, but I can honestly say that Monica and Eddie were the ones who helped me through those years.

I settle into my chair, and for the next three hours, I unload everything about Luke: the attraction, the whirlwind romance, how attentive he was when I was in the hospital, and I describe the moment he lost his cool on the guy who tried to drug me— his fierce protectiveness flooding back like a movie reel in my mind. I spill my heart out about the good times, the tough moments, and even the spicy ones. Monica listens intently, laughing in all the right spots and wiping away her own tears while mine spill over too. It's cathartic, to say the least.

"Sounds like he's completely and utterly in love with you— and you scare the shit out of him," she says, shaking her head with an amused grin.

I chuckle softly, sniffling as the snot pours out of my nose. "I don't know about that. But I do know things got tough, and he just... gave up."

"C'mon, the mowing your lawn, the little gifts, the texts and calls to check on you? That doesn't sound like giving up to me." She raises an eyebrow, her voice teasing but full of concern.

"He told me he wants to be friends, and I kinda threw a fit about it," I confess, the weight of those words hanging in the air. "I think part of him was just feeling guilty."

Her acrylic nails tap on the outside of her mug before she sighs. "Most men have the emotional maturity of a gnat. I love Ed—but... gnat." Her shoulders shrug in a 'what are you going to do' gesture. "Drop him off on a deserted island, and that man would have us eating a gourmet dinner, a beautiful hut, and weapons to take on an army. But when it comes to emotional intelligence, he's like a lost puppy caught in a storm."

"And we're just supposed to accept that?"

She chuckles, shaking her head. "No, but you can understand. Most men aren't taught all the big feelings and how to deal with them. Not like girls are, anyway. The good thing is, it's not too late. If he's smart, he'll figure it out."

"Yeah, with years of therapy," I grumble.

"Have a feeling losing you might be the thing that gets the ball rolling faster," she says with a wink.

"I'm not waiting for that. To be honest, I think I'm too much for him anyway. He's quiet, reserved..." I trail off, thoughts of last night rolling through me—Jess accusing me of being too much, demanding, and manipulative.

"Too much, what?"

"Everything," I answer honestly. "Outspoken, opinionated, emotional. He's not used to someone like me, and looking back, I tried to make my presence less overwhelming around him."

"Honey, have I taught you nothing?" she scoffed. "Shrinking yourself to be more digestible? No, we let them choke. Jess, for example. She can choke on the stick shoved up her—"

I chuckle at that and cut her off, my hands raised. "I get it—"

She leans back in her chair, a playful glint in her eye. "But seriously, you can't just dim your light for anyone. You're a force of nature."

"No, it wasn't like that—" I pause for a moment, gathering my thoughts. "I never wanted him to feel overwhelmed or suffocated by me because of my resemblance to Maddy and the hurt it caused him, so I held back a lot. I avoided him, guarded my responses. Then when we started hooking up, it changed. I shared everything with him—family, career, thoughts, hopes, dreams." I think that's what hurts the most—that I gave him everything, opened up, and then he left.

"You cared about his feelings. That's different. You were being considerate and trying to protect him from any potential pain. From the beginning, you always cared about his feelings more than your own."

"That stopped when he ended it."

"No, it did not. You still care about him—still protect him. Or else you would have told Ev or one of those Body Squad guys to make sure he stayed away."

My shoulders slump, and I hang my head down. "I know. I do still care—too much."

"But he wants to be friends. Only friends. And if I want to continue living in Three Sisters, I need to accept that."

"Are *you* going to be okay with that?"

"I think I have to be."

I've been so scattered emotionally, purposefully holding on to anger. But I need to let that go in order to let the relationship go.

We leave for the airport, and I'm even more exhausted than I was last night. It feels like the entire week is catching up with me—the time change, long hours, and emotions. I do have a new sense of resolve about Luke.

Eddie and Monica give me a hug at the drop-off, despite Eddie's grumblings.

"Security is right there, and I only have my carry-on. Promise I'll go right to the sky lounge." I do the scout's honor finger thing, and he rolls his eyes.

Monica hugs me first. "We love you! Come back sooner. Bring Dog even! He'll be fine—lots of walks." I chuckle at the thought of my big, menacing love walking through the city.

Eddie gives me a hug next, and I see the worry on his face, even if I know it's mostly unnecessary. "Be safe. Keep your head on a swivel and don't draw unnecessary attention. Are you sure you don't want me to accompany you on the flight? I don't mind—"

"I'll be fine, I promise."

"I'd feel much better if you were chartering. Why aren't you again?"

"My stupid brother said I don't care about the environment."

Eddie laughs. "Which one? Because if it's Everett, I'm not sure he's got a leg to stand on. Pretty sure that helicopter he flies isn't exactly a hybrid."

"It absolutely was!" *Bastard.*

By the time I'm actually on the plane, it's dinner time, and my eyes can barely stay open—not even for the perks of first class, dinner, and unlimited drinks. Instead, I send a quick text to Everett letting him know I just boarded.

Within ten minutes, my eyes drift closed, only to be woken up what seems like a few minutes later—because it is. Rumblings work their way through the airplane, and I realize we haven't taken off yet. The flight attendant assigned to first class confirms that we are delayed due to the pilot being stuck in traffic. *Damn my brother once again for making me feel guilty.* I could be enjoying a comfortable flight right now. Instead, I'm stuck on the ground with a hundred other grumpy passengers.

My layover from Portland to Redmond is only forty-five minutes long, cutting it close to begin with, but I assumed it'd be alright since I should be landing and departing in the same terminal.

To top it all off, I feel the migraine I had this morning returning.

When it's clear I won't be making my connecting flight home, I call Everett.

"S'up, Dess?" he answers, and for whatever reason, tears well in my eyes. *Must be exhaustion.*

"Hey," I reply back, trying not to sniffle. "My flight is delayed. I think I'm going to miss my connector."

"What? Why?" A slight panic in his tone comes through before he corrects it quickly. "Sorry, one second, let me.." He trails off but I hear movement on the other side and assume he's going somewhere more private.

"Sorry, I was at my desk and there were a bunch of people around. So what's the deal? You'll be stuck at PDX?"

"I guess. The pilot got stuck in traffic, they just let us know he's going through security now. I'll definitely miss that connector flight to Redmond.

"Shit. I'm on call so it can't be me, but I'll send someone up there."

"No, it's okay. I'll grab a shuttle to a hotel and catch a flight in the morning."

I hear a commotion in the background, and what sounds like something being slammed and then it goes quiet for a second.

"Everett?" I ask and then check my phone to make sure it didn't get cut off. Seeing that it's still connected, I put it back to my ear.

"Dess? Sorry, phone was being weird. What time do you land with the delay?" Everett asks.

His phone was being weird? If I had more energy I'd question that, but all that I can think about is the migraine creeping back in.

"I don't know; I guess nine thirty? But really, that's just an estimate."

"No worries. I'll have one of the guys there waiting. I gotta go! Don't worry about Dog; you can pick him up tomorrow! Love ya!" He hangs up before I can ask who. Something about the way he skittered around the details makes me uneasy. But before I can dwell too long, the pilot appears, and the sleeping aid I took pulls me back under.

Chapter Thirty-Two

Luke

It's been less than a week since I cornered Odessa at church —something I probably shouldn't have done, considering I didn't even get to say what I wanted. I still see the look on her face when she connected Pastor Joseph with Joe, a point I should have clarified but didn't realize I needed to. She was out of there before I could even apologize and explain. There were a hundred things I wanted to tell her, starting with how sorry I am for being such an idiot and that I love her.

Instead, she bolted as if the church were on fire and I was holding the matches. She was so angry that she didn't just go home; she left the entire state. At least she didn't go into hiding like Charlie, but leaving was enough for me to get the picture. My only hope now is that it isn't too late. I almost booked a flight when I found out, planning to track her down myself, but everyone convinced me otherwise. They told me to let her be for a week, to give her space to breathe and make a plan to win her back. I only hope she's willing to listen when the time comes.

Which, luckily for me, is tonight. Everett sent me her

flight itinerary and the go-ahead to woo his sister. Hell, all of her friends have; they even started a group chat dedicated to it.

TEAM WIN ODESSA BACK—

EVERETT ASTOR

Bring Dog!

DREW REYNOLDS

What's her favorite flowers? I have a florist.

CHARLIE CARRINGTON

I don't think she's ever said. Anything but roses 😁

OLIVIA TURNER

Maisie, do you have any special treats today?

HAYES CARRINGTON

Can't go wrong with the sugar cookies or brownies. 😊

ISLA MITCHELL

Maybe a nice bottle of wine?

OLIVIA TURNER

Don't mention wine. I've got six more weeks! 😩

CHARLIE CARRINGTON

Take her to get a milkshake!

HAYES CARRINGTON

Bring one for us too. 🙏

MAISIE PAISIE

I'll make her a little basket of her favorites. What time does she land?

ETHAN FLACCO

Happy to drop off takeout from Ponderosa too.

. . .

Of course, the only time Ethan responds is when Maisie does.

I slide over to the Safari app, double-checking—more like triple-checking—that I'm right. I already know her flight is supposed to land at nine, but the tight layover in Portland has had me on edge since I first saw the timing.

When the screen reloads, 'delayed' starkly replaces the once-clear 'on time.' A stream of curses spills from my lips as my palms slam against the desk, frustration boiling over. *One fucking thing to go right—that's all I'm asking for.*

I rise abruptly, every muscle tense as I dash for the door, heading toward the one person guaranteed to know what's going on—Everett. He isn't the problem, can't control it, and has nothing to do with it, yet part of me wants to throttle him for not coming to me right away.

Just as I'm about to round the corner of my office door, I nearly crash into the man himself, panic written on his face while his phone is pressed to his ear. I point at the phone, raising my eyebrows, but I can already feel the tension leaving my shoulders. *He'll make a damn good brother-in-law.*

He nods, pulls the phone away from his ear, and switches it to speakerphone. "Sorry, I was at my desk, and there were a bunch of people around. So what's the deal? You'll be stuck at PDX?"

He may sound confused, but the look he sends my way is a cocky mix of "what's your problem" and "I've got it handled."

"I guess. The pilot got stuck in traffic, they just let us know he's going through security now. I'll definitely miss that connector flight to Redmond." She responds and something about the defeat in her tone has my heart sinking for her.

"Shit. I'm on call, so it can't be me, but I'll send someone up there." The lie he tells is so smooth I arch an eyebrow and nod approvingly.

"No, it's okay. I'll grab a shuttle to a hotel and catch a flight in the morning." Without thinking, my fist flies into the magnet board next to the door, the cheap metal popping inward and sounding like a gunshot in the small room. The papers once attached drift to the floor as I mutter "like fucking hell," as the frustration bubbles up inside me. *I hate Portland.* Hate the hotels around the airport, hate the drugs and crime that seem to infest every corner. But most importantly, hate the thought of her being alone there.

When I look at Everett, he has a shit-eating grin on his face. "My oh my, how the mighty fall."

"Everett?" I hear Odessa ask.

"You good now?" He asks with a chuckle and I nod, breathing through my nose. He clicks the unmute button I hadn't even realized was on.

"Dess? Sorry, phone was being weird." I almost snort at that dumb excuse but keep it reigned in.

"What time do you land with the delay?" Everett asks her.

"I don't know; I guess nine thirty? But really, that's just an estimate." *Not a problem, I'll be stalking the flight tracker like it's my new job.*

"No worries," he quickly says, and then even faster he continues. "I'll have one of the guys there waiting. I gotta go! Don't worry about Dog; you can pick him up tomorrow! Love ya!" Then he hangs up quickly and smiles at me.

"Change of plans, looks like you'll be headed to Portland after work."

I barely grunt in response, turning around to my desk to grab my keys. There isn't anything that I can't handle from my phone, and Ellis is working today. I'll put him in charge of anything that pops up, but no way can I sit at my desk and wait.

I hear him cackling behind me. "Leaving now. *Shit*. You got it bad."

"Shouldn't you be giving me the big brother talk or something?"

He shakes his head but smiles, "Nah, I think you've paid your penance the last few months. Now it's all about pep talks."

I roll my eyes, packing up my work computer and the rest of my stuff.

"Odessa has always been strong for everyone and never allowed anyone, including me to see her weakness. She refuses to be soft around *anyone*. But that doesn't mean she wants to be the strong one all the time. Time to take control, don't give her the option, ensure you're not going anywhere when she's ready."

Fuck, he's right. Odessa really only let me in when I challenged her back. Since she was in the hospital, I've played it safe and tried to show her how much she means to me. Now I need to be assertive.

My phone dings, and I look at it then rolls my eyes again at Everett who starts to walk away still cackling.

TEAM WIN ODESSA BACK—

EVERETT ASTOR

Dess's flight was delayed and she's going to miss the connection home.

EVERETT ASTOR

Lover boy is packing up his desk now.

HAYES CARRINGTON

Sitting at PDX for six hours? Respect.

MAISIE PAISIE

Treats are wrapped up and ready to go, as well as a coffee!

Most of my plans go up in smoke; I can't bring Dog because I don't want him waiting in the car all day. I did manage to find an entire bouquet of yarrow at the farmers market this morning, so at least I have that. Then I picked up the goodie bag Maisie made as well as a black coffee for myself and resisted the urge to speed the entire two and a half drive to Portland. At least the drive is relaxing enough. The warm weather means the pass is clear of snow, and beautiful. Tall green trees line the winding road, a river down below, and the sun shining brightly overhead. The drive is almost so enjoyable that I almost forget about my nerves. *Almost.*

I still have six hours until Odessa's flight lands and no idea how to spend my time.

I settle on walking through the outdoor sporting store—not that I have any desire to go hiking again soon, but my therapist thinks it'd be a good idea to start small.

Christian Shaw, a former Army sergeant with multiple deployments under his belt, is now my life guru and licensed therapist. He's earned accolades for his work with veterans and first responders grappling with PTSD. Hayes set me up with

240

him, encouraging me to talk to someone who truly understands the weight of the past.

In just two sessions, I already feel lighter, as though the shadows I've carried are beginning to lift. Not entirely gone, but I'm hoping that once I convince Odessa I'm taking steps to heal, she'll consider giving me another chance.

With only two hours left until her arrival, I pull into the airport parking lot and find a spot. I plan to wait right outside of security when she gets here.

I'm amped, my fingers hitting the refresh button every ten minutes, eager for updates on her flight.

When the notification finally says "landed," I feel the breath get yanked from my chest. I stand, positioning myself where she can easily see me.

Five minutes pass, then ten. I've stood tall, arms crossed the entire time, my gaze roaming the crowd while I wait. You'd think I'd be fidgety, and on the inside I am, but on the outside, I'm as cool as a cucumber. Dan used to call me "cool hand, Luke" whenever I got this way. Damn, wouldn't I give anything to call him right now, to hear him laugh at me for acting like such a little bitch?

Then I spot her, walking out with a backpack and a roller carry-on. Her face is obscured by a hood, no makeup, and her shoulders are slumped—nearly unrecognizable. I might have missed her if I hadn't recognized my Cascadia County Sheriff Department sweatshirt. I knew she had it, but I thought she would've tossed it in the trash months ago. A tiny ember of hope sparks deep inside me.

The closer she gets, the more I realize she isn't even looking for her ride. She's just putting one foot in front of the other, her eyes barely open. It takes three calls of her name and stepping right in front of her before her gaze finally lands on me.

"Whoa," I say, my hands going to her arms to steady her as she stumbles.

"Luke?" She looks confused, but her body sags into me.

Now that I'm up close, I see the dark shadows under her eyes and the flush of color in her pale cheeks.

I press my right hand to her forehead while my free arm pulls her closer. Instantly, I can tell she's too warm. My mind races with a million possibilities the doctor warned me about while she was in the hospital—mainly infection. It's been over nine weeks, but I can't shake the fear that something might still be wrong.

"I'm okay," she insists, trying to pull away. But when she sees my look, she stops.

"And I'm not buying it," I say firmly, guiding her to sit on the nearest bench.

Once she's settled, I squat down in front of her, and she meets my gaze with tired eyes.

"Can I see your leg?"

Her eyebrows nearly shoot up to her hairline, almost making me chuckle. Even when she's sick, she's expressive.

"I just want to check where the—" I pause, struggling to say the words.

"I think it's just exhaustion."

"Humor me," I plead.

She nods, and I pull up the leg of her sweats, thankful they have wide legs that glide up easily.

Her leg is smooth, tan, and completely free of bruises or swelling.

For someone who looks like death, she still manages a smug expression.

"How are you feeling, really? Don't say fine," I say, trying to memorize every inch of her face up close again.

242

"I have a migraine, and I'm tired," she sighs. "I had some crazy hours, so it's probably just exhaustion."

"Explain the fever then."

She cringes. "Flying?" Then she adds, "I don't know. Can we go? I'd rather not stay here all night."

"I'm going to grab the truck and pull around. Are you okay to wait? I can find one of the officers assigned here or carry you." I hate the idea of leaving her there, but I'm not sure she'll let me carry her to the car either.

She attempts to shove at my chest, but it barely moves me. "I'll be fine, Sheriff. Go." There's no heat behind the nickname —almost like when she called me that before I messed up. That flicker of hope burns brighter.

People mill around steadily, but that doesn't stop me from running to the truck and calling Levi as I go. He's not a doctor, but he might as well be—smart as hell and good at his job.

He answers, concern evident in his voice. I rarely call him these days, not like before when Dan was around. I make a mental note to change that; there are a lot of relationships to repair, and his is near the top of the list.

"Vi, I'm at the airport picking up Odessa. She looks terrible —has a fever and a headache."

He doesn't talk for a moment, then says, "Okay. She's awake and talking? Do you know if she's eaten or drunk anything?"

I nod, hitting the elevator button more forcefully. "Yes to the first. Not sure about the second."

"Did she mention any pain in her leg or trouble breathing?" he asks.

"No, she didn't say anything like that. I checked her leg, and it seemed normal," I reply, urgency rising as the elevator doors finally open.

"Okay. So you're at the airport. She just flew back from

New York, where she was working? Probably crazy hours?" He sounds like he's working through all possible scenarios.

"Yeah. And?" The doors open on my floor, and I start jogging toward where I parked the truck.

"And if it's just that she looks like shit, is tired, and has a fever, it could be exhaustion from working and flying."

"That's your medical diagnosis?" I grind out.

"I'm not a doctor, dumbass." He softens his tone. "I know you're worried, but right now, that's the best thing I can think of."

I hit the locks and climb into my truck, starting the engine as I wait for my Bluetooth to connect.

"What do I do?" I ask.

"Stop somewhere and get her Tylenol and ibuprofen; she can rotate them. Grab anything with electrolytes, maybe a few snacks, and just watch over her on the drive home. Call me if anything else comes up."

I nod rapidly, trying to engrain everything he said into memory, thank him, and hang up.

When I pull up to the curb, I jump out of the driver's side and hurry around to open her door before I go in to get her. Just as I'm rounding the truck, I see her exiting the building and immediately change course to reach her. I'm there in a blink, lifting her like I did when we were hiking. The fact that she doesn't resist means she's sicker than she let on. When I set her down to open the passenger door, she quickly steps back, creating some space.

She climbs in, placing her backpack at her feet and reaching for the buckle. I'm about to close her door when she looks up. A soft smile pulls at her lips, though it almost seems painful. Quietly, she says, "Thanks for the ride, Luke."

Something in her tone sends my anxiety spiraling. I've dealt with many sides of Odessa, but I've never felt her this removed. Even when she yelled at me to stop mowing her lawn, I felt closer to her. *This? Heartbreaking to say the least.*

I close the door and hurry around, dodging cars pulling in to pick up their own passengers.

She speaks first as I start to pull out. "Do you mind if I sleep?"

I reach for the blanket I have in the back and hand it to her. She rolls it up and uses it as a pillow. It takes everything in me not to reach over and hold her hand, but halfway home, I end up doing it anyway.

Chapter Thirty-Three

Odessa

My cheek rests delicately on my Sferra pillow case and I snuggle in deeper, the smell of fresh linen enveloping me in a sense of calm and luxury.

There's still a lingering headache, but it doesn't hurt nearly as badly as it did last night when I got off the plane. A soft snore in the corner jolts my eyes open.

Luke sits in the armchair, his head tilted back and mouth slightly open as he sleeps peacefully. The morning light filters through the curtains, casting a warm glow over his features, and I can't help but smile at the sight for a brief moment, forgetting all of the heartache between us. He looked like every woman's fantasy at the airport last night, from the worn jeans that clung just right to the baseball cap pulled low over his brow.

I wanted to throw my arms around him and kiss him, feeling all the embarrassment and anger I had when I left melt away. Thankfully, I was too sick to actually follow through with those reckless thoughts. Which saved me from making a colossal mistake. *Friends, Odessa. Just stay friends.*

Vaguely, I remember him walking out of the gas station

with a bag full of meds, snacks, and drinks—his brows furrowed in concern as he rushed out. It was like a scene from a movie, one where the hero comes to the rescue, ready to save the damsel in distress. *And, well I'd be lying if I said I wasn't glad I was the damsel.*

Once we were home, he effortlessly carried me up the stairs, his strong arms supporting me when I could barely stand. I can still feel the warmth of his body against mine as he helped me into pajamas, a gentle smile on his face that somehow managed to soothe my discomfort. He tucked me into bed as if I were the most precious thing in the world. And I let him, without complaint or resistance, uncaring of the repercussions it would have on my heart the next day. Or maybe, finally accepting the friends part of this situation.

That must be why he's still here. To make sure I'm okay after I walked out like a zombie and was nice to him.

He must sense me watching him, because eyelids snap open and he startles awake saying "Achilles."

"Hi," I say, my voice coming out higher pitched than I intended.

"You okay?" He scans me from head to toe before glancing at his watch.

"Much better," I reply, pulling the blanket snugly around me.

He stands, moving through the room and the back of his hand touches my forehead. He nods as if confirming something to himself, then sits back down on the edge of the bed.

"You scared me," he admits, his voice soft.

"Oh," I reply, feeling a mixture of confusion and guilt. "I'm sorry."

He doesn't say anything, but the way he stares at me so intensely reminds me of why I insisted we couldn't be friends.

Because seeing him hurt makes me want to protect him, even if it means sacrificing my own feelings.

"Can we—" he starts to say at the same time I say "I should shower..." At first he doesn't move, but then his shoulders sag. "Take your time. I'll make breakfast."

Before I can protest, he stands up and walks out of the room. *Shit.* I should have led with, "Thank you for helping me. See you later."

I end up taking way too long in the shower, but there's something about your own shower after a long trip that hits different.

When I make it into the kitchen, there's already an entire feast.

"Holy moly. What's all this?"

For the first time in what feels like months, he gives me a half smile and it melts more of the ice from my heart.

"I didn't know what you'd want. So, eggs and bacon. Avocado toast. And pancakes,"

"Where did it come from?!"

He uses the spatula to point over his shoulder, "My house? I am a proper adult you know."

The teasing sends a waves on tingles through me. *Friends, Odessa. FRIENDS.*

"Well, it looks amazing. Thank you. And thanks for last night. Sleeping in a hotel would've been awful."

His grunt of a response has me looking up and I notice his jaw clench.

"Not a fan of hotels either?"

"Not exactly the safest place in the entire world for someone of your caliber."

I scoff and laugh, "You sound like Eddie."

"Oh, I know. Had a great chat with him last night."

My eyes snap to him. "You talked to Eddie?"

"He called you on the way home and I didn't want him to worry."

"Ahh," I say while scooping some of the eggs on to my plate.

"Did you have a good time back in the city?"

"Great." I say too quickly.

I can tell he doesn't believe me by the way he stares at me, but he doesn't say anything more.

When I sit at the counter, he makes his own plate and sits by me.

"Can we talk?" Right as I'm saying "No work today?"

He gives me the same soft smile and shakes his head, "It's Saturday."

"Right..."

"There's some things I've been wanting to talk to you about."

I feel my body shrink, I hate talking.

"Can I go first?"

He looks surprised but nods.

"I'm sorry that I went back on my word after the accident."

He rears back, and starts to protest.

"No, really. Listen, okay? I was hurt and acted poorly toward you when you were only trying to be my friend. I shouldn't have thrown such a fit when I didn't get my way."

He stammers while trying to process my words, but I keep going.

"I know that I can be a lot for people. I ran into someone from my past while I was gone and they made me realize a lot."

"Someone from your past?"

"Yeah... long story. But I just wanted to say that I'm sorry, and I'd like to be your friend."

"Can I talk now?"

I nod but keep my mouth shut, partly because I'm nervous about what he's going to say.

"I've been going to therapy for the last week. It's new for me, but after realizing what an absolute idiot I've been, it's been helping."

"I was broken—losing Dan and blaming myself for both accidents. I didn't want help; I just wanted to wallow in my misery because I thought I deserved it. You helped me break out of that, but then your accident happened, and I tried to punish myself again. I took on the responsibility as if I were the snake that bit you. I'm starting to learn how to deal with those feelings." *Damnit, one point for Monica.*

Then he hits me out of left field: "I don't want to be your friend. I want more—"

"Stop! Please, wait." I scramble, unable to hear more of his confession. *I can't do this with him again. I can't go there again.*

"The person I ran into? Kind of an ex, and well, we started —I'm... off the market." *Not true, not true, not true.* But she was an ex-employee, and yes, I am off the market, just not because I'm seeing her—or anyone for that matter.

The hurt is written all over his face, but he masks it so quickly that I almost believe him when he says, "Okay. We'll table that conversation for now."

"So, how was working again after taking a little hiatus?" The way he flows into an easy conversation nearly gives me whiplash, but I take the reprieve and fill him in on everything— minus Jess—that happened in New York.

When he leaves, it almost feels like maybe being friends will work. *Or maybe it will quietly kill me, like heart disease.*

Chapter Thirty-Four

Odessa

"Here you go, sweetheart." The server sets my iced coffee in front of me, along with one of their famous blueberry scones. The warm aroma of the freshly baked scone immediately entices me, making my already great day even brighter.

Delta and Cooper should be here any minute so we can go for an afternoon hike along one of the trails in Tumalo, but I couldn't resist stopping into the Little Corner Coffeehouse first.

The weather is much nicer now than it was the first time I found my way here. Sometimes I can't believe it's already been six months, while other times it feels like a lifetime ago.

The church sits behind me where I'm sitting at the round table, my back to it. It still hurts to look at it because it makes me miss Luke. I think I'm over the hurt I felt when realizing it wasn't our thing anymore. After our conversation the other morning—where he explained everything: his heartbreak and fears, his uncertainty about the future, and his overwhelming grief from guilt—my resolve has crumbled. I knew it would happen, and that's why I couldn't be around him. Now, I can't stop thinking about the effort he's making to heal, let go, and move forward. The question is, can I release the anxiety I feel about trying again with him?

My attention is drawn to the side. Down the road a little ways is a bustling food truck lot. Kids are running around, playing on the nearby playground, while adults chat and enjoy their meals at the picnic tables.

I sip my coffee and people-watch for at least twenty minutes, my scone completely gone and my coffee almost entirely ice.

Right as I'm about to whip my phone out to call the guys and start yelling at them for being late, they stomp up with scowls.

"What's your problem?" I ask, my mood souring with their energy.

"You know that guy?" Cooper asks as he pulls out a chair to sit, the sound of it scraping against the ground making me cringe. Delta gestures toward the food truck lot when I glance over at him.

When I turn to look, I don't initially notice anyone I recognize. It isn't until I squint that I can make out the shaggy hair of the creep who tried to drug me—the same guy Luke nearly killed. He's leaning over a table, taking a bite of his food, but I know it's him.

An involuntary shiver rolls through me, but I try to play it off as a joke. "That creepy guy by himself? Zayden Thomas. The guy from Ponderosa Pine who..." I trail off when I see the shift in their demeanor. They were already on edge, but now they look like they're ready to strike.

"What's going on?"

"He's been watching you for at least ten minutes," Cooper explains. "We were finishing up a work call with Hayes when he pulled in. He must have recognized you..."

Delta huffs, "He nearly broke his neck to make sure it was you."

"Okay?"

Delta takes the other seat; he looks calm on the outside, but I can see the vein pulsing in his neck. These guys are more paranoid than conspiracy theorists at a UFO convention.

"I think we should call Luke," Cooper continues.

"Because he's staring at me? It's not like he followed me here. YOU saw he was surprised to see me."

"He shouldn't be near you," Delta says defiantly.

"It's a free country. Don't get me wrong; I don't love that he's here, but he's not doing anything *legally* wrong."

"D—You see that?" Cooper demands in a hushed tone, nodding toward Zayden.

Rather than turn, I keep my eyes trained on Cooper. No one would ever expect that beneath that manicured mustache lies not only a trained badass but also one of the smartest people I know. I don't know if it was trained into him or if he just naturally notices things, but nothing gets by him.

"Call Luke, Dess. Make it look natural," Delta instructs, his voice calm but urgent.

I roll my eyes and grab my phone, acting annoyed with them instead of terrified on the inside. I don't even care that it's Luke I have to call—something about hearing his voice is the only thing I want right now.

He answers on the first ring, and it nearly breaks my heart with how breathy it sounds. "Achi—"

That damn nickname. Every time.

"Hey, Luke—"

"What's wrong?" I hear the shift of his body and the demand in his tone.

"I'm with Cooper and Delta. They asked me to call.

Zayden Thomas has been watching me, and something else must have happened because they both look ready to kill."

"Speakerphone," Delta and Cooper echo in unison.

I quickly switch to speakerphone and listen as Cooper explains. He looks like it's any other phone call, even smiling as he says, "White male, five feet eleven inches, endomorph, black hair under a trucker hat, no visible tattoos, dark green T-shirt and jeans. Dess—he's getting food at the Thai truck; do you recognize him?"

I glance over and spot him right away. "Nope," I say, looking back at my phone, trying to ignore the butterflies at seeing Luke's name. This is serious. And terrifying. And confusing. *But also, I miss him.*

"That's not the car he got here in..." Delta says.

I look over to see a green sedan slowly backing out of the parking lot designated for the food trucks.

"What the hell am I missing right now?" Luke growls, sounding visibly pissed off.

"Thomas arrived in a red Subaru Forester. He got food, watched Odessa, and looked like he was waiting for someone. Unsub arrived in a green Subaru, walked by his table, nonchalantly placing something down, and then went to order. Now Thomas is leaving in the unsubs car."

Meanwhile, Cooper repeats the same six-letter number sequence over and over again, his eyes fixed on the departing Subaru. It takes me a second to realize it's the license plate.

"Luke, I'd bet my ass there are drugs in that car, and it's heading straight toward Three Sisters."

"License plate?"

Cooper gives it with a smile on his face, his mustache twitching with excitement. "3JG7K9."

"Can't promise anything, but I'll watch for it."

"You either find a reason to pull his ass over and search that damn car, or I get Hayes and Drew involved, and *we* handle it," Cooper says, his voice turning darker than I knew possible. *Mad respect. Kinda hot, Coop.*

"Excuse me?" Luke asks, just as venomous.

"Don't hit me with any bureaucratic bullshit when we just watched how that asshole looked at Odessa. You made a promise to him about coming back here and if you don't honor it, we fucking will." He hits the red button on my phone with more force than necessary and I have to consciously school my features. *That. was. awesome.*

Delta nudges Cooper with his foot, but I'm still reeling from the pissing match between Luke and Cooper.

I glance over and see the other guy getting into the red Subaru.

"Get in your car," Delta says, standing up. "Drive to Hayes and Charlie's and stay there until we call."

"What?" I say, standing up so quickly that the table rocks.

"We have to go."

"I'm coming!" I say, following them down the small set of steps that leads to the sidewalk.

"Odessa," Delta groans but keeps walking.

"Don't fight me on it; it'll only slow you down, and I'll end up winning in the end."

Cooper and Delta exchange looks, trying to find a way out of it.

"Luke and Everett will kill us," Cooper says to Delta, who nods in agreement.

"You think sending me defenseless in the same direction as the creepy guy who already tried to hurt me is the better call?"

"Fuck!" Cooper exclaims, realizing it's a lose-lose for them.

"Get in the car, Odessa," Delta shouts back, and I hurry behind them toward Cooper's supercharged Durango. It's supposedly very fast, but I haven't had the pleasure of experiencing it yet. I have a feeling that may change today.

I slide onto the leather seats and buckle my seatbelt, making myself as small and quiet as possible—which isn't easy for a six-foot-tall opinionated woman. However, I'm not going to miss out on the chance to watch these guys work.

Cooper flies out of his parking spot and speeds in the direction the red Subaru went. Delta and he work in perfect sync, communicating with each other without speaking as they navigate down the back roads. Delta has a map pulled up on his phone and is tracking each turn before Cooper makes it. They may not have been trained in the same military branches, but they clearly know how to tail someone without getting caught.

I'm faintly aware of Juniper trees—which I've learned smell good in the rain but look like twisty, gnarled trees in a drab green—whizzing by in a blur. Cooper isn't driving like a madman, but I haven't stopped looking ahead at the red Subaru. They've left so much distance between us and him that I have no idea how they're even tracking him, but occasionally, a glimpse of red appears in the distance.

Slowly, Cooper pulls off to the side of the road and stops. Delta still has his map open, and Cooper grabs his phone from the cup holder to do his own digging.

I don't dare talk; whatever weird focus they have going on shouldn't be interrupted. The only time they do speak, it sounds like they're talking in code.

My phone rings, startling me out of my trance of watching them. I look down at my shaking hand and see it's Hayes.

"Hayes, should I answer?"

"Affirmative," the guys say in unison. If this weren't so serious, I might have laughed.

"Hey, buddy." I try to answer as calmly as possible, but my voice cracks with nerves.

"Where are you?" Hayes asks urgently, making me cringe.

"I'm with the guys."

"What the fuck, Dess? Where the hell are they?"

"Hunting down a drug dealer."

"Yeah, I got that when Luke called and asked me to break check some tweaker's fucking car! And when I asked why, he said to ask my employees *or you*."

"Oh, shit!"

For the first time, I see Cooper crack a half-smile, and a small laugh comes from Delta.

"Did he hit you?"

"Of course he fucking did! When the sheriff asks you to commit a crime, you make sure to do it right."

"Now tell me what the hell's going on." Charlie may call him "ruthless Hayes" when he's mad, but he sounds more like "disappointed dad Hayes" to me.

"Look, I don't know. That guy you hit was Zayden Thomas—the one who put drugs in my drink a few months ago."

"He was watching me from the food truck lot in Tumalo. He and some other guy did a vehicle exchange. Coop and Delta called Luke and informed him of what Zayden was driving in toward Three Sisters. Now we're doing recon on the guy that left in the other car."

"And you're with them, because?"

"You'd prefer I head unarmed in the same direction as one bad guy, or toward another bad guy with two trained operators who are consciously trying not to get caught?" I put as much sass and "you're an idiot" into my voice as I can muster.

"Point taken," he says with a heavy sigh. "Is that her? Is she okay? Safe?" Luke's voice sounds in the distance, as if he isn't close to Hayes but can't resist asking.

Hayes starts to respond with "She's—" but then realizes he

hasn't asked me yet. "You okay?" he asks, his tone much softer now.

"Tell him I'm good. I'm safe. Promise."

He relays what I said and then responds to me, "Alright, don't distract the guys. Have them fill me in on what they find out."

"Okay. Hey, Hayes..." I add before he hangs up. "Is Luke okay?"

"Pretty sure that man would give up his badge and life to make sure you're safe. Maybe you should think about cutting him some slack," Hayes replies before ending the call. *Yeah, I've been thinking that too.*

Chapter Thirty-Five

Luke

I practically skidded on dry pavement getting out of the police department to get to the edge of town. Cooper may have pissed me off by threatening to take matters into his own hands, but he isn't wrong. Zayden Thomas is a problem that isn't going away. Unfortunately, as much as I want to go Yellowstone on him, this isn't a situation that can be solved with brute force.

I need to approach this with a level head and figure out what he's involved in, and why he keeps coming back to Three Sisters. If Cooper is right, it's dealing drugs, and he just picked up his latest shipment.

I'll need to gather evidence, build a case, and take him down legally to ensure he doesn't get out in a matter of days again. Oregon is a little too lenient with drug users if you ask me; however, dealing drugs is an entirely different ballgame. If we can prove he has intent to sell, I'll make sure he gets max sentencing.

It takes me going down two side streets to get to the edge of town, where I can park to watch for him. Seven minutes of me watching every car pass through, staring down each one, until I see the newer green Subaru driving my way. The shaggy brown hair, hands at ten and two, looking straight ahead.

From my vantage point, I can see he's going to make this hard on me. I need a reason to pull him over, one that will hold up in court, so I need to bide my time until he makes a traffic infraction. I hit the gas, my truck lurching as I head for the small break in cars that allows me to pull out behind him.

I'm careful not to run his license plate through dispatch yet. I don't want anyone even knowing I'm on to him.

He maintains the same slow speed, stopping at each crosswalk to let the pedestrians walk. It's stop and go traffic through the entire town, the summers here are always crazy but especially leading up to the weekend of the rodeo. He may seem calm, but I don't miss the way his eyes glance into the rearview every few seconds to see if I'm still behind him.

We start to approach the other side of town, where it opens up to highway and I feel the panic rise. I need to think and think fucking fast.

Then I look over to see my saving grace pulling onto the road directly in front of us—Hayes.

I immediately call him on my personal phone, hitting the speakerphone.

"S'up, Luke," he answers in a voice that's much too chipper for how hard my heart is pounding.

"You have August with you?"

"Uh, no?" he answers like a question.

"Charlie?" I ask quickly.

"No, I'm alone. Whats—"

"Slam on your brakes! Right now!"

Without question, I see the taillights of Hayes's truck turn bright red, then I hear the crunch of metal when the Subaru hits it. We weren't going more than ten miles per hour, so the damage won't be bad, but it's enough to initiate a police investigation. Plus, it's one hundred percent Zayden's fault for rear-ending someone.

"Was that a little white dog that ran into the road? Glad you missed it."

"Don't know what it was. Only saw a flash of white, and it was gone." Hayes responds without missing a beat.

"Good. Call one of the guys, or Dess. Stay in your truck. Be there in a second."

I flip my lights on, the recording from my vehicle now beginning.

The three of our vehicles pull over, and I radio in to dispatch, requesting backup from any available deputies. I step out of the SUV with a smirk on my face.

Hayes remains in his vehicle, and I approach Zayden first. He rolls his window down, and I see that he looks visibly shaken but there's an underlying tone of anger.

"You okay, boss?" I ask, even though I'm not the least bit concerned for his well-being.

He nods, his mouth forming a flat line.

"Why don't you step out?" One brief second, and I see the telltale signs of fear mixing with "I'm going to run." *I hope the fucker tries.*

He doesn't though, he opens the door and climbs out of the low car.

"He slammed on his brakes out of nowhere. We'll exchange insurance and go about our way. You can leave." He tries to blow off the situation, but I can see the tension in his shoulders.

"How 'bout you come back here and we'll talk."

Defiance rolls off him, but he follows. "Back in Three

Sisters? Thought we were clear you weren't welcome." I raise an eyebrow, waiting for his response.

He simply shakes his head, a sneer playing on his face.

Deputy Corbin arrives, and I ask him to stay with Zayden while I speak to the other driver. He nods, but I see the twitch of his lips when he sees that it's Hayes's truck. Small towns where everyone knows everything about everyone, including what vehicle you drive.

Hayes's window is already down, and he arches one brow when he looks at me, with a finger holding up. I hear whom I'm assuming to be Odessa but I only catch "not to get caught?" from whatever she was saying.

I left the station and went right for Zayden, not even stopping to think what she was doing after he left. *Is she still with Cooper and Delta? Did those lunatics follow the other guy? Or did they take her home? Is she alone?*

"Is that her? Is she okay? Safe?" Even I can hear the break in my voice when I ask.

Hayes nods and starts to answer but then stops himself mid-word, "She—." Then he turns toward his dash and asks, "You okay?" to her.

"Tell him I'm good. I'm safe. Promise." Her voice calms the anxiety in me immediately. I turn and head back toward Zayden. Odessa probably already filled in Hayes with her side of things and he's smart enough to figure out why I had him commit a crime.

"Sheriff Haynes, you smell that?" Deputy Corbin says making an effort to sniff into the air in front of Zayden's face.

I lean closer toward Zayden who is standing between us but hasn't been detained yet.

"Sure do. You been drinking today?" I ask Zayden, smelling the faint odor of beer on his breath. Zayden's eyes widen in surprise, and he stammers out a denial before I raise a hand to stop him. "Don't try to deny it," I say, my tone firm but calm. "Deputy Corbin and I both smell alcohol. We already have probable cause to conduct a field sobriety test."

His mouth clamps shut, and I don't miss the brief glance between his car and me. In a fraction of a second, my spidey senses begin tingling, and I see the shift in his stance. The tell-tale sign he's going to run. He's caged in between Deputy Corbin and me, but there's still a foot between each of us.

At the same time my hand reaches out to grab him, he takes off running and my fingers slip through. *Motherfucker.*

My knees protest as I lunge after him, but adrenaline surges through my veins, pushing me forward. I can hear Deputy Corbin shouting orders into the radio as I take point in the chase. He runs past the driver's side door of the Subaru like he's going to run toward the businesses across the street. I'll give it to him that he's fast already eight feet ahead of me, but we train for long distance while criminals rely on short adrenaline fueled sprints.

Part of me wants to yell for Hayes, but I don't have time to get it out before Zayden surges past the bed of Hayes's truck only to run smack into the driver door when Hayes throws it open at the last second. His body collides with the door, causing him to splatter against it and fall backwards. Before he can stand up, I'm on top of him. Once again, Deputy Corbin and I work in tandem, and Zayden's in handcuffs. What couldn't have been more than ten seconds felt like ten minutes. As I look up to thank Hayes, I see the barrel of his Glock pointed at Zayden still. A look of disgust on his face as he stares down at him.

Then he blinks it away, sheaths his gun in the holster attached to his console, and looks back at me with a smirk. "Dumbass."

I let out a hefty breath, my chest constricting with the

sudden exertion, and then laugh. I hope that was caught on my dash cam, because I want to replay Zayden smashing into the door frame over and over again.

My hand clamps down on Zayden's bicep while my other goes under his armpit as Corbin and I lift him up. "Former Navy SEAL," I say, gesturing to Hayes. "Good guy. Great aim. Even better timing, it seems."

Zayden lets out a slew of expletives, but I just chuckle. Whether Hayes was there or not, Zayden wouldn't have gotten away—but for the sake of the story, I'm sure as hell glad he was.

Once we have Zayden sitting in the back of Deputy Corbin's cruiser, I grab gloves from the back of my truck and start investigating the Subaru Zayden was driving.

It isn't registered as stolen, but it also isn't registered to him. I hit the button for the trunk and open it to find three backpacks. They're all the same dark gray with orange Patagonia branded on the side. An expensive bag, but one that would be common around here, and especially at the mountain.

I unzip the first bag, and immediately it's a jackpot. You name the substance, and I guarantee it's in here, everything from cocaine to pills, even to a quart-size bag of the vials he had on him before.

It's a slam dunk arrest for him, one he won't be getting out of like the last time. I know there's something bigger going on, though, and I have a feeling he's going to be the key to figuring it out. He seems like the type of weasel that will easily roll on whoever dropped off the Subaru.

I set the bag down, remove my gloves, and grab my phone out of my pocket. The photo of Odessa and Dog stares back at me, and every inch of my being wants to call her, text her, leave this fucking scene to go check on her. But I can't do that. I'm honoring what she asked of me, and that was a friendship. The one thing I spent months begging for, and now I can't risk losing it.

Taking a deep breath, I focus on the situation before me and start making the necessary calls. First to alert the CODE team, then Sheriff Larkin, and finally my contact with the D.E.A..

Chapter Thirty-Six

Luke

My fingers ache, and my eyes start to blur as I finish the last of the initial incident report from the Zayden Thomas case. Delta, Cooper, and Odessa unknowingly uncovered one of the largest drug busts in Central Oregon history. I had enough on Zayden that he rolled over before I even offered a deal; he didn't have a name or an address, but he did agree to testify that his dealer was the one who dropped the Subaru off in the parking lot.

If it weren't for Cooper and Delta tracking this guy down, we might never have discovered Nicolas Bertleson. I'm furious that Odessa got caught up in this mess with them, but the sheriff in me is grateful they followed that asshole to the edge of his property. If it had been anyone else, I'd be plotting ways to arrest them or kick their ass. But Delta and Cooper are far more trained than I am, and I know they'd protect her with their lives.

They tracked that Subaru to a property on the border of Cascadia County and Deschutes. The CODE team had been hunting for this dealer for the last six months, and I had no idea he was operating right under my nose. He was smart enough to keep rotating through different Subarus, never revealing his name or home address—well, technically, his grandmother's home address.

Juanita Bertleson was nowhere to be found in our searches, and, given her records suggest she's over a hundred, that presents a whole different case for me to tackle. But what we did find was more illegal drugs than ever discovered in Central Oregon. Nicolas Bertleson had been running a major operation right under everyone's noses, using his grandmother's property as a front. The craziest part? From the outside, it looked like an ordinary house, with no guards or dealers—nothing protecting the property. All it housed was him, three dozen different Subarus of varying colors and models, and enough drugs to supply the entire state.

It was actually clever. One of the most popular vehicles in Central Oregon is a Subaru. Nobody knew where he lived or where he stashed the product. He'd have mules meet in a lot and switch vehicles. He'd presumably leave cash in one vehicle for the mules and product in another for the dealers. His hands stayed clean of most of it.

The contact I have at the DEA will take over the case from here. He's worked with the CODE division on previous cases, and given the quantity and complexity of this operation, he's the best person for the job.

I pinch the bridge of my nose hard, leaning on my desk as I finish the report. The usual hum of activity surrounds me— telephones ringing, deputies gossiping like busybodies, and the distant sounds of a printer churning out paperwork. In the last twelve hours, I've only left my office to use the restroom and grab more coffee. I want to capture every detail I have, except for the part about Hayes being involved in the "accident."

My phone has been ringing off the hook, but none of the

calls have been from the one person I want to hear from. I haven't spoken to Odessa since she was on the phone with Hayes in his truck.

I'm not sure I can face her, especially not when I'm desperate for her and she told me she's seeing someone else. I want to respect her decision, and if that means taking a back seat and waiting, then that's what I'll do.

A burst of laughter and excitement fills the hall, accompanied by the pitter-patter of little feet. Many employees around here have young kids and bring them by occasionally, but I'd recognize that giggle anywhere.

A smile spreads across my face before I even look up. Ellie barges into my office, her bright eyes filled with mischief and her wild blonde hair tumbling out of her bun. "Uncle Luke!" she exclaims as she throws herself into me. "You'll never guess what I get to do!"

Olivia follows behind her, her baby bump on full display since she's due next month.

"Hmm," I tap my chin, pretending to ponder while I set Ellie back on her feet. "You get to be a big sister soon?"

Ellie laughs but shakes her head. "Well, yeah," she replies with more sass than I thought possible, "but I also get to be in the showcase at the end of summer! I have to go to the studio every day and learn a special dance routine. It's going to be so much fun!"

"Wow! That's a lot of practicing," I say, turning to Olivia. "That's a lot for a six-year-old, right?"

Olivia slyly shakes her head and mouths, "Not every day." Then, a bit louder, she adds, "But there will be a lot." Meanwhile, Ellie twirls around the room, lost in her own world.

"I can't wait to see it! I'll be front row with the biggest bouquet for you," I say with a grin.

"Yeah, good luck with that," she replies, plopping into the

seat across from me. "You know Drew paid for the remodel of The Flower Shop, right? They have his credit card on file at this point."

The huff I release is mixed with humor and frustration: "If only that worked on all women..."

"Still can't get Odessa to budge?"

I shake my head, watching Ellie continue her twirling, completely absorbed in her imaginary dance routine.

"She told me she ran into someone from her past, and they're 'trying again.'" Just saying the words out loud sends another wave of disappointment through me.

"Who is? Dess?" Everett says, bouncing in and picking up Ellie mid-twirl. She squeals with laughter, and he sets her down before taking a seat next to Olivia.

"Yep. That's what Luke is boohooing about."

Everett's scoff catches me off guard, and I look back at him so quickly that my neck hurts.

"She's such a little liar. There's no way! Trust me. She's just saying that because she's being stubborn."

Olivia nods in agreement. "There are no exes she would ever go back to—we heard all the sordid details a few months ago at girls night."

I shrug. "Maybe it wasn't an ex? Just a fling she had. I don't know—didn't ask too many questions."

They both look at me as if I've said something outrageous. Olivia raises an eyebrow. "You're making excuses to make it easier to give up."

"You're giving up?" Everett sits up, looking at me in disbelief.

"What else is there to do? I told her everything and apologized. Hell, I've been trying for the last three months to get her to even talk to me. Now she is, but she's telling me it's done."

"Sounds like you've made some progress to me," Everett chimes in.

I tug at my disheveled hair, already a mess from a long night of work, and now I'm being bombarded with relationship advice.

"It doesn't feel like progress," I mutter, feeling defeated.

Olivia leans forward, her expression hardening. "I'm saying this because I love you, and I know more than you think I know..." The way she tilts her head reminds me of a kid being scolded.

"You are the most stubborn man I know. You put up with over a decade of Maddy's crap. And for most of that, it wasn't love—it was an obligation—still is, if we're being honest. You can handle a few months of Odessa reacting to how you treated her because you DO love her."

"I agree with Liv."

"Once again—aren't you supposed to be giving me the big brother talk?"

His hands go out at the side, so casually that I don't expect the words out of his mouth. "My gut says you're the one for her, and my gut never lies..."

Chapter Thirty-Seven

Odessa

"My gut says you're the one for her, and my gut never lies..." My feet come to a halt in the hallway as I hear Everett inside Luke's office.

I waited at my dining room table all night last night, hoping for a flicker of light at his house that never came on. I had a feeling he spent the night in his office, and I couldn't wait any longer. Being the good friend that I am, I stopped by Maisie's and grabbed us both a coffee and a pastry.

Of course, my brother beat me here, and of course that jerk is throwing me under the bus right now.

My shoulders instinctively square, and I tip my chin, bracing myself before I walk into his office. I've walked down a runway in ten-inch heels with more confidence than I can muster right now, but I can't stand in the hallway all damn day.

All four sets of eyes snap to me, surprise etched on their faces except for Ellie's. She sees me and launches herself into my arms.

"Auntie Dess! Guess what?!" She doesn't give me a chance

to answer. "I'm going to be famous just like you! I'm going to be a dancer! Will you come to my showcase?"

I beam down at her, silently thanking her for smoothing over this awkward moment.

"Of course I'll be there! Front row, baby! When is it?" I reply, looking toward Olivia for the answer.

Her face has at least recovered, and she wears an evil smile that matches my brother's.

"End of summer. You and Luke can sit next to each other! He said the same thing." She wiggles her eyebrows at him before she starts to stand, placing her hand on the armrest and shoving. Both guys leap to their feet in case she needs help, which causes her to roll her eyes.

"I'm fine." Then she looks at Ellie, who I'm still holding. "Time to go, Elles-Belles! We don't want you to be late for your first day."

She takes Ellie from me and winks as Ellie yells, "See ya later, y'all!"

Everett glances at me and then back at Luke. "May the force be with you." *Traitor.*

He dances past me, already covering his arm and attempting to dodge the hit I wasn't planning to send. Instead, I narrow my eyes at him and let him go by uninjured. *For now.*

"Hey, uh..." Luke runs his hand through his already rumpled hair and looks back at me. "Come in?"

His tone is hesitant, almost as if he's unsure of himself and afraid to spook me. A small smile spreads across my lips at his nervousness, and I extend my hand with his coffee.

"Looked like you had a late night," I say as he nods and grabs the cup. "Thought you could use this."

His eyebrows shoot up at my admission, but I catch the smile he hides as he brings the coffee to his lips. "You waiting up for me, Achi?"

Without hesitation, I reply, "Yep," then let my vulnerability show as our eyes meet.

"I'm sorry." He looks confused. "I wasn't sure if I should text."

"Never stopped you before." Again, his expression shows surprise and maybe some underlying guilt.

I take the opportunity to toss the food onto his desk and then sit in the chair Olivia just vacated.

He stares at the bag for what feels like a lifetime before looking back at me. I nearly expect him to beat around the bush and make small talk, but instead, he cuts right to the chase.

"Why ya here?" My heart physically aches with the sadness in his voice.

"Because I lied," I reply, then, trying to lighten the mood, I add, "This might not be a church to confess my sins, but a sheriff's department has to count for something, right?"

That earns a cheeky chuckle from him as he shakes his head. "Not even close."

"Oh, well," I say, waving my hand dismissively.

He narrows his eyes, like he's studying me, his expression growing serious again.

I mirror his somber look and close my eyes, finally admitting, "I lied about seeing someone. I'm not with anyone, and it wasn't fair for me to say that."

When I finally peek at him, he's still watching me, his expression unchanged.

The only thing that moves is his Adam's apple as he swallows.

"I'm sorry," I whisper.

"Are you saying this just because you feel guilty for lying?" he asks, his face revealing nothing.

"I'm not sure how to answer that without sounding like a jerk or making it worse."

His head tilts adorably as he processes my words.

"If I say no, it downplays my apology and makes it seem like I have other motives. I genuinely feel bad about lying to you. But it's not the only reason I'm here."

"So you do have ulterior motives?" he asks, a smirk playing at the corner of his mouth.

"I'm also here to invite you over for dinner."

He stands up suddenly and nods. "Sure, let's go."

"I didn't mean right now!" I laugh.

"Nope, I'm not missing my chance. Plus, I didn't eat dinner yesterday, so I'm cashing in on it now."

Before I can protest, he lifts me out of the chair and into his arms.

He holds me tightly, and I sigh contentedly as my arms wrap around his waist. It feels like he'll never let go.

"You're not mad that I lied to you?" I ask.

"I'm freaking elated. The unobtainable Odessa Astor back on the market? Now I have free rein to do whatever it takes to get out of the friend zone—shirtless workouts, cooking you dinner, spontaneous romantic gestures. It's game on, Achi. Prepare to be wined and dined."

I pull back slightly to catch a glimpse of the grin spreading across his face. "You look like a crazy person." His smile is so wide that the corners of his eyes crinkle, and I can't help but feel a flutter in my chest.

His laughter is melodic, and I realize how much I've missed this version of him—the carefree, playful side I only got to see for a little while.

"Not going to argue with that. I feel a little crazy—like I'm not convinced this isn't a dream and I'll wake up with drool on my desk."

"Probably because you're exhausted," I say, patting his chest. He still has his arms locked around me. "Come on, I'll drive you home. You can eat what Maisie sent and then take a nap."

His lips form an adorable pout. "But—"

"You want to have this big relationship talk when you're delirious, with no sleep and no real food? I'm not going anywhere; it can wait." I smile reassuringly at him, and I see the skepticism fade, replaced by a grin.

"You said 'relationship.' Is that your way of telling me I'm already out of the friend zone?"

"Oh my god. Get your stuff, Sheriff." I roll my eyes and move toward the door, trying—and failing—to suppress a grin.

"Fine, but you're definitely napping at my house. I really shouldn't be left alone in my current state."

His exaggerated, pathetic expression makes me laugh as he gathers his things and falls into step beside me. The relief I feel is hard to ignore; we can put the relationship talk on hold for now. I want to give him another chance. I want to be with him —I always have—but taking that leap? It's still terrifying.

Chapter Thirty-Eight

Luke

Odessa refused to let me discuss our relationship before I headed to the press conference. At first, I tried to resist, dropping hints and promises of our future together. But after she fed me a massive breakfast, I fell asleep wrapped in her arms—finally resting for what felt like the first time in months.

I rushed home, showered, and got ready to head back to the station. I'm really getting tired of these press engagements, talking to the vultures who pretend to care. But it comes with the territory of being sheriff. Thankfully, the conference room was filled with only a few reporters—not nearly the scrutiny of some past events. My report was brief, sticking to the basics. I answered questions as best I could, but my responses were limited. This case doesn't belong to me anymore, and all I can really offer the public is my willingness to share every detail with the DEA and my trust in them to handle it with care.

After a grueling two hours, I finally make my way into my office to decompress. Even though I'm eager to see Odessa tonight, I feel drained from all the attention.

"Fancy seeing you here, Professor McGonagall," I hear from the doorway. I glance up to see Everett leaning against the frame.

"Shouldn't you be off by now?" I ask, checking my watch. Shit, *it's only five.*

"Just clocked out. I, uh... well, I have something for you." He taps an envelope against the doorframe. His usual goofy smirk is gone, and dare I say, he looks almost nervous.

"What've ya got?"

He steps fully into the office and settles into the same chair he occupied this morning.

"You were pretty out of it when Odessa was bitten that day. Do you remember us talking in the waiting room at all?"

"Honestly, not really," I admit, running a hand through my hair.

"The synopsis? I'm pretty sure my house is haunted."

"What?" I laugh at his odd comment.

"Yup. By Dan."

That gets my attention, and I sit up straighter. "What do you mean by Dan?"

Vague murmurs from the hospital begin to resurface in my mind, but I can't recall any specifics.

"Drew always had crazy stuff happening to him, usually prank-related, but we always laughed it off. Don't get me wrong —I believe in paranormal stuff. But the chances of it being Dan rather than Drew just misplacing his keys? Not likely, right?"

"Right," I reply, my tone sounding more like a question than a statement.

"That is, until this..." He holds up the letter, and I can only see the back of the envelope, which is written in a scrawly font.

"And that is?"

"A letter written by my Grandma Astor—addressed to Odessa's future husband."

"I'm not picking up what you're putting down."

"Exactly!" He leans in closer, tapping the letter on my desk. "This letter was found on the ground after falling out of a completely functional lockbox. I even sent it back to the company to check for any faults, and it was in perfect condition."

"What the hell are you talking about, Astor?"

"At the exact moment Odessa was bitten by the rattlesnakes—the moment you saved her—this letter miraculously fell out of my locked safe. The machine popped open on its own, scaring Isla, who then called Drew to come check for any intruders, and out came only this letter. Nothing else. Not the cash, not the other envelope, or the SIG that had been sitting on top of it."

"You're telling me that Dan—as a ghost—opened your safe, found a letter addressed to Odessa's future husband, and threw it on the ground?"

"Exactly what I'm telling you."

"Are you high?" I can't help but ask.

"Only on life. Look, I get it; it's a weird pill to swallow. But I don't believe in coincidences, and I've got a feeling about you. Something deep down tells me this letter belongs to you. I know Dess was here earlier, and I don't know what transpired, but I promised my grandma I'd give this to the man I thought was the one for Odessa."

"And you think that's me?" I say, trying to keep my heart from racing out of control.

He lightly tosses the letter onto my desk. "Yeah, boss. I think that's you."

I stare at the letter for a moment as he starts to leave.

"Everett," I call, and he pauses, looking over his shoulder. "I'm determined to be everything she needs—the one she can rely on, trust, and love wholeheartedly. From this moment forward, I promise to prioritize her above all else—this job, the situation with Maddy, everything. Odessa will always be my number one. I know I failed her the first time; I won't make that mistake again."

He turns, but I don't miss the genuine grin returning to his face. "I know. I wouldn't be here otherwise." With that, he leaves, and I'm left with a sense of resolve I haven't felt before. The drained energy from the press conference revives just by being in his presence.

I quickly grab the letter, nerves tightening in my chest. The front reads, "To the future Mr. Odessa Astor." The back, which I can finally read clearly, is signed "Grandma Astor."

As I pull out my pocket knife and delicately slice open the envelope, it doesn't escape me how honored I feel that Everett chose me to receive this letter.

To Whom My Grandson Thinks Deserves My Granddaughter,

You don't. There is no one truly deserving of the wonder that is Odessa Astor. She is fierce, she is strong, and above all else, she is loyal. There is no woman in the world who will love you, care for you, or honor you more profoundly than her.

Now, I need you to understand this: I say this with the utmost respect and love, knowing that Everett wouldn't give this letter to just any man. You are the one he trusts to love our girl, and I'm certain that if I were still around, I would feel the same way. Unfortunately, I'm not, and I'm placing my trust in his instincts on this one.

I want you to appreciate the precious gift you have in Odessa. She has a spirit that lights up the darkest days, and her laughter is a melody that brings joy to everyone lucky enough to hear it. With that fervor, she also faces life's challenges head-on, never backing down and always standing up for what she believes is right.

You may find that there will be times when things feel difficult or uncertain. It's in those moments that you must remember the strength of her heart and the depth of her loyalty. Cherish her, support her dreams, and be her partner in every sense of the word. And remember, love is not simply about the grand gestures; it's often found in the small, everyday moments that knit your lives together.

I ask that you nurture her spirit and honor her individuality. Listen to her, respect her opinions, and allow her to be the strong woman she is meant to be. Together, I believe you can create a bond that not only withstands the trials of life but flourishes in the face of adversity.

I may not be able to guide you directly, but I trust that you will honor the love that exists between you and my beloved granddaughter. Show her every day that she is cherished, and never take for granted the warmth and light she brings into your life.

With all my love,
Grandma Astor

Chapter Thirty-Nine

Odessa

Three strong knocks echo against my door, jolting me off the couch. Luke had to handle the press conference this evening, but he promised to come over afterward so we could talk. I've been a bundle of nerves ever since—my house is deep cleaned, dinner has been resting for an hour, and I've edited a hundred pictures for my Instagram account. My followers have fallen in love with Central Oregon, just like I have. Somewhere a business idea is rattling around in my brain, I just have to figure out what I want to do with it.

When I open the door, he stands there with a bouquet of yarrow and a sexy grin.

"You look beautiful, Achilles," he says as he hands me the flowers. *Swoon.*

Dog bypasses me and leaps into Luke's arms, who catches him effortlessly. "Hi, handsome boy." The way Dog nuzzles into him almost makes me feel guilty for keeping them apart. But I know that while Isla and Everett were dog-sitting, Luke spent some time with him. *Just one more chink in the armor I thought would never crack.*

I leave the door open and spin around to take the flowers to the kitchen. *Luke's here. In my space. With flowers. Playing with my dog.*

He follows me inside, closing the door behind him, and I can feel my shoulders shaking with nerves. Before I even make it to the kitchen, he grabs my shoulder and spins me around, the bouquet bumping between us.

Taking the flowers from my hands, he sets the vase on my credenza, then places both hands on my hips, lowering his face to meet mine.

"What's wrong?"

I laugh softly, placing my hands on his chest. "That obvious I'm nervous?"

I watch as his shoulders relax, and then he pulls me closer. "Nothing to be nervous about. We can skip the whole big, deep talk and go right to the getting back together part if that makes you more comfortable."

"That easy, huh?"

"Yep!" He pulls back a touch, still holding me. "Or I can give you the bullet points: I'm sorry for being emotionally unintelligent, for being scared, and for hurting you. I am madly, deeply, irrevocably in love with you. I don't want to be just your friend. I was an idiot for ever thinking I could settle for that. Not when I desperately want to be so much more—Dog's dad, your husband, and your partner in every sense of the word." He pauses briefly, trying to sense out my reaction to him saying the word husband. If he thought it'd scare me, he'd be right. But my first reaction isn't horror, it's relief. A small smile tugs at the corner of his mouth.

"I won't lie and say I'm not terrified because I am. Terrified of creating a dream-worthy life with you and then losing it. But I promise I'm going to keep working through those issues, digging to their root, so I can be the man you need." The last of my resolve crumbles as I pull him in for a kiss.

My hands find his face, cupping his strong jaw. "I love you, too." His eyes widen, and the smile he gives me is so genuine that it nearly brings tears to my eyes.

"Oh, Achi," he says between kisses, "a man could drown happily in those words."

There are a hundred more things for us to figure out, to talk about, and to plan for, but right now, I'm taking comfort in the knowledge that he wants to make it work. For tonight, I want to let the world outside fade into a distant hum while we lose ourselves in the excitement of being together again.

Chapter Forty

Odessa

It's rodeo time in Three Sisters. I have no idea what that means, but it's all anyone has been talking about.

Almost the whole crew, minus the Turner/Reynolds clan, is in attendance. Everett and Isla are cuddled up in the row in front of me, Levi next to me, and Maisie on the other side. The 'Bod Squad' is around somewhere, taking turns grabbing beers and flirting with random girls.

The smell of dirt mixes with the scent of fried food, and excitement fills the air of the stand. I can totally understand all the hype that everyone was creating. It's packed with people, but I spot Luke before anything else. He's on the edge of the arena, perched on Scotch like all the other cowboys. He's wearing the same uniform as the deputies next to him, but there's something about him that sets him apart. A quiet confidence, a subtle authority, a sense of calm amidst the chaos. It's like he was born to be in that moment, in that place, doing exactly what he's doing.

I can't help but watch him work the crowd with ease and grace. There's an aura of respect that surrounds him, a magnetic presence that draws people in. He's clearly good at his job, loved by the town, but also feared by those who dare to cross him. He'll smile at the kids, chat with the elders, but his eyes never fail to miss a beat, always scanning the crowd for any signs of trouble.

I'd feel jealous of the way women flock to him, but he never shows them an ounce of interest beyond polite conversation. His eyes always finding mine, a small smile before he goes back to work. Like he can't resist checking on me as well.

He left my house this morning with a pep in his step and a smirk that I knew would reveal all the dirty things we had just done to the neighbors. It's not a long walk of shame, but I've definitely mentioned putting a gate between our fences.

One week in, and things feel back on track, yet I'm still a little wary. I know I need to let that go, but I'm still holding onto some doubts. Time heals all wounds, or whatever the bullshit saying is.

Until then, I'm taking it day by day, thankful he's still going to therapy and talking things out with me. I had known he was suffering, but his mask was so convincing that I couldn't see the extent of it until recently. Now that everything is out in the open, I'm... hopeful. A scary place to be, but I'm working through my own trust issues.

"Luke and Odessa sittin' in a tree..." Levi starts the teasing chant, and I can't help but smile even when all the other guys chime in as well. "K.I.S.S.I.N.G."

"That's not all we're doing," I say back and Levi laughs.

Maisie groans next to me, "Eww, he's my cousin."

"Sorry!" I hit my shoulder into her and she laughs.

For a brief moment her body freezes, shoulders straightening and I immediately know why.

Here we go.

Ethan starts to walk up the stairs and takes the seat next to

Levi. "Hey," he greets all of us with a small wave but looks forward at the arena. He knows just how to give Maisie space, yet somehow always be in her space.

"You okay?" I whisper to Maisie.

Her shoulders relax, and she nods, "I think so. The talk we had the other day made me realize a lot."

I give her a reassuring smile and then lean the opposite way, over Levi so Ethan can hear me. "Where's Jake?"

"Uhm, hello? What about me?" Ethan says faking feeling dismissed.

"You're a close second. But he's our fav."

"He's somewhere around here with my mom. She was grabbing something surely to rot his teeth and keep him up all night."

"Tough break. Last year Ellie was cracked out from the sugar high." Levi says sympathetically.

"Wish they could've come." I lean back in my seat, feeling a twinge of sadness that they couldn't make it. Olivia wasn't feeling up for braving the entire crowd tonight, so they came last night when things were a bit quieter.

The sun begins to set, and so does the action in the arena. Barrel racers fly by, kicking up dust as they round the barrels with precision. It's graceful and badass at the same time; I can't take my eyes off them. That is, until I feel more than see Luke approaching. I search him out and spot him taking the steps two at a time, the metal bleachers clanging beneath his feet.

"Move, Turner." He grumbles as he reaches our row, and I can't help but smile at his possessive tone.

"Excuse me," Levi says, throwing a hand to his chest. "Is there a problem, Sheriff?"

Luke smirks, crossing his arms. "Yeah, my girl, my seat. Or your ass in handcuffs sitting in the back of my car."

"Oh, does he always talk this dirty?"

I chuckle. "You have no idea..."

Everett immediately starts pretending to barf, in front of us, but everyone else laughs.

Levi, of course, moves a seat back, and Luke takes his place next to me, flashing a cocky grin. "Hi, Achi," he says before kissing me. In public. Not that we haven't been the whispers throughout town for at least a week now, but neither of us had confirmed or denied.

Whistles from all around us grow louder, but Luke only kisses me harder. When he pulls away, he's all smiles. "Looks like the secret's out," he whispers in my ear, making me blush.

"Yeah, no denying that kiss. You sure you're ready for that?"

"Never been so sure."

Someone's phone rings, but I'm barely aware of what's going on. Luke's declaration to the town repaired something I hadn't known was broken.

"What do you mean?!" Ethan shouts, snapping us out of our bubble.

Luke spins around faster than I thought possible, facing Ethan with his sheriff face snapped back on.

"Mom! Where are you?!" Ethan's standing, his sight bouncing around the packed arena. The panic is clear on his face, and I feel the anxiety in the pit of my stomach. Something is wrong, seriously wrong. He starts to storm down, but Luke grabs his shoulder.

"Talk to me."

Ethan tries to shake off his grip, but Luke doesn't budge. "I have eyes and ears all over this place. Tell me what the hell is going on."

Maisie's hand latches onto my arm, her nails digging into my skin as we all stand staring at Ethan.

"Jake's missing."

Epilogue

Luke

Only two more "yeses" stand between me marrying Odessa: one from Drew and the other from Odessa herself. Hayes, Everett, and Eddie have already given me their blessings. Hayes, my best friend, knows me inside and out—his approval came easily. Eddie surprised me by giving his blessing at Easter after a heartfelt fatherly talk that I wish I took notes on to share with whomever is my future son-in-law. As for Everett, he's been dropping hints for the last nearly year, clearly eager for me to make things official. In fact, he handed me that letter giving me his blessing before I even started dating Odessa.

Then there's Achilles. I'm nervous as hell about asking her, but it's not because I fear she'll say no. I've caught her talking about wedding venues multiple times, and her Instagram feed is filled with wedding content. She's as invested in this relationship as I am.

No, my real concern—my only concern—is Drew. He may not be the closest to Odessa, but his opinion looms large over me—perhaps because of the unresolved issues surrounding

Dan and my steadfast loyalty to him from the moment Drew first started coming around Olivia.

Things have been fine between us, though strained. Drew has been wrapped up in family life and the whirlwind of their baby's first year, while I've been consumed by thoughts of Odessa. We exchange casual greetings at family dinners, but we're not exactly texting buddies, which makes my decision to knock on his office door at two in the afternoon on a Tuesday feel a bit strange. As I knock, he looks up, surprise flashing across his face before he quickly masks it.

"Luke," he says, standing and extending his hand. The initial shock in his eyes gives way to a tension that hangs thick between us—definitely not the "besties" vibe Ellie would describe.

"Drew," I reply, keeping my tone casual as I shake his hand. "Sorry to barge in."

"All good, man. Did you get my text?"

"Text?" I echo, pulling out my phone, and there it is—a message from him blinking back at me.

DREW REYNOLDS

Hey, Luke. You up for grabbing a beer sometime this week?

"Just got it," I reply, raising an eyebrow.

"Oh," he responds with a half-hearted chuckle. Silence hangs between us, the air growing thick with awkward tension.

"Everything good?" I ask, following his gaze as he glances through the glass panes at Olivia's office. She's animatedly chatting with Charlie at her desk, blissfully unaware of the unease brewing between us.

"All good. Very good. Yup." His nervousness puts me on high alert.

296

I arch an eyebrow and remain silent, waiting. For a hard-ass former Navy SEAL, he looks like he's sweating bullets.

"Shit," he mutters, shaking his head.

"Look, you're a straight shooter, Luke. I admire that about you, so I'm going to cut to the chase." He meets my gaze, his expression serious.

"I know it's been awhile since I fucked up with Liv, but I'd like to apologize."

"To me?" I ask, taken aback.

"Yeah. You're like a brother to Liv. She respects you, your opinion, your friendship. I didn't handle things with her well back then, and I need you to know how much I regret that."

"You don't need to explain. I get it." Unfortunately, a little too well.

"Good. Good. I'm just trying to do this part the right way."

"What's that?" I ask, curiosity piqued.

He inhales deeply, his expression tight as he exhales. "I spoke to Zeke, Levi, Ethan, Cal, Elise, Hayes, and Charlie—pretty much everyone else in this town. You're the last one I need to talk to."

I fight the grin threatening to spread across my face as realization dawns on me; he's about to ask for the same thing I came to discuss with him about Odessa—but for Olivia.

"You asking me for permission to propose to Olivia?" I ask, trying to keep my tone serious.

"Uh, well, yeah," he stammers, shifting his weight from one foot to the other, his hands fidgeting slightly. *Why is it so fun to mess with him?*

"One condition," I say, raising my eyebrows.

His eyes widen, flickering with eagerness. "Anything."

"You give me the same blessing."

"Huh?" He raises an eyebrow, a slight curl of confusion on his lips.

"I'm here for the same reason. I came to ask for your forgiveness—for how I treated Odessa. I want to marry her."

"Why me?" Surprise etches his face as he laughs.

"You three are her brothers, blood or not. You mean the most to her. Eddie too, but I spoke to him a few months ago. You're the last on my list."

"Well, aren't we a bunch of chicken shits, saving the hardest for last?"

I let out a laugh, the tension easing momentarily. "We still have to ask our women."

He shifts slightly, concern washing over him. "Exactly."

"She'll say yes," I throw out honestly. "She loves you, and the kids love you. You're a good dad to all of them. As long as you treat her the way she deserves, that's all that matters to us."

"Same goes for you."

I walk out of his office, feeling the last weight lift off my shoulders. Now, I just need to finish planning the perfect proposal.

***

Odessa

Luke ran off early this morning, claiming he needed to check on Scotch before we went to church together. Then he texted to say he wouldn't make it home before the service but would meet me there. Something feels off, though—he's been flighty, and I can't figure out why.

With an eye roll, I sit alone in our pew, waiting for him.

We're approaching one year since we started officially dating, and it's been more than I thought possible. More fun, more laughter, more love. It's simply been more. And although I spend every day with Luke, it isn't enough. It's never enough.

Maddy has moved to Southern California and enrolled in a trial focusing on amnesia. So far, she's making progress, remembering a little more each day, but there are still moments when she forgets. Joe is there part-time to help with her care, but Luke hasn't visited. The program believes it wouldn't be good for her progress right now.

Part of me hates myself for feeling happy about that, but another part knows it's not just selfishness. This situation has allowed Luke to shed the guilt he carried for so long.

He hasn't moved in yet, and I haven't transitioned into his house either, but we did remove the fence between our properties. So, you could say things are getting pretty serious.

Luke slides in during the prayer, but I don't look up or open my eyes—just embrace the smile that's already spreading across my face.

"Odessa," he says, angling his body toward mine. I open my eyes to meet his gaze.

"Luke."

"I've got a surprise for you."

"Yeah? What's that?"

"You'll see," he replies, resting his hand on my thigh and giving it a gentle squeeze.

When the service is over, we walk out hand in hand, shuffling around the other churchgoers.

"I'll drive. Your car will be safe, and we'll get it later," he says as he leads me to his Bronco. I can already feel it—it's probably my favorite thing: going out on a trail and having a picnic. Now that summer is approaching, we've been able to get out more.

"Ooh, you really brought out the big guns with this surprise."

As if on cue, Dog's head pops up, startling me. "Holy shit. Why do you have Dog?"

He grins that same cocky smile he wears when he's up to something, and it feels like the wind gets knocked out of me.

Could today be the day?

Am I ready for that? To be engaged? To be Mrs. Luke Haynes?

Without a doubt in my mind. Yes.

He drives out of town for what feels like an eternity down the bumpy country road, though it's probably only about twenty minutes.

"Where are we? Relatively, I mean." Considering I barely know how to get from Three Sisters to Bend, I'm still pretty directionally challenged.

"About ten minutes west of Redmond."

"You going to tell me where we're going?"

He shakes his head and turns up the music. This time it's something by George Strait, who I've learned is his favorite.

We turn off onto a dirt road, driving down what looks like someone's driveway—except there aren't any houses, just fields of different crops I don't recognize.

Then I see it. The furthest field is filled with tight clusters of tall green stalks, white flowers blooming atop them.

"Is this—?"

"A friend of mine bought this seed farm a little while back. I called in a favor."

"You—called in a favor? You had him plant a field of yarrow?"

"I did." He chuckles, and I look at him—really look at him. The crinkles at the corners of his eyes from smiling so hard, his perfectly white teeth, the gold flecks in his eyes making them almost hazel. He genuinely looks as happy as I feel.

He gives me a quick kiss and rushes around to open my door. Dog and I step out, but I feel a wobble in my knees as Luke takes my hand, guiding me closer to the field.

"Yarrow is one of the least difficult flowers to grow, yet it is one of the most resilient. It thrives in a variety of conditions, adapting and blooming even in the harshest of environments." He turns toward me, dropping to one knee.

"Achi—we had a pretty harsh start, but damn if the blooms weren't worth it in the end. You've shown me what it means to be resilient, to stand tall and fight for what matters most. You are my biggest inspiration, my greatest love, and the person I want by my side for all that life brings. Will you marry me?"

Well, with a proposal like that, how could a girl say no?

Thank you, next...

Already ready for more Cascadia County? Read on for a sneak peek of Book 5 in The Cascadia County Series—Behind the Pine.

Behind the Pine

Prologue

Maisie

Seven Years After Graduation—

*W*hat do you do when your world comes crashing down
with the mere opening of a door?

"Put your big girl panties on, lace up your sneakers, and go
for a run." That's what I keep telling myself will help clear my
mind after last night. Yet, despite repeating that mantra for
every other task today, here I am, mid-afternoon, and nothing
has worked. Not my early arrival at the coffee hut, scrubbing
the floors and appliances before our 5 a.m. opening, nor the
meticulous triple-checking of the inventory. Not even the
baking of cupcakes, cookies, and a few savory treats could
distract me. The countless faces I greeted and served passed by
me unnoticed. I've been on the verge of tears all morning—so
much so that my sole employee finally sent me home.

I've owned my coffee hut for the last four years—a dream
my parents helped me achieve when they assisted me in buying

it from the previous owner at twenty-one. Back then, it was just a drive-thru coffee hut with only my friends as customers. I started working there at sixteen, likely logging more hours than I was legally allowed, and became the manager at eighteen. The prices were outrageous, and the coffee brand wasn't great, but I did my best to draw in customers. When the previous owner announced he was selling a few years ago, it felt like a blessing; I knew I could make something special out of it. And boy, did I. Once I began selling baked goods as well, it became the busiest place in town—no small feat considering we have a major franchise competitor that could easily dominate the small industry.

She wasn't wrong to send me home; I was a mess, and there was no reason for me to hover over her now that the Sunday morning rush had passed. I'd be lying if I said I wasn't disappointed, though. Maisie's has always been my favorite escape, a place where I can lose myself in the grind. Normally, I can tune out the noise, bake fresh goods, and greet customers with a smile. But today was different; it felt like my heart was breaking over and over again each time I pictured Ethan standing in my friend Olivia's doorway with a baby.

Ethan, *my* Ethan, the best friend I ever had, who I haven't been able to face in three years. Carrying not just a *baby*, but *his* baby. Talk about the gut punches of all gut punches. I hadn't even known he was seeing someone, let alone that she was pregnant. His parents didn't say anything, yet, he definitely walked in with a baby and said "this is *my* Jake."

So rather than face the heartbreak head on, I did what I do best. I bailed. I couldn't face him or the injustice I felt. I had to leave, to get out of there before he saw me and the devastation written on my face. Even though it's completely undeserved and I'm the villain in this story. *Apparently, I am still the coward I've been since graduation night.*

Thankfully my friend Charlie was there to whisk me out of the party and sneak me out the side door. I felt terrible leaving her "re-do twenty-first" birthday party like that, but I knew I couldn't stay another second.

Which is understandable, right? He was my best friend. We'd been close since second grade—him, me, and our friend Olivia.

But Ethan and I were always linked in a different way. That bond changed on graduation night, when life shifted for me—and I couldn't even bring myself to tell him about it.

A few days later, he left for college, heading straight to Oklahoma to play D1 football. He was drafted into the NFL only partway through his college career with an insane rookie contract. I've followed his journey closely—maybe too closely, if I'm being honest. It's become my dirty secret, my guilty pleasure: the one vice I can't seem to give up.

Even though I had to push him away, I'll always love him.

Of course, he's come back to town to visit his family since then, but I've always managed to be conveniently busy or disappeared altogether—even closing down Maisie's for a few days if I couldn't find anyone to cover my shifts.

I reached a point where I realized I couldn't keep losing money. So, I asked Luke, my cousin who works for the Sheriff's department, to tell Ethan to leave me alone. It felt like finality— the last nail in the coffin, my last resort to avoid him. But it worked.

I hadn't seen Ethan in person in nearly seven years. I have no idea if he's dating someone, married, or if his favorite drink is still strawberry milk. I don't know anything about him anymore. And while that may be my doing, it's not something I wished for; it's simply the only way I know how to keep my secret.

Even now, less than a handful of people know what

happened, and I want to keep it that way. No, I *need* to keep it that way. Which means I'll continue to avoid him. *And run.*

My feet hit the dirt road, and I sink into the feeling—it's one of the few things I do purely for myself these days. Maisie's consumes most of my life, and while my customers have become friends, I rarely have the chance to connect with them outside of work. But running is different; I've always carved out time for it.

The ranch where my parents live spans a few hundred acres, and my dad has been working for the owner, Will, since he was a teenager himself. This dirt road has witnessed countless runs throughout my life, winding past hay fields and up the hills toward my favorite lookout spot. From there, I can see for miles—taking in the entire ranch, the hardworking hands, the cattle grazing, and the wildlife going about their routines undisturbed.

It's peace, my comfort spot, and the place I do my best thinking. Which is precisely why I drove ten minutes from my own house, venturing out of town for this moment of solitude.

As I lose myself in thought, the sound of tires crunching on the dirt road catches my attention. A brand new white F150 approaches, one that I don't recognize as belonging to any of the other ranch hands. Will is always hiring new guys, so it could be one of them—or perhaps it's old man Will himself, always eager to show off his latest shiny pickup.

I move over to the far left side, hoping the dust will settle the other way and I won't end up inhaling most of it with my heaves.

Only the truck slows to a near crawl, stopping right next to me.

The driver being no other than the man I've been running from. *Ethan.*

He rolls his window down, looking at me with sad eyes that only make me feel more guilty than I knew possible

"Go away, Ethan," I say, turning my back to him as I walk toward the lookout. I shouldn't be surprised he found me out here; this is where we spent countless hours together—daydreaming, sharing secrets, and losing ourselves in conversation beneath the wide-open sky.

But instead of respecting my wish, I hear the unmistakable sound of his door opening as he climbs out.

"Maisie! What the hell? Seven years of a grudge isn't long enough?!" His voice carries through the air, louder than I've ever heard him shout.

"Guess not!" I reply, my heart racing as I resist the urge to turn around.

"That's it? You threw away a lifetime friendship and won't tell me why? Aren't even going to say anything about me having a son?" My knees nearly buckle with guilt. *It's all my fault and I can't even tell him why.*

With a deep breath, I slowly turn around to face him. It's like seeing a completely new version of him—somehow taller and more filled out than I remembered. The years of professional training have transformed his physique, adding strength and confidence to his stance. Yet, despite the changes, he's still Ethan. His hair, still a touch too long for most people's liking around here, only makes me want to run my fingers through it, just like I used to.

Right now, the green ring around his iris stands out prominently against the brown inner ring as he glares at me with a mix of rage and sorrow.

"Congratulations, Ethan." The words feel heavy on my tongue, a bittersweet mixture of joy and heartache. "I am truly so happy that you are happy, and successful, and have started your own little family. But please, leave me alone."

He winces, and I catch a flash of pain in his eyes—just an instant, but it cuts deeper than I expected. He shakes his head slowly, as if trying to process the weight of my words. Then he turns, retreating to his truck, and the sound of the door closing feels like a finality, echoing in the air between us.

He rolls down his window as he pulls up next to me, the engine idling softly. "You'll have to find a new place to run if you want to avoid me." His voice barely covers the crack of disappointment beneath it. He gestures toward the lookout. "We're building a house there."

We? I nearly choke on my gasp, the shock striking me like a blow. "But how? It's part of the ranch!"

"He sold it to me." His tone is steady, but there's an undercurrent of frustration that rumbles beneath the surface, something tangled in his chest that he's holding back. As he drives past, I catch sight of the baby carrier in the backseat, a stark reminder of everything that's changed.

I watch the truck drive for so long I see it crest the hill. *Our hill.* The one that's no longer ours, but his. *Theirs.*

The Day Before Graduation—

As I settled onto the familiar patch of rocks on the hill overlooking the ranch, I watched Ethan's old truck rumble down the dirt road toward me, the setting sun casting a golden glow behind him. Tomorrow marked our graduation day, a milestone cloaked in excitement but tinged with a looming sense of loss for me. I had always pictured this moment differently—a celebration of our future together—but now it felt like we were standing on the edge of two diverging paths: me staying, and him leaving.

I turned just in time to see him jogging up from where he had parked, a warm smile on his face as he called out, 'My fierce Mais!' It's always 'My fierce Mais,' or 'My sour Mais,' or 'My sweet Mais,' depending on the situation, but no matter what, he's called me 'My Mais' for as long as I can remember.

"Hey!" His hair was already ruffled by the wind, likely from driving with his window down. He plopped down beside me. "You ready for tomorrow?"

He grinned that crooked smile that made my heart flutter. "You have no idea. Finally done walking those dusty halls! Then training begins next week, along with a few summer classes." His enthusiasm was palpable, but beneath it lingered an unsteady current in my chest.

"I'm happy for you," I said, forcing a smile even as a wave of melancholy washed over me. "But it's kind of weird, right? Leaving everything behind?" *Leaving me.*

Ethan chuckled softly. "So weird. But it's the dream, right? Play college ball, hopefully get drafted, make enough money to come back here."

"You really think you'll end up back in Three Sisters?"

"Of course I will," he said, his voice brimming with certainty. "It's home. And—" He hesitated, his expression shifting as he looked out at the horizon.

"And what?" I prompted, my heart racing.

"Where you are," he replied softly. "I've got some big plans —ten-year plans," he added, turning to face me, his captivating rich brown eyes encircled by a green ring, locking onto mine.

"Ten years?" I echoed, my voice barely above a whisper.

"Yep."

The sun sank lower now, painting the sky with brilliant shades of orange and purple. A silence settled between us, my thoughts racing with questions about his plan and why he wasn't elaborating. Would it include me? Even though I would be staying here, going to community college while he was leaving?

"Do you ever think about... us?" I asked suddenly, the words spilling out before I could stop myself.

He looked surprised at my question but intrigued, his brow furrowing slightly. "Us? Like friends?"

"No, I mean... more than friends." I took a shaky breath, willing myself to keep going. "We've always been there for each other. And with you leaving... I guess I just don't know where that leaves us."

Ethan's expression softened, and for a moment, we just stared at each other, the weight of unspoken words hanging between us. I could see the flicker of realization cross his features.

"Honestly, I've thought about it a lot," he confessed, his voice quiet. "In my ten-year plan, I see... you."

My heart raced at his admission, a mix of hope and fear surging within me. "Really?"

"Yeah," he said, shifting closer. "I see the house you've spent years telling me you'd build in this spot, the kids running around—though I'm not sure I'm sold on the Highland cows yet. But everything else? All those stars you wished on out here with me? I want you to have them all. I want to be the one to give them to you."

As he spoke, a wave of emotions washed over me.

"But the best way for me to give you that is to leave," Ethan continued, his eyes serious. "Even if I don't get drafted, I have a full ride to a damn good school. I can get a solid degree and then come back to figure things out."

"You don't think being so far away will change everything? I'm staying here, working the same job with the same people. You'll be off with an entire new team, new friend group, new everything." The insecurities bubbled to the surface, and I struggled to mask them with carefully chosen words.

His gaze locked onto mine, filled with sincerity and admiration, as if he truly believed that distance and time apart wouldn't change a thing. "Not sure anything could change how much you mean to me, Mais. You've always been 'My Maisie.' You mean too much to me for me to mess this up. We trust each other, right? I'd never do anything to hurt you."

It feels like we should've had this talk ages ago, especially since we've been tiptoeing around the fact that we don't date anyone else and spend all our free time together. I might worry about what's coming next, but I trust him completely; I'd never do anything to hurt him either. Still, there's this nagging thought in the back of my mind—what if something happens that changes everything between us? Could I ever truly move on from him?

Also by TJ Deal

The Cascadia County Series

Behind the Cascades

Behind the Juniper

Behind the Larch

Behind the Yarrow

Behind the Pine

Behind the Wildflowers

About the Author

TJ Deal is a Pacific Northwest-based aspiring author who often daydreams about writing stories in the incredible places she travels to around the world. Thanks to her husband's unwavering support and her lifelong obsession with reading, she has decided to follow her passion for writing. Her days are mostly spent drinking coffee, relishing in the daily grind of motherhood, and capitalizing on every free moment to work on her latest novel.